TAUNTED

BY A KILLER

A MEN OF THE BADGE NOVEL

RILEY
McKISSACK

TAUNTED BY A KILLER

ISBN: 978-0-9913299-5-3

Published in the United States of America.

ABOUT THE AUTHOR

Riley McKissack is an award-winning journalist. Cornered gunmen, cop killers, a bomb going off in a domestic terrorism incident, Riley's covered them all. Riley spent years chasing stories involving every type of bad guy and cop imaginable, including FBI, Homeland Security, homicide detectives and arson investigators.

Riley sponged up the drama, tension and danger on SWAT operations, hostage negotiations, drug busts and countless other dangerous situations.

That passion and drama spills out onto the pages of Riley's novels, along with the personal stories behind the men and women who stand between danger and the people they love.

Riley can be found at:
https://facebook.com/riley.mckissack
http://rileymckissack.com
https://twitter .com/RileyMckissack

JOIN THE RILEY MCKISSACK NEWSLETTER
http://www.rileymckissack.com/contact

CHAPTER ONE

Orange flames clawed and scratched at the air, lighting up the night sky with a sunset-colored brilliance. Fire devoured the decrepit, broken-down house in a swirling, dominating riot of passion and power.

The beauty was unmistakable. As was the danger.

The fire screamed with a beastly delight, content in the knowledge that few could stop it or even contain its spread.

"Where are the firefighters?" Cassie Meyers tore her eyes from the spectacle to concentrate on dialing 9-1-1. But, a sudden, distant howl of sirens announced help was coming.

The fire roared louder in protest, swirling black smoke toward the night sky, filling the air with the tangy smell of a fall bonfire. It smelled like football games, wienie roasts and death.

So beautiful. So deadly.

"Shoot video," she coaxed herself away from her fixation on the swirling flames. "There's nothing else you can do." She hit the camera feature on her phone and began filming.

The flames crackled and sparked with livid anger.

The men would try to contain it. But it was too late. The beast ate ferociously, ravaging its feast.

A shuddery hand skated across her skin, teasing her nerves with an animal awareness of someone watching her from the dark wooded area.

She swiveled toward the shadows outside the fire's circle of light. *Was someone out there watching?*

The night hung back from the fire, knowing its darkness was no match for the beast. Still, shadows loomed long, bouncing toward then back away from the fire.

The eerie loneliness of the block vibrated with threat. The deserted block held mostly abandoned houses, leaving Cassie vulnerable and alone on the street.

As the dark edged closer around her, she moved nearer to the flames, stepping fully into the circle of light it threw onto the street. The warmth of the flames felt good on this chilly evening.

Still, shivers ran through her. Not from the elements.

Who had alerted her with a text about this fire, allowing her to arrive before firefighters, before police?

Why wasn't the tipster out on the street?

Tipsters usually approached her almost before she could get out of her car.

Not tonight, though.

Tonight, she was alone in this decaying neighborhood, anxiously monitoring the steady approach of the fire trucks. The fire trucks with the strapping men and a few women, heroes who would walk into a burning building to bring out anyone trapped inside.

A fire truck skidded around the corner, taking it

almost on two wheels, the siren screaming to the fire it was coming for it.

The fire roared back, stretching even higher into the night sky.

"Thank God they're here," she breathed, sucking in a deep breath, pushing back the fear.

Firefighters piled off the truck almost before it had stopped. Two ran toward a hydrant, pulling a hose behind them like a long slinky, coil after coil unfurling.

Two firefighters strapped on oxygen tanks and breathing apparatus. "Anyone in there?" one yelled at Cassie before fastening his mask onto his face.

The decrepit house looked deserted to her but homeless people often camped out in them.

She shrugged and the men bolted toward the front door. Simultaneously, the roof of the old house began creaking and groaning, and the door exploded in flames.

Staggering back from the raging fire, the men altered their path, running toward the back door.

Cassie ran behind them.

"Hey lady, stay here," a young firefighter yelled. She pretended she didn't hear. Seems he hadn't yet learned the authoritative growl that could stop someone in their tracks, and keep them from getting killed.

Or in her case, stop her from getting an Emmy.

She'd take the browbeating later, apologize and fake a naïve, innocent look. Better to apologize than to ask permission, as the saying went.

She apologized a lot.

Wasn't really doing her job if she wasn't getting kicked out of somewhere.

She rounded the back of the house at a sprint. The

firefighters beat at the back door. Flames gnawed around the doorjamb.

The firemen kicked the door and bashed at it with steel rods as the fire silhouetted them into superhero figures fighting against the fiery element.

Standing behind a tree, Cassie braced herself against it to steady the shot. The heat from the fire brazed her face; she was that close. It must be almost unbearable where the firefighters stood but still they fought on to get inside the inferno.

"This is good stuff. Good stuff." She'd laugh with joy if the scene before her weren't so horrible.

She loved when she got there before any real camera people. Her camera phone did a pretty good job.

The station always fonted it *Cassie's video* when she shot early, exclusive video. Her boss thought it made the story more "immediate."

Anything to keep a paycheck coming and her job intact.

An explosion inside the back door kicked flames out onto the firefighters, sending embers and daggers of wood rocketing at her. She ducked her face behind the tree, but kept her hands steady, still shooting video.

A fiery shard of wood his her hand.

"Oww!" she screeched, pulling away.

"Get out of here, lady. It's gonna blow." A firefighter ran toward her. If he was running, she might ought do the same.

She took off, trying to keep up with the first one as he ran toward the front of the house. The second one put his hand in the middle of her back and propelled her along in front of him. If she stumbled, they'd both go down.

"Get back!" the first firefighter bellowed at the other firefighters who were pulling hoses toward the house.

Without waiting for an explanation, all four of them ran toward the fire engine. The firefighter who was pushing Cassie, grabbed her arm now, pulling her with him, carrying her with the force of his fear.

Gasping for air, from fear or exertion she wasn't sure, she ducked down behind the truck, just as a massive blast shook the building.

The firefighter pushed her to the ground, throwing himself on top of her as flaming debris rained down on the group. When the clatter of falling fire stopped, he motioned toward the truck and she scrabbled underneath the engine. The firefighter pushed in after her and the other firefighters sought as much protection underneath the truck as they could find.

Another blast shook the building and red rain fell on the ground where they'd just lain.

She met the eyes of the firefighter through the protective, plastic screen of his helmet. His eyes were wide, like he'd just been awakened sharply.

The guy might be a hero. But he still felt fear. A normal, want-to-live, not-die-in-the-flames, human fear.

Their eyes held for a moment, then the guy grinned. "Pretty close," he said.

She laughed. The adrenalin surged through her body, making her high. "Too close," she said.

Another engine rolled up, then a battalion chief's company car followed. The firefighter rolled out from under the engine and reached back a hand to her.

She grabbed it and struggled out from under the fire truck.

"Watch out for the fiery bits," he said with a laugh,

pointing down at the flaming embers still lining the street.

Preston Hobbs, the battalion chief, ran toward them, shoving his helmet on his head. Freshly shaved, his hair in place, with a starched shirt, he always looked like he'd just come from a photo shoot. Another younger firefighter ran close behind him.

"Anybody hurt?" Hobbs yelled.

The firefighters checked themselves and each other, then shook their heads.

"Pull back!" Chief Hobbs yelled. "Let it burn out, just try to keep it from getting to those other houses."

The original firefighters ran to man their hoses, and the crew that had just arrived started the process of running their hoses.

Hobbs looked down the street at the broken-down, crumbling houses that lined the rest of the block, many with sagging roofs, open doors. Most of the decrepit looking houses seemed abandoned.

"Probably ought to let them burn, too," he said, with a harsh laugh. "Urban renewal."

The young firefighter who'd ridden with Hobbs nodded his approval.

"Hey, Clayton!" a firefighter yelled at the young firefighter who stood close behind Hobbs. "Quit schmoozing the news lady and get over here and do your job."

The young guy smashed his helmet on his head and ran toward the other guys, grabbed a hose and helped pull it.

"Ought to just let them all burn," Hobbs repeated, shaking his head. "Then, bring in a bulldozer."

As if answering his snide remark, three doors down, a front door opened. An ancient woman shuffled out, clutching her robe about her chest, one hand touching the scarf that covered her head.

"They're not all vacant." Cassie pointed.

"Save that one then," Hobbs said dismissively.

The old woman looked at them, her eyes widening, showing an awful lot of white, then scuttled back inside. She slammed her burglar-bars steel door behind her, then shut the wooden inside door.

Cassie watched the woman disappear and had a flash of herself at that age, living in a similar situation.

God, Cassie hoped she wouldn't end up like that one day. Every time she saw one of these old women living in decaying, nearly abandoned neighborhoods, she couldn't help seeing herself forty-five or fifty years down the road.

She silently vowed to work harder to keep her job, to keep the income stream flowing.

"Please God, no," she whispered.

"What?" Hobbs looked down at her.

She shook her head. "Nothing."

He followed her gaze to the old woman's house. Then, he looked back at her, his expression warming. "Sad, huh? Don't worry, that won't be you."

She met his eyes. How had he known what she was thinking? Were her thoughts written that clearly across her face?

However he'd known, she prayed to God he had the vision. That he could see her future.

A detective's fleet vehicle slid to a halt along the curb beyond the last fire engine.

The door swung open and a long, lean, unshaven,

rumpled figure emerged. He stretched his frame to its full six feet, two inches height.

The most dangerously sexy man she'd ever met had just arrived on the scene. Forrester Carson.

He met her gaze, holding it for a long moment, with a simmering heat that threatened to scorch her more than the flying embers of the house.

Hobbs' gaze followed hers toward the newcomer. He snorted. "Lookie who we got here. Your ex-husband."

Or as she thought of him, trouble. Trouble with a capital *T.*

CHAPTER TWO

Cassie's face shimmered with reflected firelight. A flush shone on her skin like he hadn't seen since…

The last time they'd made love.

A fist knotted in Forrester's belly. The same fist that always gripped him when he first caught sight of her.

Each time he glimpsed her, his heart jumped. Then, the fist grabbed hold of him, shaking him back to reality.

Reminding him with a solid punch that she wasn't his wife anymore.

She could put a room between them the way she had at first, sleeping in the spare bedroom.

She could put a whole lot of paperwork between them, in the form of a divorce, officially claiming the title of ex.

That didn't change the fact he'd seen her naked, had her beneath him, open to him, with that flush on her face that said she was his, as consumed with the flames of the moment as he'd been every time he'd ever made love to her.

"Damn," he muttered. "Just damn." He shoved the car door closed, then sucked in a deep breath, preparing himself for the moment he'd speak to her.

"Hey, you're pretty presumptuous, coming out to the scene of my fire," Hobbs said to him out of the side of his mouth as he watched the firefighting of his men. He keyed his radio, responding to something one of the other firefighters had said on the handheld radio.

He and Hobbs had come up the ranks together, joining the public safety department at about the same time, one as a firefighter, the other a cop. They knew where all the bodies were buried on each other. Poked at the other's weak spots all the time.

But, Hobbs had never poked at him about the divorce.

Even though Forrester knew of the attraction Hobbs had felt for Cassie when she'd first come to town as a new, hot, young reporter.

Before Forrester had gotten her all tied up for himself. Before it had then come unraveled.

He'd seen the way the guy had checked out Cassie, looking her over when her head was turned, from head to toe, as if taking a full inventory of all she had to offer.

Couldn't blame a guy for looking. Especially at a woman like her.

Those curves, with a body that could have been used as an advertisement for a fitness club. But, he knew she worked out more to stay healthy than for her looks.

Girl had a thing about not wanting to be old and feeble. Seemed to constantly be working against the clock.

She might do it for her health, but the results had just as powerful an effect on him.

So, yeah, he'd known what Hobbs had felt—the same drive to get close to her as had driven Forrester.

But, once he and Cassie were engaged, Hobbs had respected that fact. He'd never said anything smart when they'd gotten divorced either.

If Forrester's own inner critic didn't keep calling him a fool for screwing up the best thing that had ever happened to him, he would be all set.

Except for the way that woman looked. That red hair, those hazel eyes. That lush mouth that always seemed about to crack some smart-ass remark. That body that looked as if she was designed with every man's fantasy in mind.

Damn.

He'd never get over that.

"Whadda ya got here?" He turned toward the fire, tearing his gaze from Cassie.

"Probably a standard issue, urban outdoorsman's campfire getting out of control," Hobbs snarked dryly. "The free housing in this part of town doesn't come with utilities."

Forrester shrugged. "Guess a guy's gotta make do sometimes."

Hobbs shot him a look, like maybe Forrester was talking about himself since Cassie had moved out on him.

Damn, she couldn't even be like some of the wives of his buddies, wanting to take the house from him to punish him. If she'd done that, they'd have had time in the house together, fighting over who'd get the house, buying him time. Time to work on her. Maybe to heal the wounds?

Cassie wasn't like any other woman. She'd just moved out.

And moved on.

Took that big paycheck of hers and got herself another place.

A better place, he'd heard.

On a more fashionable street, in a more fashionable neighborhood.

And closer to work.

Like she wanted to emphasize what was really important to her now. Cause it sure as hell wasn't him anymore.

Not that he deserved to be her priority.

He bit the side of his mouth, to make sure he didn't slip up and say anything inappropriate for their new situation.

Cause he didn't even have the right to that little kick of resentment that her job had moved into first priority.

The divorce was his own damn, stupid fault.

He wanted to be angry at someone. It just wasn't as much fun when the person you were angry at was yourself. Couldn't go have a beer and talk about *the bitch*, as so many of his friends did about their exes.

"I'm a stupid, damn fool," he might say over a beer. But, that would just bring a chorus of "we know" from his brother cops.

They all knew he'd been a stupid, damn fool. They'd told him so to his face.

And he couldn't even get drunk and punch 'em. Cause they were right.

Cassie.

Cassie, Cassie, Cassie.

With that flame-colored hair reflecting back the fiery colors of the burning house. He turned to her, forced himself to look right at her, and could feel her noticing his gaze on her.

Then, he turned away from the vision that was her. Enticing, make-you-want-to-take-her-now hot.

He forced himself into cop mode, glancing around the area, looking for anything out of place. Once the fire was out, this would become his scene, he already knew. "You're beating me out to these scenes," he said, shooting Cassie a sideways glance.

Better not to look directly into the light. She'd already almost singed his eyeballs when he'd first drove up.

"What can I say?" she shot back. "I'm good at my job."

"You always were." He felt more than saw her head swivel on her neck to see his expression. He kept it bland. Purposefully so.

Fighting wasn't going to get her back. And if it wouldn't get her back, what was the point?

"I guess it's too soon to know if there's a body." He looked at Hobbs.

Cassie started, then turned fully toward him and Hobbs. "Body?

Damn. He figured Hobbs would have already said something to her.

He didn't say anything else, cause he'd be an "unnamed source close to the investigation" in her story if he did.

Hobbs turned, gesturing with his finger to follow him.

Cassie's eyes narrowed. But, she just took her phone and began videotaping the firefighters and the general scene.

One of her TV stations's live trucks pulled in at the far end of the block, and she quit filming and headed that way.

Forrester watched her go, noticing Hobbs doing the same, probably with the same hungry looks in their eyes. Then, Hobbs glanced toward the ground, and scuffed his boot on a piece of grass, wiping off the red clay that covered both of his boots.

The same red clay that surrounded the house.

"You have to help pull lines?" Forrester asked.

Hobbs jerked his eyes up to look at Forrester. "Gotta help out however you can."

Forrester nodded. Hobbs was one of the best firefighters he'd ever known. Rising in the ranks faster than Forrester had risen in the police ranks, that was for sure.

He dressed the part, he acted the part. The guy was going places and you could tell by just looking at him.

Forrester looked down at his own wrinkled clothing, the same stuff he'd worn yesterday, hastily yanked on when his cell phone rang.

He wasn't TV-ready like Hobbs. But, then hell, he didn't care.

Making rank wasn't his top priority. Never had been. Never would be.

He'd only left undercover and returned to the detective unit when Cassie left him.

Which was a sweet piece of irony. Cause if he'd done it a long time ago, they'd probably still be married.

He turned to watch Cassie as she climbed into the live truck to begin editing her story for the early morning show.

Those hips turned, directing that rear end straight at him. The image wasn't meant to taunt him with the desire to touch what had once been his to touch whenever he'd wanted.

If anything, she would have meant it as a reminder of just what he'd been.

A real horse's behind.

Ass, just say it. Cause it didn't matter how much he cleaned up his language anymore. He wasn't ever getting her back.

The foul language he'd brought back from his undercover work was the least of what he'd dragged into their lives.

Cassie leaned out of the truck to grab the live truck's heavy door. As she did, their eyes met.

The moment held too long, cause looking at her reminded him of everything he'd lost. And would never have again.

Everything he should have treasured and protected.

But clearly hadn't.

CHAPTER THREE

Cassie unhooked her microphone. "Another live shot down," she said to JoJo.

He pulled a video card from his camera. "They want me to feed back some fresh stuff for the next half hour."

She nodded, then headed toward the nearest house to the fire site. As she climbed the front porch steps, she checked for signs of the old woman who'd stuck her head out earlier. She knew the woman was still up, had seen her peeking out of the curtains numerous times.

The television set projected the audio of Cassie's station all the way onto the front porch. She'd probably been watching the report to learn what was going on in her own neighborhood.

Rather than coming outside to find out, the woman huddled inside the decaying house.

"Hello," Cassie called, as she tapped on the front door.

Like a mouse nervous a hawk was outside, the woman inched the curtains back to look out.

"Hey." Cassie fluttered her fingers.

The woman pulled the curtain back further and nodded at Cassie. But she didn't come to the door.

Cassie walked closer to the window. "Just wanted to

know if you saw anything before the fire, know anything about how it started."

The woman looked beyond Cassie toward the burned-out house.

Firemen rolled up hoses. One hosed down hot spots, while another poked at the debris, making sure the fire wouldn't revive. A small crew would remain until the beast was completely dead.

That familiar, burnt wood smell wafted in the air, acrid, sharp.

"It went up fast," Cassie said.

"Uh huh, sugar, it sure did." The old, black woman looked Cassie over as if comparing Real Cassie to the image on the news almost every day.

She'd gotten used to that sharp, assessing eyeballing, so they could report back to their friends on the redheaded "news lady."

"I was so glad when the firemens showed up. So glad." The old woman sighed. "It were terrible scary out here alone with that fire. Ablazing how it did."

Cassie nodded. "I bet." The woman was going to talk to her, was already starting to warm up to the conversation. She motioned to JoJo to bring the camera. She usually had better luck if she approached people without a camera already to go off in their faces.

"Hey," a shout sounded from inside the charred skeleton of the building.

Cassie turned toward that voice. The intensity of the fireman's tone riveted her attention, the way people often sounded when they were talking on the phone to 9-1-1.

Alarm, alert, pay attention. This is important.

Several firemen moved toward the sound. Cassie's

cameraman turned, focusing his camera on the house again.

"There's a body in here."

A screech of alarm sounded in Cassie's belly. Like a knife turning in her gut, in her mind, all of her senses went into high alert.

Her heart jumpstarted into breaking news mode. The station would want her live again with this news.

"Oh, lord, lord, lord," the old woman gasped. Cassie turned to her. The woman covered her mouth with a wizened hand, as if to hold back any more outbursts. Her eyes rounded and darted from the fire to Cassie.

"No, baby. I ain't seen nothing. Nothing a'tall." She shook her head back and forth like a pendulum, denying what was written all over her face. She clutched her throat with that bony hand, shielding her jugular vein.

The old woman let the curtain fall shut, hiding the haunted expression on her face. As if she'd seen her future.

Her expression reminded Cassie of the middle of the night feeling she awoke to often since the divorce.

The alone and scared feeling that surged through her when she awoke from haunting dreams, sitting straight up in bed.

Dreams of herself old and alone. And scared.

Cassie looked at the swaying curtain. And instinctively knew the old woman would be watching the news reports all day long.

Watching to see what information she could glean about what had happened in the middle of the night just a few doors down from her home.

It was a homicide investigation now. Everything had changed in an instant.

"Okay, everybody pull back 'cept the EMS guys!" Chief Hobbs bellowed.

A look passed between the chief and Forrester. That look said it would probably be a case for the medical examiner. No one could have survived that raging inferno.

Hobbs walked around back toward the sound of the fireman's voice who'd found the body. Two EMS guys raced back there, too.

Forrester lifted the crime scene tape and started to pass underneath it.

But, as Cassie walked toward him, he dropped the tape. As if alerted by some internal security sensor to her presence, he turned toward her.

His eyes swept down her body, taking a full inventory.

Yeah, she thought, *everything's still here*. Just as he'd left it.

"I'm up here," she said, hearing her own dry, cutting tone of voice.

He smiled lazily and looked up to meet her gaze as if he hadn't just checked her out like some guy in a bar.

"Sorry," he said, not sounding sorry at all, "haven't had much sleep. Came straight from the mountains and had hardly fallen into bed when the call came."

The mountains. Where they'd had a lot of good times with Forrester and his buddies.

"That'd explain the hiking boots." They were covered with mud. "Visiting your cousin?"

"Yeah, Luke and I went out hiking and did some fishing. The guy's in bad shape.

"Hmm," she murmured. And suddenly, her snarkiness just seemed petty, compared to Luke's loss, his wife succumbing to her long battle with leukemia. "That's so rough. I think he really lost his soul mate when he lost Mazie."

He tilted his head, but the casual gesture didn't match the sadness in his eyes. A deep, yawning grief for his cousin ate at him. She knew, because it ate at her. If anyone had deserved a happy ending it had been Luke and his wife Mazie.

But, they hadn't gotten it.

"They made it to 'till death do us part'." Forrester's body seemed to sag, though he kept his tone deceptively light. "They just thought that death would separate them much later."

She sighed, pushing the air out of her body as if the sadness could go with it. "They were so sweet together. The way he sat at the hospital with her so many hours, sleeping there. I really thought she was gonna make it."

"She did make it," he said softly. "Over and over again, she won more time with Luke, beating back the leukemia. The first time she went into remission, we all thought it was gone. But that damned disease just kept sneaking back, battering her defenses, till she couldn't fight it anymore."

"Till death do us part," she said softly, wistfully, "not many people make it to that anymore. They were something special."

He didn't say anything, his face blank. Hiding the pain he felt over his cousin's wife's death? It felt like it was something different.

"What?" she said, knowing something was simmering below the surface when he kept his face that decidedly expressionless.

He shrugged. "Hearing you wax poetic about staying married seems kinda funny."

She met his eyes, wanting to say exactly what she thought, that he had some nerve acting like there was anything wrong with her. She wasn't the one who'd given up on the promises they'd made to each other.

But, they both were sad about Mazie. And, he was tired. And she was tired. Getting first video on stories might be a notch on her career belt, but it was seriously cutting into her sleep.

So she let it pass.

Cause it was all in the past now, anyway. Their past.

She looked down at her reporter's notebook, flipping a page, clicking her pen, making it clear that their conversation about the fire was going on the record.

"You still believe in marriage?" He said low in his throat, his voice deep, gravely, that early morning growl she'd heard so many times before. But, she concentrated on his question and fought against the kick in her lower belly.

He was gonna push it?

Okay, then.

She looked him straight in the eye. "Just cause we didn't work out doesn't mean I don't believe in marriage."

He winced. "Ouch."

"I believe in love, lasting love that will endure a lifetime. I want that. Thought I had it. But, just because I was mistaken, doesn't mean I'm going to hang up my dating shoes." She sucked in a long breath, looked down at her notebook, sighed and flipped it closed.

"I miss sleeping next to my husband, waking up with him." She closed her eyes, remembering everything they'd had together, seeing their nights together and their early mornings in bed like a movie, a 3D movie with sensory effects. "Making love to a man I believe loves me. Having breakfast with him, kissing him before I leave for work."

She could see it all, the life they'd had, with so much good about it. "I miss having someone to come home to." Then, like a slap in the face waking her up, she remembered how it had all ended. She opened her eyes and looked him in the eye. "I want that, all of that. I believe I can still have it."

He stepped forward, reaching for her hand. A shot of adrenaline kicked in and she jerked her hand back, out of range to him. Like her heart.

She shot him a dark look, infused with the anger that so many sleepless nights brought, nights she lay awake missing what they'd had.

What she *thought* they'd had, she corrected herself. Cause that was another middle of the night conversation she'd had with herself over and over again. How could she have been so blind?

"I didn't mean with you again," she said, keeping her voice low.

Honesty. They'd promised each other honesty. That was their new policy.

His eyes narrowed and he tilted his head toward her hand. "I just noticed you've got a burn there." He slowly edged his hand toward hers, as if she might yank it back again. Taking it, he turned it over so that the burn showed.

"That's gotta hurt," he said.

"Hurts like the dickens." Hurt almost as much as losing him had hurt. Hurt so bad, she almost couldn't help crying.

But, she was tough, could stand the pain.

He turned toward his jeep, pulling her along the few feet to the side of the vehicle. He opened the back seat, pulled out the smaller cooler he took along when he went fishing for food and drinks, and opened it.

He grabbed a handful of ice and laid it on her wrist.

The soothing cold sank into the burn, pushing back the pain. She sighed with relief. "Oh my gosh, that feels so good."

"You just gotta ask for what you want, Red." One of his hands held hers in place while the other hand secured the sent-from-heaven ice on her wrist. "You don't have to suffer."

His tone was low, seductive, as if talking about another type of need, the man she spoke of sleeping next to her.

The place that had been his.

She cut her eyes up at him, looking through her eyelashes. The man could make her want, that was for sure. The desire he inspired had never been the problem.

But, like this house fire, she'd gotten too close, too near the flame, and gotten burned badly.

The pain from the destruction of their marriage was still there, like a memory, burning just underneath the skin. If she got burned by him again, she wouldn't survive.

The Grady Burn Center wouldn't even be able to save her.

She placed her hand over his, taking control of the ice. "Thanks. That feels so much better."

"Just gotta ask, Red. Just gotta ask." His voice flowed over her like honey, sweet and gentle.

But, she wasn't tasting what he had to offer. Never again.

She stepped back and shook back her hair. "I must look like hell. Got up out of bed, without even a shower."

He looked her over. "That makeup's hiding the worst of it."

"Thanks. I guess." She laughed roughly. "Honesty, right?"

His eyes met hers with a directness, a hard edge. "That's right. Honesty always. I promised I'd never lie to you again." His expression hardened into steel, knife-edge sharp, a look that could almost cut through her defenses, almost convince her to climb back into his bed. "And I never will lie to you again."

Their gazes held for a long moment, then she forced herself to turn away. To focus on the smoking carcass of the house, the reason they were together this morning.

"So, why are you out here before the firefighters even had a chance to call you?" she asked, flipping her notebook open again with one hand while balancing the ice on her other wrist. "Before they informed you there was a body."

She looked directly at him. "You knew there'd be a body, didn't you?"

"I said I wouldn't lie to you, Red. I didn't say I'd tell you everything." He grinned that grin that always made her want to lean in, lean into his mouth and take what it had to offer.

"I can't tell you everything when it comes to work. You know that."

His smile faltered then. As if he was remembering work had been part of the problem.

His work. Her work. But mostly his.

He leaned back against his car, a casual shrug causing his shoulder muscles to flex underneath his shirt. "I just had a hunch." He tapped her notebook. "And that's not for reporting on the air."

She closed her notebook. "Okay. Why are you here and what do you know?"

He gave her a sideways glance. "It's not what I know. It's what I feel. What I sense."

He pushed away from the car and sauntered toward the house. She followed him, closing her hand over the ice again, holding it in place against the pain.

At the curb, he folded his arms across his chest. "Something's going on, Cassie. Something bad."

As if a wind had blown across her skin, her skin prickled. Earlier, when she'd been alone here, it had felt as if something evil had crawled down the street, circling the house, a tinge of danger creeping around the edges of the house, teasing the flames higher.

Now, it felt as if it crawled around just beyond her vision, that she could almost see it out of the corner of her eye. If she turned around fast enough, she would catch something ugly leering from the woods, like a coyote, waiting, watching, yearning hungrily for a piece of flesh.

She shivered and Forrester looked down at her. "You need a coat?"

"No."

"Someone died here," she whispered, her throat raspy and suddenly dry.

"Maybe. Gotta wait to see what the arson investigators and the medical examiner say."

A human had been inside that house, maybe dying even as she videotaped the fire. Had she heard them screaming, merely interpreting it as the sounds of a house under attack by the flames? Another shudder ran through her that had nothing to do with the weather.

Forrester wrapped an arm around her shoulders, pulling her into his side.

It felt good, comfortable, like the old days. When his arms had been where she went for comfort.

After a long day of other people's tragedies, she'd find forgetfulness in his arms.

When he was home, that is.

The words came from deep inside her memories of all the nights when she'd wondered where he was.

When he'd worked undercover. Deep undercover with the people who'd seemed to matter most to him, other police officers.

Finding bad guys and bringing them to justice had become the driving force in his life.

He told so many lies undercover that he'd seemed to forget what the truth was.

Until finally, he'd lied to her.

As if it had become part of his nature, he'd lied for no reason sometimes.

Until the night he really had a reason to lie to her.

She shoved away from his side.

"Hey, Detective," one of the firefighters called. "You need to see this."

The two EMS techs walked away from the building, returning to their ambulance, announcing with their actions that it was indeed a homicide investigation, no one to take to the hospital.

Forrester glanced at her. "You okay?"

She squared her shoulders, standing straight as much to reassure herself as him. "I'm fine." She would be fine. Eventually.

Forrester gave her a long assessing look, then nodded and turned away toward the firefighter. "Whatcha got?" he called as his long legs covered the ground quickly.

"You're not gonna believe who this is."

CHAPTER FOUR

"City councilwoman Betty Farber was found dead in a burning building this morning." Cassie spoke into the camera, in a professional voice that belied the deep level of shock that had hit her when she'd learned the identity of the body. "John," she spoke to one of the anchors. "In this run-down neighborhood, where most of the homes are empty, firefighters found the councilwoman's body inside a burning house."

"That's unbelievable, Cassie," the anchor said.

Tell me about it, she wanted to answer.

"Yes, it is, John. Investigators want to know how she came to be there and under what circumstances," she stated calmly as if people all over metro Atlanta weren't just nearly choking on their first morning cups of coffee.

JoJo, her usual cameraman, waved to her they were clear. She took out her earpiece and stepped out from in front of the camera.

JoJo pointedly disconnected the microphone from the audio cable before they started talking. As if he knew neither of them wanted the station folk to hear what they were about to say.

"What the…" She squinted her eyes at JoJo. "Did you hear him ask me was she naked?"

JoJo threw his had back and howled. "I wanted to laugh out loud. Almost did. But, I could tell by your face you'd lose it if I did."

"I was *this* close to losing it." She held her fingers up just a pinch apart.

JoJo threw his head back and laughed again like he was listening to a stand-up comedy routine.

A laugh bubbled up in her in response to his. When JoJo laughed, she could forget the circumstances, forget a dead body hadn't even been hauled out of the burned-out hulk of a house yet.

She shook her head. "Oh, those people. I wanted to say how about a little respect for the dead. A city councilwoman at that. Let her family at least digest the news she's dead before we start reporting on the air with salacious details, like whether or not she was naked."

She lifted her hands toward the sky. "And why is that always the first question he asks about a dead woman? He never asks that about a dead guy."

JoJo chuckled. Nothing in this business ever upset him.

An impossible deadline? Almost missing slot for their piece on the air?

"Long as nobody's dead that we know, we're fine," was his usual response.

He shuffled his big old Alabama frame back to the live truck and began wrapping up cables. "I just wanna go to my crib and get some sleep, home girl. None of this means nothing to me," he repeated his second most used saying.

She turned back to the scene of the fire, where all sorts of officials were circling the body, literally and figuratively.

Arson investigators, the medical examiner. And circling outside of them, a covey of homicide detectives murmured, their heads together.

Even the District Attorney's office had sent people.

Word was the mayor was on his way.

A city councilwoman was dead.

A settled woman, not known for partying or hanging out with the bar crowds. There wasn't any reason for a woman like her to end up dead down here on this sad street.

"Pretty pitiful end, huh?"

She turned. "Hobbs," she said.

The battalion chief took a step forward, bringing himself level beside her as she faced the house. Crossing his arms, he rocked back on his heels.

"What can you tell me so far, chief?" she asked, using his title to indicate it was an official question.

"Not much, missy. Not much, yet. The mayor's going to make a statement in a bit. He's up for reelection, you know." He narrowed his eyes with a glint of dark humor.

"Is nothing sacred, Hobbs?"

"Not really, Red."

Red? A squirmy little pulse swirled through her stomach. He'd never called her that before.

That was Forrester's pet name for her. It only sounded right coming from him.

The chief didn't look at her, as if knew he'd committed a faux pas, the awkwardness putting a distance between them that she'd never felt before.

He'd always treated her with a professional joviality. But, something about that comment had just felt wrong. Too intimate.

She opened her notebook, and clicked her pen. "Nothing?" she said. "You got nothing for me?"

Preston smiled, the smile not quite making it to his eyes. "This is above my pay grade, too big for the likes of little old me. The mayor, the district attorney, the fire chief and the police chief are gonna have to release information on this one."

He blew out a breath. "Whoowee, don't want to get my tail caught in the news machine that's surrounding this story, at least not this news cycle."

He gave her a real smile then. "I'm handing it over to the day crew and going home to get some sleep. I suggest you do the same." He waggled his fingers and walked away.

Yeah, she wouldn't be going back to sleep anytime soon. Her day was just getting started. With one of the biggest stories of her career.

A text came through on her phone, about the hundredth text since she'd first gone on the air. "Good work, girl," the executive producer texted.

They'd worked together down in Columbus, Georgia, a much smaller television market than Atlanta. Climbing the ladder together, with the shared history of mistakes in the smaller market, bound them closer than any of the producers she'd met since she'd gotten to Atlanta.

"Just doing my job," she sent back her standard reply.

You were only as good as your last live shot.

She glanced around at the crowd of people that had

gathered as the day had dawned. The news had spread and everyone within walking distance had come down to check it out.

Cassie scanned the crowd.

Who had tipped her to the fire?

Who had killed that woman?

A scarier question played in her head. Was it the same person?

And if so, were they still here, lurking in the crowd, watching the ruckus their handiwork had created?

She'd stood alone on this dark, deserted street with only that one inhabited house with the elderly woman. A shiver shuddered through her. She'd felt watched.

Was the phone call a tip? Or had it been meant to lure her here?

Lure her to a lonely, deserted spot where another woman had already been murdered?

She pivoted, putting the scene behind her. It wasn't certain the councilwoman had been murdered. Like hell it wasn't, even if the authorities didn't make it official yet.

She took out her phone and began quickly videotaping the people who lined the street.

Was the murderer there amongst them?

The high was incredible. Flames shooting toward heaven with a beauty beyond belief, the house bending in supplication to the fire.

What a success.

Taking down that woman. That councilwoman, who had no idea what the world should look like.

She'd thought she had the power to shape the world.

But, she'd learned she was powerless.

Ha, the way she'd looked bound and gagged, eyes wide, almost bulging out of her head.

If she'd been a properly moral citizen of society, this would never have happened to her.

She'd chosen. She'd determined her fate.

Life was all about choices.

Make the right ones, you had a good life. The wrong ones, eventually you had to pay.

She'd paid.

Now, it was time to move on. To keep cleaning up this city.

With a burning, cleansing flame.

Much later that day, Forrester stood on the front sidewalk, looking at Cassie's new home. The trim needed painting. Left much longer, it would start to have wood rot, termites might get in.

Wood damage at the least. And, that'd cost a whole lot more than just a couple gallons of paint.

Typical of Cassie, throw some money at her problems. She'd moved out of their home, spent a hell of a lot of money to get this new place.

But, she wasn't keeping it up. Later, when the problem got too big for paint to fix, she'd throw a bunch of money at it, hire some pricey hotshot contractor to fix the place up.

Throwing her money away.

The front door opened, and Cassie stepped out onto the front porch. She eyed him up and down.

She spread her legs in a feminine imitation of him,

legs apart, her arms crossed. She narrowed her eyes and surveyed him.

And waited for him to speak.

"That wood needs painting," he said, without thinking. He'd known that was a mistake even before her eyebrows shot up.

"It's not *your* problem," she said through lips so tight he was amazed she could even get the words out.

"You're right—sorry." He raised his hands in surrender and took a step toward the front porch. Her eyebrows shot up.

He lifted his chin in acknowledgement of the nonverbal communication and stepped back.

"I'm here on business," he offered. "Cop business."

Her eyebrows lowered. "You should have said so."

He should have said a lot of things. While they were still married, when there'd still been a chance for them.

Hell, don't go there, he cautioned himself.

"I'm saying so now."

She nodded, then gestured with her hand toward a couple of rocking chairs sitting on her front porch. He followed her toward them.

"Nice," he said. "Your granny's?" He already knew they were but wanted to try to get her to talk about her granny. Start a conversation that might lead back to them?

She nodded, but didn't say anything further about the rocking chairs. "Want some ice tea?"

"No. I'm fully caffeinated." He lowered himself cautiously into one of the ancient, wooden rockers. Gingerly, he rocked back and forth. A loud squeaking accompanied the movement. "I can fix that squeak for you."

"I can hire someone to do it." She sat in the other, then turned toward him, her eyes issuing a direct command to get down to business.

Okay, then. He rocked back and forth to the sound of the insistent squeaking. Then, as if he couldn't help himself, he stood, flipped the rocker over and jammed the wooden rocking bottom onto the leg, with one bang of his fist.

He pulled out a pocketknife, opened it to the screwdriver component, and turned a screw that helped keep the chair leg fastened to its rocker bottom.

He flipped it back over and sat in it, giving it a push backward. No squeaking. "There, all fixed," he said with satisfaction.

He looked over at Cassie for a nod of approval, her method of rewarding him for a job well done around the house when they'd been married.

Those little nods filled him with a sense of accomplishment more than any words could have ever done. Just a nod and a little smile, like she knew she could count on her man for things like that.

He met her eyes, and the glacial stare she gave him.

It clearly said, what are you doing on my front porch, messing with my granny's rocking chairs?

She looked away, rocked a few times, then said, "What cop business did you come about?"

A squeaking of disappointment began in his chest, keeping time to her rocking. That internal squeaking was much more irritating than any real sounds from the chair could have been.

He didn't belong here, she wasn't his woman, get to business, the rocking chair beat out the recriminations as it hit back and forth on the wooden slats of the front porch.

"You were out there at the fire scene awful early, Red."

"You know that how?" She looked at him, an arched eyebrow said she was waiting for him to admit he'd been checking out her television news reports on their website, or seeing them on television.

Watching your ex-wife on TV, like any other schmo in this town who thought she was hot, who lusted after her. That's what he'd been reduced to.

"That video you shot didn't have any fire trucks in it. In fact, I could hear the fire sirens, hear the engines showing up."

"Maybe I didn't video the firefighters who were already there, focused on the fire instead."

"You can't miss the sound of those heavy engines if they'd been there." He tilted his head, raised his eyebrows. She wanted honesty from him, then she should give it to him as well.

But, honesty hadn't been her problem. It had been his.

She met his eyes levelly, as if reading his thoughts. She'd always been able to do that, had read the lies easily.

What sort of an undercover guy was he if his wife could read his face like that? Her ability to read him had started to make him nervous, like everyone else could read him that easily.

Had started to undermine his confidence, make him wonder when a bullet would find him.

But, that hadn't been the reason he'd gotten out of undercover. It had been the reason they'd gotten divorced.

Damn, don't go there, buddy, he talked himself

away from the ledge. Like he was doing a lot these days.

"How'd you get out there so quickly, Cassie?" He lowered his eyebrows, studying her. "Before the fire guys?"

She looked away, pushing the rocker back and forth. "I'm gonna get some ice tea." She pushed out of her chair and went inside, leaving the front door open.

Was that an invitation? He'd take it as such.

He followed the sounds of ice cubes falling into a glass. A newly renovated kitchen with all that money could buy was nothing like the beat up, old kitchen they'd had. A top of the line, stainless steel refrigerator stood beside a top of the line, stainless steel oven.

"Nice," he said.

She whirled around to glare at him. "Thanks," she said with absolutely no inflection in her tone, as if he were some guy on the street, commenting on her body.

Placate the jerk and move on, had been her motto for guys who thought they had a right to comment on her, to check her out, to ask her out, and more.

All because she was a public figure, a person on the news, who came into their living rooms, their bedrooms. Wherever they had a television set. Nowadays, even on their phones, computers, tablets.

Guys could leer at her wherever an electronic device existed.

Hell, probably guys in China and Europe were booking tickets, applying for visas, all to try and meet the woman whose news reports could be seen on the Internet now.

She was highly visible, highly desirable.

And as far as she was concerned, Forrester was just another jerk who thought he had a right to some part of her.

All because she was doing her job. And because she looked like that.

Man, the way she looked. She'd changed into soft cotton yoga pants and a T-shirt that showed everything he'd been missing. The curves underneath those clothes so enticing that they aggravated the want he felt every time he saw her.

He had to clear his throat before he could speak. Didn't want hoarseness to reveal her effect on him. "You want to go back outside?"

She shook her head. "We can talk here." She pointed at a little Formica dining table in the corner of her kitchen that looked oddly out of place with all the other expensive touches.

He laughed as he settled into an old chair upholstered in checkerboard plastic that matched the table. "Your granny's."

She smiled and nodded. "Brought it up from her place. I'm gonna fix up her house, just haven't had time to yet. Thought I'd bring it up here till then."

"Cute."

A look of satisfaction crossed her face.

"We could have brought this stuff to our home," he said. Again with the not thinking first.

"We could have done a lot of things different in our home," she said bitterly. Her gaze jerked to his, her eyes rounding at her sudden reference to their failed marriage.

So, he wasn't the only one who spoke without thinking.

He leaned across the little table, with its homey red-checkered pattern, and took her hand. It all looked so right, the image that haunted his dreams, them together at the kitchen table, his hand grasping hers.

But, nothing about the situation was right.

"I'm sorry, Cassie," he said, his voice coming from low in his chest, the knot in his throat making it hard to push the words out.

She nodded. "So, you've said."

She slowly pulled her hand from under his, reached for the chilly glass of ice tea and took a long gulp. Her throat worked to get the liquid down, as if he weren't the only one who'd felt the moment, felt how things might have been, should have been.

"Coulda, woulda, shoulda," he said as lightly as he could, in as joking a manner as he could muster.

She took another swallow, avoiding his gaze.

"Ah hell," he sighed. "Let's talk business."

She smiled weakly. "Let's."

"Can I see your raw video?"

She looked at him and shook her head. "You know the rules."

"Okay then, will you give me the number that your tipster call came from?"

Again, she shook her head, her face blank, expressionless.

"Cassie." He leaned forward, meeting her gaze with a softness that didn't speak of husbandly reproof, of any sort of a husband's right to complain about a wife's behavior that might get her killed. "I don't like the idea of you being out there, in that neighborhood, alone at night."

She blew out a gust of laughter, her face relaxing into normal lines. "I didn't like it particularly myself."

"So, who's your tipster?" He fixed her with a hard cop stare. "Who knows there's going to be a fire before the 9-1-1 call even comes in?"

She rubbed at a drop of moisture running down her glass.

"I don't know, Forrester," she said the words earnestly. "Wish I did."

"But, you won't give me the information that might help me find him."

"I don't think it will help." She looked him in the eye. "I called the number and it says it's not a valid number." She shrugged. "The person probably bought one of those little disposable phones, then tossed it afterwards."

"Maybe I can trace it to where it was bought." He tapped the table. "Get a video of the guy from some security camera."

She looked up at him. "You sure it's a guy?"

It was the first time he'd even thought about it. "Probably. Can't see a woman doing this."

She shrugged. "Don't rush to judgment, you always told me. Don't go into an investigation with preconceived notions that will bias your view."

Hell, he'd told her a lot. But, that she remembered?

Their eyes met with some of the connection they'd always had. They'd loved this back and forth, this talking stories and cases over, exchanging ideas.

A smart, hot woman, with a mind of her own.

A sizzling combination.

The idea of this woman at the beck and call of some

weirdo, summoned out to a dark, lonely street at night, scraped across his skin like a knife.

Cutting at his nerves, every instinct telling him this wasn't going to turn out well.

CHAPTER FIVE

Cassie looked across the table at the man she'd lived with, loved with, and broken up with.

She could read all the fears running through his head, all the worries for her safety. The same ones she'd had about him, knowing the danger he'd put himself into in his undercover work.

"Well, it's not really all that safe a job, when you get right down to it." Had she purposefully thrown his words back at him?

Was she enjoying being able to make him squirm a little bit, make him feel the gnawing pain she'd felt when she realized that all his lies hadn't been just to spare her some worry?

To keep the details of his undercover role on the down low.

Down low? She couldn't help laughing to herself over that choice of words.

Hell, yeah, she was enjoying him worrying just a bit, enjoying sticking it to him that she didn't need him, didn't need to consult with, or get his permission, or his approval on anything.

They were divorced, and he could just damn well get used to it.

Live with the consequences of his choices.

His eyes narrowed. As if he, too, were able to read her thoughts, the slightly mean thoughts running through her head.

Then, his expression leveled, returning to a professional gaze. Was it as hard for him to push back the personal as it was for her?

"Look Cassie, do you think we can work together on this case? I'll help you and you help me?"

She looked at him, weighing his words. "How can *you* help me, Forrester? Seems like I've got the inside track right now."

He nodded and sat back. "That could change, though. I could give you inside information about the results of the autopsy, the arson report."

He raised an eyebrow. "Inside contacts are invaluable to reporters, to beat the other guys with facts."

Now, look who was parroting who, repeating back her own words.

She should treat him just like any other police source, do the give and take that she would do with any other detective.

She nodded. "Agreed."

He stuck out his hand. For just a shake of the hand, like she might do with anybody else. This was business.

But, it didn't feel like just business.

That hand was waiting to be shaken. But the thought of the contact with him rattled her.

That hand that had touched her so intimately, brought such pleasure, such passion.

To think of it as just any other hand? That was something else. Something beyond her ability right now.

It was too early.

"You've got my word on it." She pushed back her chair, its legs scraping noisily on the floor as she stood up.

He raised an eyebrow, but pulled back his hand. "So, you'll let me see the video?"

She nodded. "I've got it downloaded to my computer."

"You'll give me a copy?"

"No." She shook her head hard. "You can subpoena it for court, if it becomes relevant. Otherwise, you can look at it here."

She wanted to just give him a copy, send him out the door, with all the pull he exerted on her. How much more self-restraint could she exert, resisting the attraction he still held for her?

But, she wasn't handing over her "notes", as her working video was called in a legal sense. If she did that, it could be argued she had no right to keep any of them out of his hands.

He and the department could demand all notes she'd taken on the story. Any story, in fact.

How many sources might be compromised that way? She couldn't just roll over for him. She had to maintain her professional ethics.

If a reporter became known as someone who couldn't be trusted, then they were done in this town, heck maybe in the whole business. Word tended to get around on that sort of thing.

She could feel him following her to the living room, his large frame taking up way too much space in her house. This new home had held no memories of him, no trace of his presence.

Now, it was as if he was dropping pheromones everywhere he went. She'd be able to detect his essence, breathe in traces of him once he was gone.

Once she was alone in this house. Again.

Oh, man. She sucked in a long breath and braced herself for sitting next to him on the couch, showing him her video.

She'd attached the computer to the television, so she could view a bigger image, could study it better.

Because she'd wondered herself if there were some hidden clues in it.

The thought of the councilwoman alone in that burning house. Had she been alive as the flames surrounded her?

Cassie had listened over and over to the video, wondering if could she detect screams through all the ruckus as fire consumed the house.

Was that a scream, she'd asked herself, rewinding the video again and again.

She was alone in that house with him. That man who was no longer her husband.

What were they doing in there for so long?

Scalding rage burned the inside of the punisher's eyelids, leaching out onto the punisher's skin. The punisher began rubbing at his skin, fingers curling into claws.

The reporter had been the messenger, delivering the news of the fires, of the deaths, the retribution.

Maybe she should become the message. That woman with her flaming red hair. Those locks would blend with the fire that would consume her.

The fire that would cleanse her.

Maybe before long, she'd become a clear message to the people of Atlanta—make the right choices, don't end up like the redheaded woman.

Perhaps the red-haired woman could still be led to the right path so she'd get a bit of a reprieve. For now.

She needed another example of what happened to wrongdoers.

A new victim was needed, a new person to pay the price for their evil choices. An example to show the world the righteous way.

To show the red-haired woman and other unchaste women the righteous way.

The thrill erupted, the thrill of punishing The Wicked.

Sliding away into the greenery of the nearby park, the punisher went looking for the next person who didn't live by the rules, who flaunted their evil choices in the face of good people.

The world needed the punisher. This society had gotten out of control, strayed away from the right path.

Someone had to bring them back to the way.

The punisher was merely the rod that brought the children back into line.

CHAPTER SIX

Peering out her window, Mary could see him slipping around in the shadows. The white boy's skin stood out against the inky blackness like the moon against the dark sky.

The mayor had been here yesterday, speaking on the corner of her street.

It had been the death of a powerful woman that had brought him out here. But, the mayor and anyone else who could make a difference had long ago forgotten about this street.

They'd forgotten about old women like her, with no power, no money, no one to speak for them at city hall.

She glanced at her television set. Yesterday, the face of the woman who gave the news had beamed from her TV, looking so sympathetic. So reassuring.

Would the news lady help an old woman like her?

She'd called 9-1-1 so many times the operators knew her by name. "Hello, Miss Mary, how are you tonight?" they'd ask. They'd think it was just another *scary something* out there on her lonely street that had her calling them.

"Yes ma'am, Miss Mary. We'll get a cruiser out

there to check it out," they would say, sweet and kind every time.

But, she knew they'd begun to put her low on the list of priorities, low on the list of the needs in this under-policed, over-crimed town.

She was just another scared and nervous old woman to them.

That was a good description of her. Cause, right now, she truly was a scared old woman.

That white boy didn't belong on her street. The only time white boys came down here was for something bad.

Looking for drugs, looking to sell something stolen, or looking for a girl who'd go off into one of these abandoned houses with them for the right price.

She saw that white boy sneaking around out there. He was going from house to house. But she couldn't see what was in his hand.

The way he slinked through the shadows, like his skin didn't stand out like a nightmarish print on her brain, told her he wasn't doing no good out there.

What was he up to?

Looking for something to steal?

He wouldn't find much of anything to steal at her place. The television was all she had left of any value, if the old set could be considered "of value."

Her daughter up in Tennessee had come to see her and had offered to buy her a new one. But, she'd said no. That would only bring the bad people round looking to get it.

Her old set didn't tempt nobody.

From a dark room in the back of her house, she pushed aside the curtains barely a whisper's worth. She felt more than heard, felt more than saw the white boy creeping round the back of her house.

Every nerve tensed as the white boy crept behind her home. She held her breath until he went on to the next house.

Then, he disappeared on down the block and was gone.

"Thank the Lord," she prayed out loud as she shuffled back to her living room, her soft slippers cushioning her almost eighty-year-old feet. Nothing cushioning her mind from the fear.

What would she have done if he'd broken in that back door? If he'd gotten the burglar bars open, he might have come in and killed her.

It would be too late when he realized there was nothing here for him to steal. She'd be dead and gone to meet her maker.

Her husband's photo sat by the couch, his reassuring face solid and dependable the way it had been for their fifty plus years of marriage. "Oh, lordy, Harold, I'd move out of here and go on up to Tennessee if your ghost wasn't here for me in this house, baby."

Fifty-three years, living here with him. She couldn't go and leave all those memories behind. As long as she was here, it was like he was just off in the next room.

And might walk in at any moment.

Sometimes she thought she heard him mumbling in the other room.

Like now.

Noises crackled from the back of the house. "That you, baby?" she called. "That my baby out there?"

She cackled an old woman's laugh, hearing the age in her own voice. How'd she ever get so old? Seemed like only last year, she was a young bride, happy in this house with her Harold.

Another noise came from the back of the house, like something breaking. Nervous apprehension crawled up her spine. It wasn't Harold out there.

Was someone trying to get in her back door?

If she called the police, they would take forever to get here. She couldn't call her daughter. Besides, she was way up in Tennessee. Asleep now, cause she had to get up early and go to work. "Lord, I just want to speak to another human being on the phone."

Sleep hadn't come to her cause images of the flames consuming that council lady just a few broken-down houses away popped into her head every time she closed her eyes.

9-1-1? No. They wouldn't believe the old lady who'd called wolf every time she saw a stray dog slink by.

She picked up the card the reporter lady had left on her front door, wedged into the burglar bars. The news lady's cell phone number was printed on the back.

Cell phone—that meant she'd have it with her always.

She took the phone receiver in her hand, holding it to her ear, listening to the dial tone. Would that reporter lady come out now if she said she wanted to talk?

It rang so many times that it went to voice mail. Then, she looked down where the news lady had printed her home phone number and dialed that number.

———

Cassie sat straight up in bed. She'd been in a warm,

safe place where she lay with her husband's arms around her.

Where'd she'd had everything that could protect her in life—youth, a good job with plenty of money, a husband, good looks. The police would come in moments if she called.

But, something had awakened her to this dark, lonely bed where she slept alone.

She peered through the dark at her closed bedroom door. Had the noise come from out there?

Was someone in her house?

Her heart beat at a breakneck pace. She listened, trying to hear over the blood pulsing in her ears.

Was that footsteps in her hallway?

She sucked in air, then held her breath to listen.

A brushing came from the back of her home. Was that someone sliding a window open, slipping in, coming for her?

She reached into the bedside table and pulled out her pistol.

Checking to see if it was ready, she loaded one bullet into the chamber. Now, she was ready.

Ready for anything that came through that door.

She swung her legs over the side of the bed and stood.

A little, blinking light on her phone flashed in the darkness.

Her phone. Of course. It had only been her phone.

A shaky laugh slipped from her lips, taking some of the fear with it. Her legs began to shake with a weakness that came after the panic. She sank onto the bed and waited a minute for her hands to stop quivering.

It had only been her phone. Set to vibrate, it had cut into her sleep, rattling on the nightstand. She'd been so tired, the vibrating sound of her phone hadn't registered in her mind.

Overreact much?

Yeah. But, thank God it had only been her phone.

She hit the button to wake it up and a missed call message popped up.

Then, she glanced at her home phone and saw a missed call there. She'd turned its ringer off as well. She checked her caller ID. The same number as on her cell phone. Harold Jackson?

She punched the recall button and waited. Would someone answer or had she missed a tip?

If she hadn't been so exhausted from yesterday's sleepless night, she would have heard the rattling of the cell phone. Sleeping the sleep of the dead. The expression sent a nervous shudder through her body.

Damn. Why had she set her phone to vibrate and silenced her home phone?

"Hello," a shaky, high voice quavered. The way Cassie's would have sounded if she'd called out to the person she'd thought was in her hallway. An old woman's voice.

"Hi. This is Cassie," she said. "I think you just called me."

"Miss Cassie," a woman croaked in a used-up voice. "This is Mary Jackson. I stay over by the fire you covered last night. You asked if I seen anything?"

Instantly, Cassie was wide awake. She looked at the clock. Three thirty. She'd gotten enough sleep. That was good, cause she probably wasn't getting any more tonight.

"What can I do for you, Miss Mary? Do think maybe you saw something you want to talk about?"

"I don't know how useful I might be. But, we can talk."

Something in the woman's voice sounded needy. Sounded like her granny had seemed at times, not wanting to ask for anything.

But, needing something.

"Do you want me to come over?" Cassie said. "I can come now."

"You wanna, sweetie?" The woman's thin, frail voice fairly begged for company.

"I'll be there in fifteen minutes."

"Okay, sugar. But, take your time. No need to hurry." *Come as quickly as you can*, her tone said.

That tone her granny's voice had gotten sometimes.

An instant pulse of guilt beat out from her heart. Hot moisture rushed to her eyes.

You did your best, sugar pie. You did your best, she heard her granny saying.

I don't want you 'membering me this way, with guilt, sweetie pie, a faint whisper echoed from the hallway.

Her loving, kind, forgiving granny wouldn't want Cassie to keep beating herself up for what had happened at the end.

You were young, living like the young do, building a career. Give yourself a break, the whispery voice rasped. Then, the sound faded away.

And all Cassie heard was a branch brushing against an outside window that led to her hallway. That was all the sound was.

Miss Mary needed her now. She could make up a

little bit for what she hadn't done for her granny by being there for this old woman. Had that been her granny she'd heard padding down the hallway, beckoning her to awaken for another old woman?

Hot, burning tears scalded her eyelids. She missed her granny so much. She blinked her eyes rapidly and pulled on some pants.

Harold Jackson, the caller ID had read.

Harold probably wasn't around anymore.

Otherwise, Miss Mary wouldn't be calling some strange, white lady reporter in the middle of the night.

A door opened, then closed with a crack. The punisher narrowed his eyes.

The streetlight illuminated that red hair, flaming into the night as she rushed to her car. In such a hurry to get somewhere.

Sliding the car into gear, the punisher readied to follow her. Far enough behind that she wouldn't notice, close enough not to lose her.

Where was she going at four in the morning?

A middle of the night booty call?

A flare of jealousy burned through his body.

He crawled through the night, his car slipping along in the darkness behind her, her rear lights pulling him on.

CHAPTER SEVEN

As she approached Mary Jackson's street, a sheen of orange shimmered in the nighttime sky, like undulating waves of death. She turned the corner and saw snakes of fire crawling from one broken-down house to the next.

Another fire ate at the houses on the same block where the fire had burned a city councilwoman's body nearly beyond recognition.

A shiver coursed through Cassie's body.

Someone had returned, demanding their presence be acknowledged.

But, she'd gotten no tip this time. Why?

She'd been given enough notice on the last two deadly fires to arrive on the scene before the fire fighters even.

Tonight, no call.

There'd been a similar fire with a female body found inside only weeks before. The police weren't saying it was connected to last night's fire but you had to wonder. Though starting a fire to cover up evidence in a murder wasn't unheard of.

It didn't necessarily mean they were connected.

Was there an arsonist-serial killer waiting out there

for her? She'd assumed before that a different tipster had texted each time. But, after both tips, no one had approached her to lay claim to the tip. Was the tipster even the same person? The arsonist himself?

A shudder wracked her body. Had he decided it was her time to die?

If it was a serial killer, it had to be a man.

Had to be.

The way he'd fixated on women.

Inky night surrounded her car. Was he lurking out there, waiting for her?

Burning alive? Pretty low on the list of how she wanted to go.

There was no moon tonight, and no street lights on this poor street.

But, the fire lit up the street like a fairgrounds on opening night, with sparkly, bright fireworks exploding with each crackling burst of flame. Several houses already burned like a fall festival of bonfires.

The fire line ran down the street to two houses beside the burned-out hulk from last night.

"Oh no," Cassie gasped, the words tearing from her throat like a jagged knife. It couldn't be. Miss Mary's house was also on fire. Miss Mary had just called her from that house.

A scream tore from her mouth, bouncing around in the car like the flames from house to house.

Cassie jumped from her car. Her gun. She needed her gun. She turned back for it and clasped it tightly between her two hands. She was ready for anyone who came at her out of the dark.

The fire blazed on her right, the blue-black night pulsed on her left.

Which was more terrifying? The visible danger on her right? Or the unseen, possible threats out there in that black landscape?

She gulped in a lungful of air then ran toward Miss Mary's house. Was the elderly woman still inside?

"Miss Mary," she called. "Miss Mary, where are you?"

The flames ate at the back of the house, chewing along the sides toward the front. The old woman's home would be but a snack for the monster that was already devouring the two houses before it.

"Miss Mary!" she screamed. "Miss Mary?"

Taking out her phone, she dialed 9-1-1. "There's a fire on Maple Street. Where the councilwoman's body was found in that fire last night. Do you know the one?"

"Are you calling from your house?" a voice said, dispassionately.

As if Cassie hadn't just reported something almost unbelievable. A second fire on the street where a homicide had taken place.

"No. I'm outside on the street."

"Okay, sugar. Is your house on fire?"

"No. But Mary Jackson's house is."

"Miss Mary's house?" The dispatcher's voice rose several octaves higher. "Is she out of her house?"

Oh, yeah, the dispatcher's voice had given up any pretense at professional self-control on that last question.

"I don't know," Cassie answered. "Are you calling the firemen?"

"Yes, dear, of course." Her voice regained the usual it's-all-in-a-day's-work tone. "Do you need an ambulance out there?"

"Get everything out here. Police, fire, EMTs." She gasped for air. "This is huge, several houses already, and it's still spreading."

"We will, dear," the woman's overly calm voice stated, as if to make up for the earlier emotional response. As if she knew these tapes might be used on a newscast later. "Can you stay on the line with me until they get there?"

The front door opened and Miss Mary stood there, in her housedress, her feet in slippers, her hair in a kerchief, and a five-alarm expression rounding her eyes.

The steel burglar bars of the front door caged Miss Mary in, as if holding her captive for the fire's consumption. The old woman rattled the doorknob, turning it uselessly. The bars were designed to keep danger out but firefighters warned that the wrong type of burglar bars could be as dangerous to homeowners as any home invader.

"No," Cassie said into the phone. "I can't stay on the line. Miss Mary's still in the house. I'm going to help her."

"Tell her to get out of the house," the dispatch operator said needlessly.

Cassie didn't take time to answer, but just hung up.

"Miss Mary, your house is on fire! You need to get out."

"I know, sweetie. I can see it. It's already coming in the back door. I need the keys to open this here burglar gate. But, they're in my purse, in my bedroom. I'm afeered to go back there. So much smoke back there."

The old lady's creaky voice quavered and she began

to cough. It sounded like she'd already breathed in a lot of smoke.

"Do you have another set of keys?"

Miss Mary's eyes watered, trying to push back the smoke. "My daughter in Tennessee took my last spare set. Said she'd get another set made for me but must have forgot. They weren't in the drawer." Her eyes narrowed and she darted looks past Cassie, her breathing quick and raspy.

"Are the firemen coming?"

"Yes, yes, they're coming," Cassie said, trying to sound reassuring. "Should be here any moment."

But, the fire's glow was showing down the hall, flickering against the walls. A crackling echoed from the back of the house.

Trails of smoke crawled along the ceiling, coming ahead of the flames. That smoke could kill as surely as the flames. Those deadly, toxic fumes could put a person down before their body was even touched by the fire's heat.

An image of the councilwoman's death flashed through Cassie's brain, shocking in its vividness. She could see her lying on the floor, with flames flickering all around her body.

Cassie prayed she'd passed out from the fumes. Of course, she had. *Please God, let her have passed out.*

Miss Mary gasped and Cassie looked into the old woman's eyes. She didn't deserve to die like this.

Neither the fire nor the smoke would get this frail, little old lady.

"We're getting you out, Miss Mary."

She grabbed the burglar bars and began shaking them, pulling at them. They barely budged. It looked like someone already had tried to wrench the bars apart. Probably some strong young man wanting to burglarize the place. If they couldn't get in, what were her chances?

Miss Mary gazed at her, hopelessness in her eyes, her lips working around her teeth.

"Oh, honey, you ain't gonna be able to pull them loose."

But, she had to get Miss Mary out. She had to. She looked desperately around. "Where are the firefighters?"

Miss Mary breathed a ragged seconding of that sentiment, "Uhuh, baby."

"I'm going to my car to get a something to wrench this open with. I'll be right back, Miss Mary."

"No, no, baby." Miss Mary reached through the burglar bars, her bony, old hands clutching at Cassie's shirt, her hands latching onto her like she was carrying away her final supply of oxygen. "Don't leave me."

Cassie gripped Miss Mary's hands tightly for a moment, willing her strength, trying to reassure her with her touch that she would save her, then pulled them free of her shirt. "I'll be right back."

Miss Mary turned toward the fire, her back against the burglar bars, as if facing her enemy.

"No, Miss Mary. Face this way, breath through the bars."

The old woman looked over her shoulder at Cassie, fear wracking her features, turning her into a wraith from Dante's Inferno. The seventh hell.

That was where whoever had done this needed to go, not Miss Mary.

But, as if unable to turn away from the danger, Miss

Mary looked back down the hallway at the approaching smoke, carrying death in its fumes.

Cassie pivoted and sprinted toward her car, popping the trunk as she ran, then she stuck her gun into her waistband. She clawed through the contents of the trunk until finally, she found the steel bar that went with the jack. "Oh, thank you, Jesus," she mumbled.

Then, she whirled and ran back toward the house, ran as she'd never run on her early morning jogs, ran as no race finish line could prompt her to do.

A house burning down around an old woman—a real finish line. Miss Mary's figure silhouetted dark against the flames licking at the walls of her living room. Miss Mary's life depended on her ability to wrench that burglar door open.

Sliding the steel tool into the burglar bars she began prying, trying to loosen the bars that held Miss Mary firmly captive in the inferno of her house.

"Oh Lord, help me," Miss Mary prayed. Over and over, repeating the words, "Help me, Lord, help me." As if she could no longer think, as if she'd already given over to the inevitable, now was just praying for quick admittance through the pearly gates.

It was a pitiful sound, an old woman praying to the God she counted on to save her.

"Give me strength, God," Cassie joined in the praying as she leaned her weight into the door. She groaned with the effort. "Help me, God," she turned the groan into a prayer.

Her muscles burned with the effort. Or was that the heat of the fire closing in on the front door? And Miss Mary.

"Lord, Jesus help us." Miss Mary grabbed the steel

bar, and pushed at it with her feeble old hands. Together, Cassie and the old woman struggled to win against the flames.

"Lord help us, God." Forrester pulled his car next to the curb.

Just behind Cassie's.

Flames consumed half the block, roaring and screaming into the night air. Where was Cassie?

He jumped out of his car, immediately pulling his gun. "Cassie? Cassie, where are you?"

Running along the street, he looked for any sign of her, for any sign of the person who had to have lured her here.

The buildings were going up like a firefighters' demonstration of what can happen if you're not careful.

Was Cassie inside one of those flaming infernos?

His mind almost exploded at the thought. The cracking and sparking of the fire-tormented houses made it hard to know if he'd missed Cassie's cries for help.

"Cassie!" he bellowed. "Cassie!"

"Over here." Through the roar of the fire, he heard a distant voice.

He pivoted toward it. Cassie stood silhouetted against a burning house.

The flames had topped the house and were set for a flashover. If that happened, she could be a flaming ember in a matter of moments since she was standing so close to the building.

"Get away from there," he yelled as he ran toward her.

"There's someone inside," she yelled, her voice sounding inhuman, with a desperation that said she knew how close to death that person was if they didn't get out right away.

Beyond Cassie, he saw a small woman inside the burning house, bent over, coughing.

Smoke billowed around Cassie and she coughed too. Still, she pushed at a bar that was wedged into burglar bars.

Damn those burglar bars! How many people had been held captive inside their own homes by protective barriers meant to keep them safe?

He bolted up the steps, holstered his weapon, then leaned into the bar, adding his strength to Cassie's. The bars began to creak, moaning in resistance.

Beyond Cassie, beyond the bent over figure of the old woman, the fire burst into a fury, scrambling up the walls.

"Oh, Lord!" the old woman shrieked, her voice mingling with the scream of the flames. She slid to the floor, instinctively knowing that was her last gap position before the fire and smoke would overtake her.

He wouldn't watch that old woman burn alive. He wouldn't.

With a superhuman strength, adrenaline coursing through him, he pushed against the steel bars with all his might. Pushed for everything he was worth. He wouldn't investigate this old woman's death tomorrow.

Wouldn't watch her die tonight.

With a desperate strength, he strained against the bar, feeling every muscle in his body exerting.

Until finally, finally, the wood splintered, and the constricting door broke away from the doorframe.

He squeezed into the gap, forcing the door open further with his body.

"Yes, thank you, thank you Lord," the old woman moaned.

Forrester leaned down, scooped her into his arms, and pulled her through the gap, away from the flames. Then he stumbled down the stairs, Cassie running beside him, trying to help support the woman's weight.

But, the woman was tiny, a little, bony woman encased in a housedress.

Behind them, the fire yelled in frustration, clawing through the front door toward them, determined to get its due.

He ran across the street, then collapsed to his knees, lowering the old woman to the ground.

"You okay, Miss Mary?" Cassie leaned down to look into the old woman's face. But, the old woman didn't look back at Cassie. Her gaze was on the house behind them.

The orange glow of her burning home reflected on her face.

"None of these houses were inhabited yesterday. Is that your understanding?" He looked into the old woman's face.

"Shouldn't ought to be." She shook her head. "Well, one of them used to be, had a fellow sort of camping out in there, but he told me he was moving on down to another area after the fire. Spooked him," Mary said in a raspy, smoked out voice.

"Do you have a hose?" he asked.

"No." She turned toward the flames, and Cassie's gaze followed hers. There wasn't much more they could do, so together the three of them watched the house burn, watched the doorway where they'd been only seconds before as it was consumed by a swirling wave of fire.

The old lady patted Cassie's hand, her other bird-thin hand reaching to Forrester's, patting it also. "I'm okay, children. I'm okay, because of you. And the Lord. He ain't ready for me yet. Got more for me to do down here."

Children? It had been a long time since anyone had referred to him that way. But, he looked at the old woman's face, and knew she'd lived long enough to call them children.

Cassie looked at him and smiled. The beauty the smile brought to her face made up for the fatigue that lined her hazel eyes, the lack of makeup, and the hair that hadn't been washed or "done".

She looked more beautiful than he'd ever seen her.

More beautiful than the night he'd first met her, seen her across the room and known he'd wanted her.

More beautiful than the first time they'd made love, with all the passion he'd seen in her eyes.

She was more beautiful than on their wedding day. When he'd thought they'd had a lifetime together.

More beautiful even than when he'd made love to her that night, the first night as husband and wife. And that was saying a heck of a lot.

The strength in her face and the joy of knowing she'd saved Miss Mary was transformative. That expression would make her beautiful at eighty, when she was as old as this frail old woman in her housedress.

God, he hoped to see Cassie's face then. Hoped to get back what he'd screwed up so royally.

But, those were thoughts for another day. Tonight was about the bastard who'd killed before, who'd tried to kill tonight.

He looked down the burning street. Had someone tried to lure Cassie out tonight to make her the next victim?

The hell if this woman would be anybody's victim.

He'd kill the person who tried to hurt her. Was the sick bastard out in the dark, plotting even now?

Angrier because he'd been denied his victim? Hell, his victims, if both Cassie and the old woman had been killed.

CHAPTER EIGHT

Firemen, cops and every type of investigator you could imagine filled the street. And on both sides of them, cushioned in around them like marshmallows, news trucks lined the curbs just outside the perimeter of the yellow tape, moving in as close as the cops would allow.

Cassie walked up beside Forrester, inside the yellow line for once, since she was part of the crime scene. She'd crossed the yellow crime scene tape to talk to her photographer and the reporter they'd sent out to cover the story.

He felt her presence there beside him in the early morning light. So right. It felt so right having her this close.

He wanted her closer. Damn it. Those thoughts just naturally followed whenever he was near her. When he wasn't near her. Hell, anytime. He really had it bad for his ex-wife.

"Did you follow me from my house?" Cassie turned to look at Forrester as if the thought had just occurred to her, her hazel eyes turning more of a green in the early morning light.

"No." He pivoted to meet her gaze. "Why would you ask me that?"

She shrugged, not meeting his eyes. She watched the investigators for a moment, then said weakly, "Someone followed me out of my neighborhood."

He reached for her shoulder, gripping it. "What?"

She pulled out from underneath his hand, stepping half a step away. Something that would never have happened before—before he'd been such a damned fool.

A prickling pain ran along his hand up into his body, as if a shard of glass had been stabbed into it. The distance between he and Cassie was filled with chilled air, no matter the simmering remnants of the fire's heat.

He concentrated on her words. Someone had followed her?

"Did you get a look at them?"

"I thought it was you, so I didn't really pay much attention. Thought you were watching me, gonna follow me if I got another tip."

"Someone followed you, and you didn't pay much attention? If you thought it was me, you should've called me."

"I was too pissed at your for following me to want to talk to you." She turned to meet his gaze, and a shock shot through him. The simple honesty in her eyes always shocked him.

For a man who'd spent so much time undercover, mingling with the type of people he was sent to infiltrate, a woman like her could fill him with awe.

A woman with no pretenses, who didn't put on airs, even if she was touted by one local magazine as the *sexiest woman on Atlanta television.*

Her no-nonsense earthiness always shocked his senses.

He flipped a lock of that red hair over her shoulder. Though he wanted to do more than that, wanted to touch her, wanted to feel her alive in his arms.

He wanted to take her home to his bed. For more than just sex.

More than anything, he wanted to ensure that she would be alive until they put this son of a bitch away for life.

"This bullshit is getting all too close to home for you, Red."

She didn't deny it, the corner of her mouth working, that tick she had when she was seriously bothered by something. She turned and began to pace.

When she finally looked back at him, her face scrunched up the way she did when she was thinking really hard, that corner of her mouth tensing and releasing as she bit at the inside of her lip. "How is burning Miss Mary out of her house connected to me? The tipster didn't call me. Miss Mary called me."

"She called you instead of 9-1-1?"

"No, no, no." she waved her hands. "She wanted to talk. When I got here, I saw the fire. I don't know if she called them, but I did as soon as I arrived."

He tilted his head. He'd try to make sense of that later.

"The firebug." She looked up at him. "I guess we can call him that now."

He tilted his head in acknowledgement of her logical conclusion, without exactly confirming it.

"The firebug didn't use his usual method. Unless I just interrupted him." Cassie's eyes held a million questions.

And a vital life force that he was determined to preserve.

He stepped closer. "I'm not sure this is the same person tonight as the other times," he said in a low voice, making certain it wouldn't carry to the other reporters and photographers staring hungrily at him and Cassie. "It's different than usual. The last two fires have been just one house. Just to cover up a murder, in my opinion."

"This." He waved his hand at the destroyed street block. "This is massive damage. The fire investigators haven't had a chance to search extensively. But, so far, no bodies."

She arched an eyebrow, her face scrunching, her mouth quivering as if she might burst into tears at any moment. "You forget about Miss Mary. She almost was a body."

He stepped forward, reaching for her, wanting to pull her into his arms and comfort her. Comfort himself?

But, she stepped back, straightening her face. "I'm okay. I'm okay."

She pointed a finger, like she was about to give a lecture. "Maybe the tipster isn't the firebug. Maybe this person doesn't kill someone, set a fire, then call me." Her expression faltered, a quiver around the mouth before she tightened it by latching onto the inside of it with her teeth.

"And maybe this isn't scary as hell." He pointed a finger back at her.

She looked at him. "Tonight could have been a copycat. The MO is different, as you said."

But, someone had followed her, driving behind her. For what reason?

"What are you doing out here in the middle of the night?" Her voice sharpened. "If you weren't following me here?"

"I wanted to see what the place looked like at night, wanted to get an eye on it the way it was when the crime occurred." He shrugged. "I went home and slept a while. When I woke up, I decided to come on out here. Couldn't get it off my mind that things might look different in the dark, that I might see something I'd missed."

And maybe a sixth sense had brought him here? "I just got the thought that I needed to scope the scene out tonight."

She laughed raggedly. "How right you were, eh?" Her eyes darkened, the color turning more of a honeyed brown. "Thank God you got here when you did, Forrester." She met his eyes for a long moment, emotion shivering in her gaze. "I don't think I ever could have gotten over it, if I'd had to watch that little old woman burn to death. Miss Mary." She said her name softly, reverently, as if a member of her own family.

Then, she shivered. "Like the witch burnings of old days."

"Like the witch burnings?" He narrowed his eyes.

She narrowed her eyes in a mirror image of him, the last flickering flames of the house mirrored in her pupils. "What? You getting an idea?"

"There's been two murders in the last few weeks." Should he say anything, take the risk of divulging too much? He had to, because it seemed this sick bastard was involving her. Her life could depend on knowing. "Just between us?"

71

She nodded, and he took a deep breath. "A few years back, there were a couple of prostitute murders. All found in burning buildings."

"What? You didn't say anything about this before." She stepped closer, putting her hand on his forearm. "You think they're connected?" Her voice rose several octaves higher in tone but she kept it quiet. "Oh, my God, like witch burnings. Like I said."

He looked down at her hand, and she quickly pulled it back, leaving a cold imprint on his arm.

"Don't know if they're connected." He shook his head. "No one ever got charged or arrested. The murders stopped. They were prostitutes, and the news quickly dropped them. But I didn't forget. They were strange."

"That's putting it mildly." She shivered again, wrapping her arms around herself.

A quick impulse to pull her close, chasing away the cold, keeping her safe, gripped him. God, he had to concentrate on the murders, the fires. Cause something told him, if he didn't, Cassie could be next.

That bastard would not take her.

"Strange? I'll know I've been in the business too long when that doesn't strike me strange," she said emphatically.

He smiled darkly. "The thing that was *strangest*?" He waited until she looked him in the eye. "They were fully clothed, and no sign of sexual assault or sexual contact."

"Hmm," she conceded, narrowing her eyes and turning toward the firefighters as they hit hotspots along the fire line. "That isn't what you would expect with dead prostitutes. Now, that's a dangerous profession, hooker. Makes news reporter seem plumb safe."

He didn't laugh. Cause he'd never liked the idea of her running out to meet just about anybody who called her and said they had a tip.

He wasn't laughing now, when she'd been alone on a street where a killer had walked just moments before.

No laughing matter at all.

Who had followed her when she left her house in the middle of the night? Someone was watching her. And, they knew where she lived.

———————

She looked around the street, which had become a busy enclave, with all sorts of professionals traipsing up and down.

Assistant district attorneys, firemen, arson investigators, every sort of journalist and cameraperson. A network crew was setting up shop down at the end, muscling in, trying to push the local crews back.

She ran her fingers through her hair, fluffing it.

"I've got to get home and get cleaned up," she said, not meeting Forrester's eyes. "I can't go on the air like this."

"What?" His eyes rounded with disbelief. "You're going in to work today? Surely they'll give you a day off, considering what you've been through."

She tried to work the kinks out of her neck, rolling her head around, shrugging her shoulders into the air.

"You don't want to take the day off," he said definitively, narrowing his eyes.

"What business is it of yours?" Her voice was sharper than she'd meant it. It was so wrong to speak to him like that, after what he'd done, coming to the rescue. Miss Mary would have burned if it hadn't been for him.

No doubt.

And, here she was snapping at him, like the divorce wasn't even final yet. They were a divorced couple. Time to get over it.

"Sorry," she said.

"It's okay." His tone was neutral and he didn't look at her. "You're right. It's not my personal business."

Then, he looked at her directly, a hard expression in his eyes as he said, "I'm speaking as a cop. This guy has fixated on you. The more times he sees you reporting on his fires, the more obsessed he'll get." He bit the words off as if he were speaking in a courtroom under cross-examination from the defense. She'd heard that tone from him before when a defense attorney asked him what he considered a stupid question meant to get some scumbag off the hook.

His words were scary, with the premise that the killer was out there watching her. But, you didn't get into this business if you scared easily.

She didn't scare easily.

She smiled at him, wanting to ease the bite from her earlier words. "The day I let this guy, or anybody who's not my boss, tell me how I can do my job, scare me into doing what they want, is the day they've won. I've got a job to do. My boss wants me on the set for the morning show. Then, the network wants me live after that."

His eyes flickered with something he wanted to say but held back. You weren't married to someone and not get where you could read them to some degree. Not even if his chosen profession had been as a liar. When he'd been undercover. Cause that was his real love.

"The network?" He licked his lips. "I thought you gave all that up. You thinking of going back?"

That rat race? She'd let her network job in New York keep her away from her granny for so many years.

"Hell no," she bit off. "Just doing a hit for their morning show. I'm a big hero reporter, saving a woman from a burning house. Surprised they haven't asked you to do a live shot for them yet."

"Oh, they've asked. Got a message from the police chief himself. I told him what I always tell him. I don't do TV. Or newspapers, for that matter." A leftover from his undercover days.

She laughed at him. "Not very politically savvy. You won't get to wear one of those white shirts if you don't play the media game."

She waggled her eyebrows. "Become a major, or a deputy chief? With the big paycheck and the ability to call the shots."

He gave her that sardonic grin she'd always liked so much when they were married, and leaned in. "Don't you know yet, darlin'? I don't ever plan to join the white shirt club."

The white shirts of the upper brass of Atlanta Police. The white shirt squad that Forrester and all his undercover gang loved to make fun of.

"They show dirt too easily, don't ya know?" Forrester said close to her ear.

She pulled back, away from that teasing breath of his brushing against her neck. "I'm heading home."

She waved at the police cars lining the street. "I gave them my full report. Now, I gotta get home and pretty myself up for the television cameras."

"I'll follow you," he said, without missing a beat.

"You'll do what?"

"You heard me. I'm gonna be your tail for a while until we get this guy."

"You are not." She tapped his chest with two fingers. "I can't do my job with a cop following me."

He looked down to where her fingers still touched his chest, and she pulled them back, feeling as if they'd been singed by the contact, feeling a heat crawling up her arm into her entire body.

"It's not stopping you, I'm thinking of," he growled in that low, sexy voice that reminded her of early mornings waking up to him in her bed. When he'd climb on top of her and sink into her.

Darn, don't go there.

"It's this weirdo who seems to be involving you in his drama," he said. His eyes dropped to half-mast, narrowing. Was that heat behind them, or intensity about the danger he was implying threatened her?

She couldn't have him tailing her. She looked at him hard, and narrowed her eyes back at him. "Well, we have security at the station for just this kind of situation."

He laughed darkly. "What? A killer who might follow you to the front gate?"

"No," she threw over her shoulder as she turned. "An obsessed-cop-ex-husband."

He arched an eyebrow at her as she whirled away. But out of her peripheral vision, she saw him go to his car. Ready to follow her?

"Damn, I do not need this." Her ex-husband hanging around. And with a good excuse for it, too.

CHAPTER NINE

Forrester slid his car along the curb in front of Cassie's house.

She swung those long legs onto the driveway and headed toward the front door. "Come on in." She motioned to him with two fingers.

He got out, and damn if he didn't follow his ex-wife into her new house. Two times in as many days.

The best smell in the world filled the living room. The smell of her. It lingered in the air.

Damn, he missed her scent. It had vanished from his place. His place that used to be *their* place.

A racket came from the kitchen, water running, the fridge door opening. "Making coffee!" she yelled.

He looked around the room. Hardly any personal touches. No photos of him, that was for damn sure. Why would there be?

Still, it bugged him that she'd so completely eradicated any sign of him from her life.

On a side table, there was a grouping of photos. He walked over and picked one up. He remembered it. Cassie had told him about that special day.

Cassie was only about six years old. Her granny had taken her to Stone Mountain Park. They'd ridden the gondola to the top and had an attendant take their photo.

Cassie was leaning against her granny's side and smiling like it was the happiest moment of her life.

Damn, the image of the two kicked his guilt in the gut, waking it up. Just damn.

A shuffling noise coming from the kitchen knocked him out of guilt land and he quickly set down the photo and turned before she emerged with two steaming cups.

She glanced toward the table, noting the slightly askew photo of her granny. She handed him a mug, then straightened the photo of her granny.

She turned without meeting his eyes.

"Feel free to watch the news, see what they're saying about this," she said as she passed by him then disappeared down the hall.

A door closed, then the shower began running. And so did his imagination. Imagining just how good she'd look in that shower. Wearing nothing.

And remembering when he would have gone in to join her. Hot sudsy water everywhere, and his hands following it all over her body.

"Damn it. Imaginations ought to have on-off switches." He grabbed the TV remote, hit the power button and covered up the shower sounds with a news anchor giving all the news that fit into the first seven minutes at the top of the news hour.

"In our noon show, we'll bring you our own hero reporter, Cassie Myers, telling what it was like to stand inches from roaring flames, fighting to save an elderly woman from her burning house."

"But, coming up, some special dogs get a new home," another anchor, a male, chirped cheerfully. As if they hadn't just been talking about someone almost burning alive.

"Eat up those Cheerios, kids," Forrester mimicked the tone. "And don't have nightmares about all of this."

Just then, the shower turned off. All his attention was immediately on that door, behind which she was naked and toweling off.

Before he could get hold of his imagination, Cassie padded down the hall, passing the living room doorway, wearing nothing but a towel.

"Just damn," he breathed under his breath.

"You want in the shower?" she yelled, almost as if in response to his muttered words. Was she enjoying this? Just a bit? Well, he'd certainly given her the right to enjoy punishing him. "I'm done," she added. "I can do the rest in my bedroom."

"I think I will," he yelled back. His skin felt crusty with sweat and a film of dirt. Being a hero was dirty work.

He walked into the bathroom. Steam swirled around the ceiling, and Cassie's scent was everywhere.

He pushed the door fully open and hit the fan to suck out the steam. And her scent. If only he could vacuum her out of his mind.

He yanked his shirt over his head, kicked off his shoes and unbuttoned his jeans, shimmying out of them. Then he slid off his briefs.

A noise from the hallway caught his attention. He looked up. Cassie walked past, still in a towel, a mug in her hand. As she passed the bathroom, she turned her head toward him. And met his eyes.

As he stood naked in her bathroom.

Her gaze did a quick once over of him, leaving a

trail of heat along his skin as if she'd touched him with her hand.

Her eyes met his, reading his reaction there, as surely as she must see it on his body. As his body reacted the way any guy would to a woman like her, nearly naked.

She averted her eyes, walking a bit faster than before.

"Sorry," she threw back. "Didn't mean to be caught looking."

"No problem." No problem at all.

But, that was his mind talking.

His body had a totally different reaction.

He flipped the water to cold and stepped in. "Yowser," he said as the needles of frigid water stabbed into his skin. "That's the ticket."

"What?" Cassie yelled from the living room. She turned down the audio on the television. "You want more coffee?"

"Yeah, keep it coming!" Cold showers and hot coffee. As the cold water tortured his body, his mind began working on overdrive, trying to process all that had happened the last week.

He couldn't help thinking these two dead bodies in burning buildings had something to do with those other two unsolved murders a few years back.

What was it about them that struck him as related? There had been almost a year between the last two.

Now, two in a week.

Had something set this guy off? Was he on a spree now, whereas before he'd taken longer to work up to killing the prostitutes?

Was this a serial killer? A serial killer and a firebug? Those didn't necessarily fit together.

Firebugs seemed to need the thrill of the roaring flames. Whereas serial killers, that was another whole level of evil.

What was he missing? How many lives would be lost if he didn't figure this out fast enough?

"Coffee," Cassie trilled, setting a fresh mug down on the bathroom sink.

"You're enjoying this, aren't you?" He looked around the curtain.

"Little bit." She smiled with an evil arch to her eyebrow. "Can't say I'm not. Since we're being honest and all."

Honest? Hell yeah, this was her version of payback.

She'd picked the perfect poison for him.

That walk down the hallway in a towel that had hit mid-thigh. Mid, well-toned thigh.

The woman knew what she was doing to him. Torturing him, letting him see all that he'd lost.

Due to his own stupidity.

"I'm an idiot, okay," he said, leaning out to get the coffee. "I admit it." Then, he leaned a bit farther, so that the curtain almost revealed more than was just *friendly*.

Her gaze slid down his stomach, across his abs, to the curtain that still hid the basics.

He grinned and reached for the curtain.

Just before he could whip it back, she pivoted and left the room.

The grin slipped from his face. She was definitely in charge in this area. If she wanted to tease, to taunt him with what he'd given up, she had that right.

Only thing was, she'd picked the perfect punishment for the crime.

As he wrapped a towel around his waist, he heard a blow dryer from the bedroom area. "You got any extra razors I can use?"

No answer. So, he flipped open the medicine cabinet. Toothbrush, toothpaste, extra toothbrush.

He moved aside a few hair product bottles. And there behind them was an unopened box of condoms.

Like a slap in the face. Saying she was on the market, all ready for any eventuality.

She was a free woman and could do what she wanted.

But, hell, he didn't need to see that reminder of what she might be doing with her new freedom.

"That's what you get for showering in your ex-wife's bathroom," he growled under his breath.

He slammed the cabinet shut and looked at his morning stubble. Maybe it was a look he could live with.

When he'd been undercover, a day-old beard was kid's play.

And he'd ended up looking through another woman's medicine cabinet.

While his wife had slept alone, innocent of just how dirty his life had gotten.

He'd had Cassie at home, the stuff of countless men's dreams. Sure, she'd already moved into another bedroom. He should have been working on getting her back. Instead, he'd chosen to sleep in another woman's bed.

Told himself his wife had technically ended the marriage. Had felt angry and justified, unappreciated.

He'd put his life on the line for *society's* benefit.

And that's how his wife had chosen to repay him.

She didn't *get* him, didn't *get* the job.

What a big baby he'd been.

Hadn't appreciated just what a prize he had in his wife. Once he'd gotten her, he'd taken her for granted. Going on longer and longer stints undercover. Wanting to be the guy who brought down Bones and the guy he worked for.

His hatred of Bones had become an all-consuming thing. Bones was the man who sold drugs, pimped out young women as sex slaves. And had caused the death of his buddy Weston's sister.

The hunt for Bones' conviction had taken over his life to the point he'd neglected his wife, leaving her lying alone in bed night after night. When they'd been virtually newlyweds.

He didn't deserve another chance. Not that she was about to give him one. And he couldn't even resent her for it.

He wouldn't have wanted his sister to give a guy another chance who'd treated her the way he'd treated Cassie.

"Ah hell." He snapped his shirt over his head, grabbed his shoes and walked out of the bathroom.

Cassie came out of her bedroom, her purse in hand, clicking across the wooden floors in high heels.

"Shut the door behind you when you leave, okay big guy? It locks automatically." Her face was closed, tight.

Almost as if her train of thought had gone on the same tracks as his.

He nodded. "Thanks for the coffee and the shower."

"No problem, big guy." She turned, pulling the front door behind her as she left.

And suddenly, the room that had felt warm and homey became empty, cold, bleak.

The way his house felt without her.

"Just damn," he cursed, taking a long swallow of coffee.

He picked up the remote and flipped the channels, stopping on one that had a reporter standing in front of the scene of the burned-out block.

Morning had fully broken, lighting the scene.

"I'm getting reports," the male reporter said, his face intense, his gaze seeming to come right through the TV set. "Reports that the elderly woman who lives in that house." He turned and pointed toward Miss Mary's house. "Saw something last night before the fire broke out. Sources say she saw a man lurking about. The same man she'd seen the evening the councilwoman was found dead a few doors down from her house."

"What the hell?" Forrester jumped to his feet. "Why are you telling the killer that? Do you want him to go to the hospital and finish that old lady off?"

Forrester flipped open his phone, hitting speed dial. "Hey," he said. "Do we have an officer outside Mary Jackson's hospital room? Good. Make sure one stays there until we figure out what to do with her."

He hung up. "Jesus. That guy's trying to get that old lady killed for sure." He glared at the television.

Then, he looked at the front door. He'd let Cassie walk out of here, with no one watching her.

It was daylight now. Still.

If the killer thought Miss Mary had seen him, he might think Cassie had seen him, too.

He tied his shoes then ran out the door, yanking it shut, checking to be sure it locked tightly.

CHAPTER TEN

Cassie turned left at the corner, instead of turning right toward the station. She felt a little bad about the head games she'd played on Forrester to give her a chance to give him the slip.

But, not all that bad. The guy deserved some payback.

And if she hadn't, there's no way she'd have been able to get out of that house without him on her like a second skin.

No reporter could fully do their job with a cop on their tail.

Dial a cop. That's what she needed. A cop on speed dial for when she needed him. Like last night when she hadn't been able to pry Miss Mary's burglar bars apart.

Forrester had come in handy. There were also a few other situations where she wouldn't mind calling him up for a bit of assistance.

If she could then send him on his way when she was done with him.

Like those nights when memories of the two of them heated her body with want and need.

They'd fit in bed like an advertisement for marital

bliss. She couldn't forget how he'd felt inside her. What they'd had had been wanton and hot.

Their heat for each other had been like a switch that got turned on just by the sight of one another.

So, yeah, she'd known what she was doing to him, trotting down the hall in that towel. Known it would send his head for a loop.

The glimpse she'd seen of him naked had done a number on her head too. She hadn't been with a man since they'd split up.

She'd bought a box of condoms with a sense of rebellion. Telling herself, she didn't need Forrester, that she was still young and attractive.

But, that box of condoms sat unopened in the cabinet.

She bet Forrester had his own box. And she doubted if it went unused. She felt her eyebrows furrowing into a ridge that would soon require Botox if she wanted to stay in the business of looking good on TV.

With a decided effort, she smoothed it out, running a finger across the area, just to be sure.

She turned the wheel, piloting herself to the meeting with Battalion Chief Hobbs. He had some theories he wanted to run by her.

She'd agreed to meet him. And she didn't need Forrester hanging around, listening in on every word.

Besides, Hobbs had said he had some ideas for where she could do her six o'clock live shot. An area of town where many homes sat abandoned.

Much like the neighborhood that had burned last night.

It would make a great live shot location, different

from everybody else that would be clustered around the burned-out buildings near Miss Mary's house.

She would intro her piece with a live shot saying, "Is this the next arson spot?"

The news director loved that sort of thing.

Take the average audience member where they wouldn't go themselves, into a different world where the criminals stalked.

"Good stuff," she hummed to herself. Her phone lit up with a text message. "Forrester," she glanced down at the name that came up. "Imagine you texting me," she said with a laugh.

She bet he would blow up her phone all morning long with messages or calls. She'd get back to him after the meeting with Hobbs. Hobbs had become a battalion chief pretty quickly. And she foresaw the day when he might get the top spot of fire chief of all Atlanta.

He knew how to court the media, get himself on TV by being helpful to reporters.

Media whore? Some of the photogs called him that.

"What's the most dangerous place in Atlanta?" JoJo joked. "Getting between Battalion Chief Hobbs and a television camera."

She couldn't help but laugh when JoJo had said it, but she wouldn't say that about Hobbs. At least not to his face. The guy was an invaluable source.

Finally, she turned her car onto a street that looked every bit as forlorn and rundown as Miss Mary's neighborhood.

A skinny dog dodged in and out of the bushes, stopping to nose a bag of discarded fast food wrappers. Broken beer bottles lined the curb as if someone had used them for target practice.

An unmarked SUV sat along the curb in front of the house where the chief said he'd meet her. Guess he was off duty, not in his work vehicle.

It was nice of him to offer to meet her anyway.

"Media whore," JoJo's voice chimed in her head. No. The guy was on the ball.

She parked, got out and walked up the sidewalk.

"Hey," Hobbs called from the doorway of the broken-down house. "Come on in."

The wooden front steps creaked and moaned underneath her feet. One step shifted, and she wobbled to the side. "Whoa, there." Hobbs stepped forward and stuck out a hand to grab hers, steadying her as she climbed the rest of the way to the front porch.

"Guess high heels weren't the best choice for this assignment," she said with a laugh.

"That's all right. That's why I'm here to help."

Even off duty, he looked polished. Recently shaven, his hair with a nice cut, and he wore a pair of black jeans with a collared cotton shirt. The guy was handsome in a not too polished way.

He could stop into a country club for breakfast and a chat with people who could help his career. Always camera ready. Handsome and genial. A guy on the way up.

Another firefighter walked around from the back of the house, the young man who'd arrived with Hobbs at the fire where they'd discovered the city council woman. He was in uniform, contrasting with Hobbs' off duty attire.

She nodded at him. "Hey."

Hobbs motioned at the firefighter. "This is Clayton

Randolph. He's a real up-and-comer, came from Tennessee to be a big city firefighter."

"Mornin' ma'am," Clayton said with a drawn out drawl that sounded like Elvis Presley. Did all the guys from Tennessee sound like Elvis?

She smiled and the guy gave her a winning smile back. Kinda like Hobbs with his charm. Was that what had caught Hobbs' interest in him?

He saw something of himself in the young firefighter?

"He's just trying to see what we can do to make some of these places fire-safe in the short term until we can get a better long-term plan."

Clayton walked on around the perimeter of the building. She couldn't help following the guy with her eyes. Good looking guy. Built like a guy who could throw you over his shoulder, drag you out of a burning building and then dazzle you with his smile, making you forget any inhaled smoke.

She looked back at Hobbs and found him grinning at her. "He's a good looking boy, huh? Would look good on television later on when he gets on up in the ranks."

She laughed. "Good looks are always a plus for the viewer." Hobbs did see something of himself in the new, young firefighter.

Hobbs smiled and waved her into the open front door.

She glanced around at what had once been a living room.

"Looks like somebody's living in here now," she noted. Empty cans of food littered a corner, along with some beer bottles. A sheet of tin blackened in the center seemed like a makeshift fire pit.

"That's the point," Hobbs said. "These old, empty houses are a haven for all sorts of shady activity. Encourages bums to move into the neighborhood."

He shrugged. "Then, when the few people left in the area go to work, these guys are right there to break in their houses. They hang around, looking for easy pickings. Good honest people who are just trying to get by don't have a chance."

He grimaced. "Don't mean to sound unfeeling toward the urban outdoorsmen, but I reserve my sympathy for the working poor who live out here, barely earning a living. And these bums take what little they have worked so hard to get."

"I know." She agreed with him to a point. Some of these homeless guys were military veterans who'd turned to the bottle after tours of duty, or guys who'd lost their grip on the lower rung of the economic ladder when times had gotten particularly hard.

Others had mental problems that had never been diagnosed or treated. Maybe just some medication could get them back on track in life.

Though she didn't say anything to contradict Hobbs, especially since he'd been nice enough to meet her at this location.

"What if I bring my photographer out after the noon show. Do you think you'd be able to do a walk through with us?"

"Sure." He half smiled. "You're going to be on set for the noon?"

"Yeah. They want a firsthand account of helping Miss Mary out of that house."

"Very heroic of you, saving her." Respect and

admiration shone from his eyes, as one lifesaver to another. "You were busting down doors, dragging people out, and you didn't even go to the academy."

"Oh, shucks, it was nothing." She flipped her hair dramatically over her shoulder.

He looked down at her for a long moment, something flickering in his eyes that wasn't exactly professional. And she remembered he'd seemed kind of sweet on her before she'd started dating Forrester. But, maybe that was just her ego talking.

Big time reporter with her big-time ego.

"What's in here?" She turned toward the back of the house.

"I don't know." His phone buzzed on his belt. "You can look around. See what you want to shoot video of later." He pulled his phone off his belt and began thumbing through it. "Be careful though."

She walked into the kitchen. More trash lay strewn across the floor. Someone had been hanging out in here as well. Maybe they moved from room to room as one room became too littered for their comfort.

She stopped and listened. None of the normal sounds of a neighborhood reached her ears. She looked out the back window and saw overgrown weeds, tangled vines reaching out from the woods that backed up to the house.

The area wasn't that far from being able to declare itself a wildlife sanctuary.

But, it was the quiet that got to her.

This neighborhood should have been kept up, had families with kids and dogs, baseball games on the front yards.

Instead, there was eerie silence, a quiet just waiting

to be filled up with screams. From this building, as the house burned down around a victim?

The image erupted so strongly in her mind that she jumped when a noise came from the doorway. She spun around.

Clayton stood there. He'd come in from the open back door and she hadn't even noticed. He'd walked in as quiet as a stray cat slinking through the weeds.

He looked at her, stared actually. This time, she didn't feel the slight attraction she'd felt when she'd first met him. This time, his expression sent shivers creeping up her skin.

He just stared at her, his expression blank. Then, as if painting it on his face, he smiled that charismatic smile that he'd first given her minutes earlier. His gaze moved past her.

Cassie turned to follow his gaze toward the door coming from the living room. The chief stood there, looking back and forth between her and Clayton.

"Sorry if I startled you guys." He gave one of his TV-ready smiles. "Listen, we're gonna have to leave. You 'bout done here? Got enough of a look-see that you'll know if you want to come back?"

She looked over her shoulder as Clayton disappeared out the back door, then back at Hobbs. "Oh, I'm definitely coming back. What time can you meet us out here?"

He tilted his head. "My day has just gone into flux. Don't know if I'm able to get back until later this afternoon. What's your absolute deadline?"

"Well, we have the video from the other night's fire. My photog can come on out while I'm doing the noon show on set, get some video here. Then, we just need some sound. If you don't make it in time, we'll just use some neighbors from around here."

"Questions like, does it make you nervous with these abandoned homes in your area? Do you want to see these vacant homes cleaned up? That sort of thing."

He looked distracted, barely listening. "Emm, hmm. Sounds good. Three o'clock too late?"

"Perfect," she said, turning to walk out with him. Suddenly, she didn't want to be alone in this house. She was leaving when he and Clayton did.

"Anything you can tell me about what's going on with the investigation into the fires?" She looked at his phone. "That text you just got?"

"Oh, there's always something going on when incidents as big as these happen. We're waiting for reports from the medical examiner. That sort of thing."

He seemed distracted. That was to be expected. The guy probably was thinking nonstop about the fires. Like her. Last night, she'd hardly been able to sleep. Just remembering the first fire over and over.

When she did sleep, she'd awakened feeling like she'd been working all night long, processing her memories in her dreams.

Then, before she could get a good night's sleep, she'd been at the second fire.

With Miss Mary standing in the doorway like a wraith from hell.

A shiver ran through her, imagining what would have happened if Forrester hadn't arrived just when he had.

Hobbs glanced at her as if the shiver had been visible. He reached for her car door, pulling it open for her when she hit the unlock button. "You be careful, girlie. Don't be out in any of these neighborhoods by yourself. Especially not at night."

He arched an eyebrow.

She got into her car before looking up and smiling at him. "I won't."

He started to close the door, but then stopped, still holding the door open, and leaned slightly in through the open door, getting into her space.

Something about his expression said he might just lean in further. A queasy shiver ran through her. As she looked up at him, she suddenly wondered about his ready availability for her.

Was the attraction still there for him? Even though he was married now.

Though a marriage certificate didn't always buy fidelity. She and Forrester were the living example of that.

His gaze locked onto hers and he tilted his head. "You and Forrester were out there together at the fire scene this morning. And you left together." His eyes strayed toward her body, taking the scenic route back up to her face.

He was a married man. This was disgusting.

He raised an eyebrow. "None of my business, of course. But you two crazy kids getting back together?"

It sounded light, the way he said it. But, underneath, a deeper emotion pulsed. It was just a vague feeling. But, it felt like he was asking for reasons other than just a casual curiosity.

It felt almost like he was asking to find out if she was available.

Was she?

Of course she was. But did she want to admit that to a married man?

A little kick of irritation hit her that he'd even make her have to ask that of herself and she reached for the door. But he held onto it with just enough power in his grip that she couldn't pull it closed.

And for the first time, she felt a queasy bit of discomfort with him.

Something said, don't cross this man while you're all the way out here alone.

With nobody to call to for help if she needed it.

That was ridiculous, though. Clayton was just ahead in the chief's car. If she screamed, he'd come to her rescue.

Or would he look the other way, afraid to cross his boss, the man who held his future in his hands?

Clayton stared straight ahead.

A little dig of anger hit her and she looked pointedly down at Hobbs' hand on the door. A long scratch mark slid like a red beacon across the top of his hand down to his ring finger. His wedding ring was missing.

Had he removed it cause he planned to hit on her?

She looked up at him from underneath her eyelashes. Was he offering her a quick hookup, something on the side that his wife didn't need to know about?

Revulsion filled her and she was glad she'd only had coffee. Her stomach roiled at the idea that he'd thought she might even consider something like that.

With a quick motion, Hobbs stepped back and shoved the door shut. "Like I said, none of my business. Forget I asked."

He flashed that killer smile. But, this time, it didn't

work on her. The fact that he'd thought he could hit on her, though he was married, ticked her off.

Surely, he'd heard through the grapevine the details of her and Forrester's breakup. Why would he think she'd ever be the other woman?

She hit the lock button, turned the key in the ignition, then smiled up at him again with her best professional smile. The one she gave to every guy who hit on her on the job.

Attorneys or bums, she always gave them that same smile. That TV-ready smile.

Hobbs didn't have to come all the way out here to help her with her story. He probably had a score of reporters calling him up for sound bites. But, he'd agreed to meet her. She lowered the window.

"Thanks again, chief," she said.

"Oh, it's back to chief. That's what I get." He laughed, with a jovial sound, looking again like the guy she was used to seeing at scenes in the middle of the night.

He waved and turned toward his car.

Her phone lit up with a call from Forrester. She put her car in gear and eased away from the curb, then hit the connect button for the blue tooth speaker mounted in her car.

"Where are you?"

"Always good to hear from my ex-husband," she said lightly, looking into her rearview mirror as Hobbs got into his SUV.

"I'm at your TV station," Forrester said, his voice low in his throat, the voice he'd used when they were in an argument and he was purposefully not raising his voice. "A producer called down to the front gate and says she has no idea where you are."

She turned right, heading back the way she'd come. "That's the standard information they're told to tell all exes. Basically, nothing."

"I got that," he said dryly. "Listen." He hesitated for a long moment. "Miss Mary's gone missing from the hospital."

"I thought she was being watched." An alert screamed through her body.

"She was."

She could almost feel his frustrated shrug through the phone.

CHAPTER ELEVEN

Cassie was standing in front of the camera, ready to go live for the noon show when her phone started blowing up. She could see the light going on and off as it sat in the door of the live truck where she'd put it so the vibrations wouldn't distract her while she was live. Somebody always thought it was a good idea to call her on a non-related matter exactly when she was talking live on the air. Look at the monitors, she always wanted to say, I'm on the air.

"Can you answer my phone and tell me what they're saying." She nodded to JoJo while she continued looking over her lead in.

JoJo turned toward her phone, but his own phone buzzed on his hip. He answered it, then his eyes shot to her face. He hung up and tossed her phone at her. "Call the station," he said. "We're leaving."

He disconnected the cable from his camera to the live truck.

"Leaving? You've got to be kidding. We're the lead in the show."

"Not anymore." JoJo shook his head, taking his camera off the tripod and stowing it in the live truck.

"Hello." Cassie hit the connect button when it began lighting up with the station's number.

She listened for a second then hung up. "I got your sticks," she said to JoJo. She lowered the legs and stuck the tripod in the truck.

Then, she turned to unplug the lights, unplug the microphone and begin rolling up the audio cables while JoJo turned the microwave mast to lower it.

Neither she nor JoJo spoke until the truck was broken down, and they were in the front seats. While JoJo had rolled up the long cable that connected the truck to the camera and microphones, she'd programmed the address into the GPS, as well as looked up the address in the map book.

JoJo was old school and liked to look at maps. But, the GPS was useful once they started winding into complicated neighborhoods.

JoJo climbed in his side of the live truck and immediately picked up the map book she'd left open to the right page. "Right there," she pointed, then turned to her phone.

JoJo glanced at the page. He knew this town like the back of his hand, and only needed a second to get his bearings before he peeled out like a cop. The ungainly live truck roared and rumbled away from the curb.

She called up the station's website on her phone, and began reading what the station was putting out there. Then, she read the wire stories they'd forwarded to her phone.

Only then, as she was dialing numbers, trying to check contacts, did she give JoJo a sideways glance.

"I know, girl, it's big," he drawled. "Big."

"God, please don't let Miss Mary be in that house."

Another fire in an abandoned house. And Miss Mary had gone missing from the hospital. Would the firefighters find a body when they got inside?

Would it be Miss Mary?

———————

Forrester walked to where they'd found the body. Slowly, almost not wanting to see, he forced himself to look down at the female figure that the firefighters had found huddled in the smoking ruins of the structure.

Duct tape had bound her wrists and her ankles. The EMS guys had cut it loose and tried to work her for a bit, before they realized there was no saving this woman. She'd been dead too long. Then, they'd retreated, leaving her for the homicide squad.

It looked like she'd originally lain on her side, because the left side of her body was blackened from soot. Something covered her head. The EMS guys had probably replaced the cloth, as a sign of respect, he guessed. No matter how many times you dealt with something like this, you were still human.

In these instances, humans had a tendency to act with compassion, wanting to give the dead their dignity. Or maybe they'd just wanted to put her back the way they'd found her for the investigation.

The figure seemed to be a black woman. It didn't look like the fire had actually gotten to her, just the smoke. The deadly smoke.

This woman looked larger than Miss Mary, the slight, little woman who'd felt like a child as he'd carried her in his arms away from the fire scene this morning.

But, he could be wrong. It could be her.

He sucked in a breath, bracing himself, then gingerly, with gloved hands, he pulled back the damp cloth that hid her face.

A shockwave shot throughout his entire body. Seeing a dead face was always bad. But seeing a dead face you knew?

"Is it Mary Jackson?" Preston Hobbs asked. He'd apparently come up behind him.

"No." Forrester looked up at him, turning away from the sad image of the woman's face in death. So pretty before. "It's that radio personality, the one who was in the news lately."

Hobbs looked at him blankly.

"They said she broke up that football player's marriage. Got involved with the quarterback from the Falcons, and his wife went public with all the gory details."

"What was her name?" Hobbs pulled out his phone.

"Stephanie something." She didn't look anything now like she'd looked in all those glamour shots plastered on billboards and then later on the news at the time of the scandal.

"Stephanie Green," he remembered.

"That's right." Hobbs leaned forward. "Damn, I hate to see a beautiful woman end up this way."

"It's better if they're ugly?" Forrester asked the required question, the only reply any man who'd ever been married knew to ask.

"Don't go all politically correct on me, dude." Hobbs shook his head. "This is just a damn waste."

"Yeah. I met her at the heroes awards last year. She sat at one of the tables of honorees." Forrester looked down at the once beautiful face now contorted in terror and had to agree. "Real nice. Funny. And down to earth, the way she just sat there jawing and laughing with that cop who took a bullet at that SWAT standoff. Man, what a waste."

Then, he looked up through the charred bones of the building and saw Cassie standing behind the yellow tape with the other reporters and camera people. And he was ticked off all over again that she'd given him the slip this morning.

She'd done it on purpose.

But why? Did she have a death wish? Her own personal police escort ought to sound pretty good when notable women were showing up dead.

A shiver of apprehension crept down his spine.

A reporter had ended up dead. Well, not a reporter exactly. This woman was more of a radio celebrity.

Still, it hit too close to home, too similar to Cassie. Suddenly, his mind went to a strange place, suggesting things that might have nothing to do with reality.

Was there any connection between the women who'd shown up dead in burned-out buildings and Cassie?

The way she kept getting to the scenes before anyone else.

Was Cassie on this guy's hit list? Or just the pretty reporter the monster liked to see at scenes?

He scanned the cluster of people that lined the streets, looking for a face he might have seen at one of the other fire scenes. Was he out there now in the crowd? Watching the devastation he'd caused?

Or hidden further away, leering out from a wooded area or another broken-down, decaying building.

Hobbs followed his gaze toward the reporters lined

up behind the yellow tape, their bodies pulsing against it, as if at any moment they might rush forward with their microphones and their questions. "What are we going to tell them?" Hobbs growled, cause he knew as well as Forrester that they had to feed the news beast something to assuage its endless hunger.

A hungry beast was a mean beast, as the saying went. And you sure as hell didn't want a starving pack of news people snapping at your heels. They had to give them just enough to fill their gap for the next newscast, to keep the people at the station who snapped the whip satisfied.

A snarling bunch of hungry lions. But, hell, they were just doing their job. Like him, he guessed. The people of Atlanta would also be howling for information on who was killing women and dumping their bodies into burning houses. Or leaving them there alive. Which was much more horrifying.

"Hell if I know what to tell the news people," Forrester said. "We have to notify the next of kin before we tell them anything about who this is." He looked at Hobbs. "Is that guy who had the affair with her the next of kin now?"

Hobbs shrugged. "Hell if I know," he mimicked Forrester's previous comment. "Guess we need to call the radio station to find out." He turned away, motioning for the medical examiner to come on in. "Sometimes this job really sucks." He glanced back at Forrester.

Forrester met his gaze and nodded. "Can't all be like this morning, I guess, pulling people out of burning buildings."

"Yeah, that old lady definitely didn't deserve to die."

Hobbs blew out a puff of air. "Little old lady just trying to survive in what's left of her neighborhood. Those bums moving into those vacant houses, starting fires. Punks breaking into homes. She was purely innocent."

Forrester knew what he was trying to say, even if it didn't come out exactly right. A huge percent of the people who got prematurely and nefariously dead in Atlanta were involved in something that got them dead. A scorned lover, a drug deal gone bad, or someone breaking into a drug dealer's house to steal his drugs, his guns or his money.

Very few people got dead without knowing the reason why.

"You think it was her lover who killed her?" Hobbs nodded with his head toward the body.

"I'd say that's the first person to start looking at," Forrester conceded. "Or an ex-lover who's ticked off she cheated on him with her married lover."

"Maybe a copycat murder?" Hobbs said. "Just a plain, old-fashioned love triangle they're trying to pass off as the work of a serial killer?"

Yeah, they'd both been in the business long enough to know the score. When an ordinary person died, someone not in the criminal business, it was usually the ex or soon to be ex. It's always the boyfriend or husband, the gospel went, even if you can't prove it.

Forrester turned to look back at the gaggle of news people. At least it wasn't Cassie. "Just damn."

"Yeah, just damn," Hobbs agreed.

Forrester's pulse began slowing from the all out sprint it had hit when he'd first gotten the call. He'd never been so freaked in his life. Something inside of him had said it was going to be Cassie this time.

He didn't know why he thought that. But, his gut had pumped that message to his brain.

Thank God he'd been wrong.

He turned away from Hobbs and walked a few steps, pulling out his phone.

"Call me before you leave here tonight," he texted Cassie. He started to hit send, then added, "Please." Cause she was his ex-wife, not his kid. Something he was certain she'd point out, if he didn't remember it himself.

Touchy working with an ex.

But, everything inside of him said this investigation was moving closer and closer to her all the time.

CHAPTER TWELVE

Forrester's soulful eyes reproached her without his ever saying a word.

"I don't feel bad about giving you the slip this morning so that I could do my job," she stated flatly.

He didn't say anything so she found herself continuing to talk, words just pouring out of her mouth.

"We may have taken a vow of absolute honesty." She paced across her living room floor, which seemed to have become their usual convening spot. "But, I never took an oath to tell the truth, the whole truth, and nothing but the truth, so help me God."

He half smiled at her imitation of the courtroom oath then stood and walked to within a foot of her. His voice was low when he said, "I'm not mad, Cassie. I'm worried."

He met her eyes with a level gaze. "I'm worried about your safety."

Oh heck, he had to go all nice guy on her?

"Not everyone wants to be seen talking to a reporter, Forrester." She rounded her eyes like he ought to understand, since he'd been married to a reporter.

"I get that. We both have to do our jobs." His voice was matter of fact.

"Exactly."

He kept his gaze on her, running over her face, as if assessing her temperature. Gauging his words for their best effect? "How 'bout we agree to tell each other when we need space. Then, check in within a certain amount of time?"

"Are you using the royal *we*, really meaning me?" She pointed her finger at her own chest.

He kept his gaze trained on her, his eyes going all cop, watching, noting her reaction, assessing her for lies.

Why was he getting so obsessive?

"This isn't like you, Forrester." He'd always worried about her, but kinda laughed off the danger, saying he trusted her common sense.

"Don't you still trust my judgment, Forrest?"

He met her eyes with a hard, direct gaze. "Sure, I do, Red. Under ordinary circumstances."

"There are no ordinary circumstances in news, Forrest. Kinda like working undercover."

His eyes skirted away. He turned toward the couch, taking a step, leaning over for the remote. He turned on the television, then changed the channel to a competing station.

He knew she liked to keep an eye on the competition. Said if it was on her station, she'd already know it.

He watched for a second, then muted the sound.

Man. She hadn't meant the undercover comment to sound like it did. As if she were reproaching him.

She leaned forward and caught his sleeve.

His eyes went sideways to where her hand held his shirt, almost touching his skin.

She dropped the contact and stepped away. Suddenly, she was ticked off. Here he was in her living room again, breathing her air, putting his opinions onto her life.

They were divorced. Yet, here he was in her house. Again.

As if having him take a shower here this morning wasn't hard enough on her conviction to keep him out of her life.

Suddenly, the thought occurred to her.

She turned, surveying him from across the room. Was this another one of his self-serving scams?

She jabbed a finger at him. "You say you're afraid for me. Ooooh, it's all so scary, Red." She waved her hands in the air.

He didn't grin, didn't respond, just waited. Cause he had to know there'd be more. And there was.

"How come this reminds me of every time I've heard you tell a lie before?"

His right eyebrow arched. "I'm not gonna ever lie to you again, Cassie."

"No matter what?"

That eyebrow worked itself hard trying to get higher. But, it was okay, cause she got the message. He was expressing self-righteous indignation. As if he had a right to it.

As if she'd really affronted him this time, hurt his feelings.

"I think you're biologically incapable of telling the truth." There. She'd said it.

"I'm what?"

This confrontation had been a long time coming. She'd agreed to be friends, pretended to sort'a accept his stupid vow that, he'd "never lie to her again."

Those were words to live by for liars, drunks, gambling addicted people. Anyone with a problem, always vowed to "never do it again."

When their lives had fallen apart, they'd reached their lowest point, and then they'd started up the other side of the ditch.

She'd be crazy to go back into that whirling maelstrom of paranoia and doubt that life with him had become. Crazy. And she wasn't crazy. She took a deep breath.

"I think lies have become an intrinsic part of who you are. Telling lies, prevaricating, bending the truth, just a little white one." She held her hands up like a scale, weighing the difference.

"You worked so long undercover that lying became a part of your nature." She shook her head. "Sometimes, I wonder if you even recognize when you're lying."

His jaw tightened, and his mouth began straining as if he was struggling to hold back a string of curses. They were probably chewing at the inside of his mouth to get out. Cause he could really let some loose when he wanted to.

"Go ahead, let it out, Forrester. Cuss if you want." She stepped closer. "It won't offend me, cause at least it will be an honest expression of your true feelings."

"An expression of my true feelings?" He stepped forward, taking her shirt, fisting it gently in two hands. "You want my true feelings? Okay, then."

It became a struggle to breathe. Not from his hands clutching at the front of her shirt, but at how near he was to her. His hands there, in the material of her clothing, reminded her of other times when he'd stripped her bare.

Literally and figuratively.

Undressing her slowly, touching her all over until she'd quivered.

She couldn't take this now. Not while some crazed firebug was setting buildings on fire around women.

A killer was stalking Atlanta. Her senses were already on overdrive.

"What is the truth, Forrester?" She took the front of her shirt and slowly pulled it out of his grasp.

He let the material slip through his fingers, all the time looking down at her chest as the cloth released itself from his grip.

Then, he looked into her eyes. His gaze heated, simmering with memories of the hot stew of their past, the nights spent swirling in each other's arms, their skin heating to the point of almost spontaneous combustion.

His lids lowered as if the heat was consuming him now, his mouth opened. And a bunch of honeyed words hovered just on the tip of his tongue?

She didn't give him time to roll out some of his sweet talk. He'd never had a problem with that. Only with the truth.

"Was it the truth when you told your mother we'd just gotten married, that time we met them for dinner?"

His jaw clenched and he looked away from her. She'd hit home.

"You acted like our elopement was a spur of the moment thing that had just happened the week before."

She shook her head, leaning in an inch or two to try and make eye contact. But, no luck on that. The guy knew the first rule of lying to her was not to make direct eye contact when he lied. "You lied straight to your mama's face, Forrester. Who does that?"

"Furthermore," she felt herself getting worked up, ramping up to a good rant, "she couldn't look at you and tell."

His eyes flashed with recrimination and pain. As if he had a right to it.

The hell with that. This was about honesty and finally getting it off her chest.

She turned her back to him and began to pace, ignoring the hurt that still lingered in his eyes. Because she'd been hurt too. By his lies.

"I'd like to think that if I had a son," she said, "that when he was grown, I'd be able to look into his eyes and know what the truth was."

She pivoted back toward him. "You lied to your own mama, Forrester. What does that say about your chances of ever being honest with me?"

He'd practiced lying to women on his own mother, perhaps from birth.

He walked to the couch and collapsed onto it. He leaned forward, took the glass of ice tea she'd brought him.

He tilted the glass up and let the cold liquid run down his throat.

She watched as his Adam's apple moved as he swallowed.

Nothing 'bout him didn't do something for her, she paraphrased the county song in her own head.

But, that'd never been their problem, so don't even go there, she reminded herself.

"I lied to spare my mama's feelings," he said as if he

believed it, setting the wet glass down hard on a coaster on her coffee table.

"You lied to prevent her knowing you didn't even tell her we'd gotten married until months after the fact." She tried to meet his eyes but he looked away, running his hand over the wetness on the outside of the glass.

"You lied to her to keep her off your back."

He shook his head and looked up, meeting her eyes with an intensity that said this conversation was pushing a lot of his buttons. "It was to spare her feelings," he said slowly, separating each word distinctly.

A red pulse of rage shot through her. Just like he'd lied to spare her feelings?

"I guess when you didn't want me to know you'd slept with that bartender, it was just to spare my feelings."

She'd gone right back to that night, the feelings erupting from the back of her mind where she'd pushed them. She usually tried not to think of that night when he hadn't come home, when he'd lied saying he had to work undercover.

Lied and slept in another woman's bed.

Do not visualize it, she said to herself. But, the woman's face flashed fully into Cassie's mind, a bartender at Miguel's, the cops and media hangout, a beautiful, spirited, funny woman.

A roaring anger filled her as the image fully erupted in her mind of Forrester making love to that woman, followed by the usual chaser emotion, the urge to slap his stupid face. She pivoted away.

Forrester stood quickly, stepping in front of her.

He'd anticipated rightly that she was about to slam out the front door.

"Get out of my way," she said quietly. She would not go back there, to the yelling that did nothing to erase the anger, the hurt.

She was not going back there.

"The weekend we got married," he said with a voice that came from deep in his chest. "My mother was in rehab."

Rehab? He'd never said anything about his mother and rehab.

He dragged in a ragged breath. "And not for the first time." He laughed harshly, with a sound that had nothing to do with humor.

He turned and collapsed onto the couch. "The million man march? That was my family trucking back and forth to rehab."

"Forrester?" She sank down onto the opposite side of the couch, her anger ebbing away with the shock. "You never said anything about that before."

He looked at her wryly. "Would you have?"

She just waited, afraid if she said too much that he'd shut down.

"Undercover?" He laughed darkly. "I was born for undercover work, trained as a child for it. My whole life was one undercover operation."

He glanced at her, black smoke filtering through his eyes, the kind that could kill. "Forrester is a pretty classy name, huh?"

He picked up his mostly empty glass and toasted the air, the ice tinkling along with his next words. "Sounds like the kind of kid whose parents hang out at country clubs. Can you believe kids at school used to actually make fun of me, say I was putting on airs with how high class I thought I was?"

"I never set them straight." He laughed harshly, his voice sounding like he'd breathed in a lot of smoke, gravelly, ragged. "Anything to keep them from knowing the truth. Red, my parents used to be drunk on their asses by six o'clock Friday night. They'd drink and brawl all weekend long."

Pain flashed in his eyes and suddenly, she could see him as the little boy he'd been. Those sweet eyes, chocolate colored hair flopping down over his forehead. The photographs of him as a kid never revealed he'd had to deal with adult-sized pain.

He waggled his hand. "By Monday morning, they'd get it together enough to go to work. One of them was always getting on the wagon, giving up the booze."

He eyes narrowed and he nodded knowingly. "Then, the fun would really begin. One or the other would sneak around, having me lie for them. Heck, my mother used to have me go pick up booze for her from her "guy" down at the liquor store, bring it home and hide it so that as soon as my dad left for AA, she could start drinking. Said she liked to go it her own, didn't need no groups."

His parents didn't talk like that but she thought it was ironic that he suddenly started pretending they were low class. As if he considered their behavior as such and thus put that kind of grammar on them.

"Vodka," he said with a wink. "That's the drink when you don't want your on-the-wagon-spouse to figure out you're only lying about how hard it is wanting a drink."

"By the time I was fifteen, I was sneaking booze

myself. I'd lie if either of them asked, and say I didn't know what had happened to the liquor."

"Wow," he blew out the word and rounded his eyes. "You have never seen such fights, when both of them thought the other was lying."

"Undercover? Red, my whole life was an undercover gig."

She stood up and walked to the window. That revelation had felt more intimate and raw than anything that had ever transpired between them in the whole two years of their relationship.

Forrester stood up and walked up behind her. He didn't touch her, but she could feel him there, inches away, his breath almost lifting the hair on her neck.

Her skin shimmered with the effect of his closeness. She wanted to turn, pull him into her and do everything they'd done in the past.

But, this time with the knowledge that there were no lies between them.

Would that moment ever come?

CHAPTER THIRTEEN

"We can talk about everything else later, Red. Or not." He attempted a grin at her, the muscle in his cheek twitching with the effort. "But, at least believe me tonight when I say I'm not lying about being scared for you."

"Okay?" Her hazel eyes looked up at him, so full of life, vibrant. Her life could depend on being aware of the danger swirling closer and closer to her, a gut feeling told him.

His gut had never lied to him before.

"Why do you think that, Forrester?" She twisted her mouth. Not fully convinced, but not dismissing it outright. She had a sixth sense feeling, too. He could see it there in her eyes.

"Well, let's look at this, Red." He began to pace, counting off the deaths on his fingers. "The other night, the victim was a city council woman. Today, it was a radio personality. Both very high profile women."

He pointed back at her. "He wants to be noticed. He's sending a very powerful message."

"Why is he doing it though, Forrester? Why these women?"

She didn't comment that he'd just revealed it was a

radio personality. The media underground network had already started whispering that it was Stephanie Green.

She'd known, he was certain.

"What do these women have in common, Cassie?"

She shrugged. "I don't know. Stephanie Green was a very beautiful woman. That council woman was quite attractive."

"Oh, don't let it be just that," he said with a curse. "Cuz if it was just attractiveness, Red." He stopped and ran his eyes up and down her body, raised his eyebrows and tilted his head.

"Thanks, I think."

"You're welcome." He smiled, then he got serious again. "I really don't think it's just that simple. Seems too easy."

What were they missing?

"What do these women have in common?" Cassie began pacing. "The prostitute, the councilwoman, and the radio personality."

"Let's pretend the murders of those two prostitutes before you got to town were connected also."

She whirled to face him. "Do you really think they are?"

"I can't prove it. But, as soon as that prostitute was found dead in that burning building, the hair on the back of my neck stood up." He met her eyes. "I thought, he's started up again."

She just looked at him with those eyes that could say more than words, raised an eyebrow, and waited for him to continue.

"Three years ago, a week apart, two prostitutes were found murdered. They were found in abandoned buildings. In almost an exact replica of each other. Not naked. No one knew anything about their final night. I thought we were going to be having one a week after that. But, they stopped."

He remembered the horror on those young women's faces and shuddered. "I thought he'd been passing through, found himself a couple of easy targets, then moved on. When that prostitute was found dead three weeks ago, I said, Holy God, he's back."

She met his eyes, horror roiling in her eyes the same as it did inside of him.

"Why didn't you say anything?"

"Because we need to hold back some information that only the killer would know. That way, we can figure out if it's the same guy or a copycat murderer."

"Who cares?" she spit out. "Women have to be warned. Maybe if we'd got the information out there after the most recent prostitute murder, these other two women wouldn't be dead."

He felt the accusation in the pit of his stomach. Cause he'd thought the same thing when the city council woman's body was found. But, it had gone all over the media, and still the radio celebrity had been murdered.

"It's not that simple, Cassie. This guy has some method he uses to get these women to trust him. Like Ted Bundy and some other murderers, he is probably a charismatic guy. These type of women, these last two, they're not getting into cars with guys they don't know."

"How do you know that?"

He looked her over. "Not for reporting, okay?"

She nodded slowly.

"There weren't a lot of bruises on them, not like they

got into hand to hand combat with someone dragging them into a car or something." The image of trusting women caught unaware sickened him. At least the prostitutes had known the risk. "He's tricking them into submission somehow."

"He could have just put a gun on them. Or jumped them, putting a knife to their throats. The real question is why these two women?" Cassie looked at him hard. "Why them? What do they have in common with the prostitute?"

"Just what I've been trying to figure out."

Cassie began to pace again. "A prostitute. A city councilwoman, and a radio talk show host."

"Sounds like the start of a bad joke."

"Oh man, Forrester," she laughed darkly. "Gallows humor?"

It had been one of the hallmarks of their relationship, laughing at the exact wrong time about something that was really terrible if you thought about it.

So, he'd tried not to think about it too much. And tried to teach her the same coping mechanism. If you thought about this stuff too much, you'd go crazy.

Suddenly, she picked up the remote control and turned up the sound on the TV.

"Breaking news on the arsons that have been on the minds of everyone in Atlanta," a young male anchor at a competing station said. "Authorities think they might have caught the arsonist who's been terrorizing the nighttime streets of Atlanta."

A picture of a young black man flashed onto the screen.

"Police are saying this man was spotted walking with a gas can in his hand in the general neighborhood of two of the last fires. When officers tried to stop him for questioning, he ran."

The anchor turned to look at his female co-anchor. She sighed and replied, "I bet a lot of people will be sleeping easier tonight in those neighborhoods."

The male anchor smiled back and nodded. "I bet. There'll be a news conference in a few hours. We'll bring you all the latest in our newscast. Now, we take you back to our regularly scheduled programming."

The two anchors smiled out from the television as if they'd just solved all the problems of the world.

Cassie looked at him and lifted one shoulder. "Can it be as easy as that?"

"Don't know. But, I'm about to find out."

She grabbed her go bag, with makeup, snacks, and a change of clothes. Everything she might need to go on the air if she had to pull an all-nighter on a story.

"Meet you at police headquarters?" She arched an eyebrow.

"You and every other news person who can be brought into work tonight," he said dryly.

She turned toward her purse, but he reached for her hand, taking it, stopping her.

"Breathe, Cassie." He looked into her eyes. "Don't go out into the night on any more tips without giving me a text or a call. Make sure I text you back that I know, cause reception can get pretty sketchy inside the headquarters building. Okay?"

"I won't go anywhere alone, okay?" She was bargaining with him, not giving him exactly what he wanted, dodging the question.

A horrible shiver ran down his spine, and he pulled

her into him, pressing her living, breathing body against his, feeling her alive and vital. Savoring her scent.

If she weren't on the planet…

"I want you safe, Cassie."

He looked down into her eyes and registered her seriousness.

"That's what I always strive for, Forrester."

Cassie took the elevator up in the safety headquarters building, which conveniently housed the top brass of both Fire and Police. Homicide was also in the same building. A regular think tank of law enforcement and fire safety.

When she entered the conference room, she saw one advantage of having so much top brass in one place. It was easy to assemble a large group quickly.

Every official who was running for reelection stood around the fire and the police chiefs. The joint news conference to end all news conferences.

The mayor beamed reassurance toward the cameras that were stacked several deep in front of the podium. The city council members all lined up behind him, their faces downcast. One of their own had been brutally murdered.

Behind the police chief, all the upper police brass in their white shirts stood, ready to be noticed for when it was their turn to vie for the police chief position.

The fire chief took the microphone first. Many of his battalion chiefs lined the wall behind him.

A covey of detectives stood near the door, because they'd been told to by the police chief.

Beyond them, standing just outside the doorway,

nearly obscured by the dark, Forrester stood, technically meeting the order of his boss.

His slight removal from the room sent Cassie a message. He wasn't convinced they had the right guy.

Hopefully it would make the fires stop. Maybe the arsonist would see this as an opportunity to throw the police off, let another guy take the fall.

He'd been on a spree. Had killed three women within ten days.

Surely that had to satisfy any bloodlust, any need to kill he might have felt.

She'd read these guys could remain dormant for years, then something would set them off.

What had set this guy off between the prostitutes of two years ago and more recent killings?

She didn't really care, as long as he was stopped.

CHAPTER FOURTEEN

Miss Mary watched the television from her daughter's condo in Chattanooga, Tennessee. Maisey had come down and fetched her out of the hospital in Atlanta.

That was fine with her cause as they said, "When you get hurt bad, you want to go straight to Grady Hospital", the best trauma hospital in the state of Georgia. The rest of the saying was, "When you start getting better, you also want to get the heck out of there as soon as possible." Cause it was also the biggest charity hospital around, taking in every poor or homeless sick or injured person in the city. Waiting for treatment if you weren't really bad off was a given.

Maisey had slid into that hospital and fetched her out. She'd sent the officer outside of her mama's room to get a Coke, said she'd watch over her 'til he got back.

Then, Maisey had almost literally dragged her out of the building, without even checking out. Maisey had referred to herself as a family friend to the hospital staff, wouldn't even identify herself as her daughter.

Maisey was terrible scared of that man who was setting fires. Had a right to be, too.

Miss Mary watched the news conference down in Atlanta. CNN was carrying it. It was national news. Said they'd caught the man setting fires.

"Oh, Lordy." She leaned forward to get a better look at the photo they put on the television. "Oh, Lordy." She had to tell somebody.

But, who?

She got up from the couch, shuffled over to her purse and pulled out that news lady's card. Thank the Lord for those firemen who'd brought out her purse after they'd put out the fire. She'd refused to go to the hospital until they brought her purse with that money she'd taken out of the bank only days before to pay her water and her electric bills.

Hadn't gotten a ride down to pay it before the fire. Cash. That was the only way to pay your bills. And in person. Get a receipt. Then, they couldn't say they hadn't received it.

She looked down at the card with the news lady's cell phone number. "She saved you, she'll help you," she muttered to herself.

She punched in the numbers and waited while it dialed. It rang over and over, until finally Cassie picked up.

"Hello," the news lady whispered.

"Miss Cassie, honey, is that you?"

"Miss Mary?"

"Yes, baby, it's me."

"Hold on." After a minute, she spoke again, a bit louder this time but still quiet-like. "Are you okay, Miss Mary?"

"Oh yes, sweetie. I'm just fine. Thanks to you." She cackled a laugh. She heard it even as she did it. She was getting older by the minute, sounding just like her mama and her aunts had in their later years.

Luckily, she was going to have a few more later years, thanks to the news lady.

"Sweetie, I don't know who to call, so I called you." Maisey would kill her if she knew she was making this call. "You won't tell anyone where I am, will you? My daughter's afraid for my life."

She heard a gentle muttering that could have been acknowledgement that she wouldn't tell anyone where Miss Mary was, or that her daughter was right to be afraid. Miss Mary didn't want to know which.

"Why are you calling me, Miss Mary. What's wrong?" The room got quieter behind the news lady.

"You at that news conference?"

"Yes, ma'am," she said. "I just walked out when you called. Now, I'm walking farther down the hall so nobody will hear us."

"That news conference's why I'm calling." She waited for that information to register before continuing. "That black boy they got locked up down there?"

"Yes." The news lady's voice was tense, almost as if she knew what Miss Mary was going to say.

"That ain't him. The one that set my house on fire. It ain't that young man."

The news lady waited a beat, a long silent moment. "Why do you say that, Miss Mary?"

Here went nothing. Here went the information that could get her killed. Get her daughter killed? Could she risk her daughter's life? No.

"Now, you can't tell nobody where I am, Miss Cassie."

"Miss Mary, I don't know where you are and you don't have to tell me."

"Don't let them be tracing my phone number. I know they can find my phone."

"I'll call you an unnamed source," the news lady's said in a voice that was steady, reassuring. Guess you had to have the know-how to reassure folks, doing what she did. And you had to be strong of spirit. Going out into neighborhoods at night where the news lady would probably never consider living.

Coming out to help pull her out of her burning home.

"I owe my life to you, Miss Cassie." She sucked in a deep breath. "And I can't live with myself if any other woman, or man, goes through what I went through inside my burning home, when I thought I'd never get out."

The memory flashed through her mind like a fire, with an accompanying streak of smoky terror trailing after. Choking smoke, the flames getting nearer. Wanting to cook her flesh, roast it like a hamburger. Flashing orange flames in her hallway. And the bars holding her captive.

"That's what we all want, Miss Mary. We all want it to stop," the news lady agreed, her voice bringing Miss Mary back into the present, where she was safe. Unless that monster found her. And burned her baby girl's house up with her little grandchil'rens.

Oh Lord, oh Lord. She had to tell. Had to.

"That man what set my house on fire? He…" She sucked in another deep breath, forcing it into her lungs then blowing it out again. What she had to say next— could make her a target. "He were a white man."

Miss Cassie sucked in a long breath, too, as if she couldn't help herself.

"White?" the reporter said.

"Yes'm, a white boy. His skin stood out in all that night like he were bleached out."

The reporter didn't say anything for a long moment. Then, said very low, very quiet, as if whispering to be sure no one heard, "What else did you see, Miss Mary?"

"I'm afraid, Miss Cassie. Afraid. Don't you trust anybody, you hear me? Anybody. Don't go out in them neighborhoods by yourself. You hear me?"

"Yes…, The news lady broke off her comment with a gasp. Then, she whispered, "I'll call you back."

The line went dead, and Miss Mary looked at her phone.

Why had the news lady hung up so quick like for?

———————

Cassie whirled to face him. "Preston. What's up? Why aren't you in the news conference?"

His face remained impassive as he looked her up and down.

How much had he heard? Had he heard her say Miss Mary's name?

"I figure they got enough chiefs and Indians in there to solve any problems. I saw you duck out and wanted to tell you myself how courageous I thought you were last night."

She met his eyes and smiled. "Thanks, Preston. Never fancied myself a hero before, but okay." She dramatically blew on her nails and polished them on her shirt front.

"But, honestly," she said in a more serious tone. "I just happened along at the right time. No one could have heard that pitiful old lady's pleas and not helped."

He nodded. "You were facing some danger though. Never know what can happen when a building is on fire. That took some courage out there. We'll have to make you an honorary firefighter."

She smiled.

His dark eyes met hers, then almost involuntarily swept down across her body, before returning to meet her gaze, with a very serious expression. "I'm going to nominate you as a civilian hero to be honored at our yearly awards banquet." Again, his eyes dropped to her body, then back up to her face again. "Maybe I can be your date."

Date? That was a word a man used when he was hitting on a woman. Not accompany her, not meet her there and have her sit at a table with other honorees alongside him.

"Your date?" She looked down at his ring finger. "Aren't you still married?"

He glanced away. "Actually, not. Me and the missus are getting a divorce. Amicable, gonna be friends still and all that."

His eyes still didn't quite meet hers. "Still not planning on asking her to be my date to the awards banquet, though. You know how it is being divorced." He laughed lightly.

Then, he looked down, making direct eye contact. "You and your ex seem to be handling it pretty well, though."

A little flash of empathy filled her. The hitting on her seemed a little more desperate now, rather than invasive of her personal space at work. Just a guy wanting reassurance that he was still attractive, could get a girl, wouldn't be alone for the rest of his life.

She remembered the first few weeks after she'd finally moved out of her and Forrester's home. Long, lonely nights spent looking at the ceiling, tossing and turning, imagining Forrester with that bartender. Wondering if he had already moved her into what had been their marriage bed.

It had been pure hell. She looked up at Preston, gentling her gaze.

"I'm sorry about your marriage, Preston. That's rough. The first part of the process is pretty hard. Me and Forrester weren't all that polite or said 'we're gonna still be friends' at first. Me, especially," she acknowledged with a small laugh.

"Good to see you were able to get past all that and move on," he said, his voice tight, as if it took a lot of effort to get air out of compressed lungs.

"It can be done, Preston," she said gently. "People do it every day in this country. All too often, in fact."

He ran one finger across his eyebrow, almost in a nervous tic. Maybe talking about such personal stuff was too much for him.

With his hand right in front of her, she couldn't help but notice the scratch she'd seen earlier.

Then, he met her eyes and quickly dropped his hand.

As if he'd just realized he'd put the hand with the scratch up on display.

"That scratch from a domestic *argument*? Not a completely amicable divorce?" She laughed, trying to make light of it.

His eyes dropped then back up to meet hers.

"Actually, yeah. It was stupid. Over my dog."

"Your dog?"

He shrugged. "Yeah, I've had the mutt since way before we got married. And the day I left, she pulled him to her and held onto him when he tried to come to me, like she was gonna keep him." He laughed awkwardly. "I know it sounds silly but we found ourselves almost fighting over the dog. I went to take him by the collar and she tried to stop me. Ended up scratching the dickens out of me."

"She got really vicious for a moment." He looked down at his hand, turning it to the light coming from a window, a deep sorrow filling his eyes. "I can see why cops say domestic calls are the most dangerous. People get a bit crazy when their hearts are broken."

Then, his face flushed, as if he couldn't believe all he'd just divulged about this personal life, dirty details. He pushed out a rough laugh that was probably meant to diminish the magnitude of what he'd just said. But, it only made it seem more real, more personal. And she could see it, two broken people fighting over the last living remnant of their time together. The family dog.

"My ex apologized for it," he finally pushed out. "Said she didn't mean to do it. She started crying, saying the only good thing left from our marriage was the dog."

Yikes, that had to hurt.

"She said the dog loved her like I never did." He shrugged, but a little bit of hurt still burned in his eyes. "I ended up letting her keep him since she was home more often than I ever had been. I'd felt a little guilty at times leaving him home alone before I got married."

He held up both hands like a scale, measuring the dog's fate. "So, it all worked out best for Fido."

"What's his real name?"

"Fido," he said straight faced. "Thought it was kinda funny."

She smiled. "Maybe you can pick yourself up another one at the dog pound and call him Spot."

"Spot." He laughed obligingly. "Maybe I'll get a Dalmatian this time. Anyway, I'm over the divorce, figure if the worse that happens is we fight over who gets the dog, then I've come out pretty well."

"Good attitude," Cassie said. They smiled at each other for a long moment, two people commiserating over the miseries of divorce, then something different slid behind his eyes, something male.

"So, you figure your divorce is gonna take?" he said in a non-threatening manner, as if they were in the same boat. Which they kind of were.

Just two wounded warriors comparing notes?

"Oh, yeah, I believe divorce is forever." She laughed, a bit painfully. "Marriage may not be until death do us part. But, divorce? Once someone has crushed your heart between their hands. It's hard to ever look at them the same."

He gazed down at her with no expression on his face. That kind of blank expression always made her want to fill the silence.

"Once you've gone through that much heartache over someone, it's really ridiculous to go back down that same road." She shrugged. "And what? Experience the heartache all over again for something you already proved once wouldn't work?"

He murmured in agreement and patted her shoulder.

Then, he leaned forward. As if he were going to say something quietly in her ear.

Or kiss her?

Her instinct was to jump back. He was a great source, a great asset in her job and she didn't want to complicate that with any sort of dating stuff when she didn't really feel it. She already had enough man-work complications with Forrester.

"You hitting on my ex, Preston?"

Thankfully, the interruption came just in time to save her from doing something that might embarrass Preston.

They both turned toward the voice, Preston dropping his hand from her shoulder and straightening up.

"Ex, Detective," Preston said, recovering quickly. If he had anything to recover from. "I believe the operative word is *ex*."

Preston looked at Forrester with a challenging look that Forrester gave him right back. Male dogs peeing on trees.

Preston laughed. "Actually, I was just telling your girl here what a hero she was helping that old lady out."

Forrester looked past Preston at Cassie. "She's a pretty kick ass broad, that's for sure." Then, his eyes slid back over to the battalion chief.

They looked at each other for a long moment, neither one of them smiling, just standing there surveying each other.

Then, Forrester tilted his head. "Can I talk to you for a moment, Red?"

"Sure."

Preston half turned back to look at her.

"Thanks for the compliment, chief," she said lightly.

"Thanks for helping save the fire victim, *Red*," he said, slightly emphasizing Forrester's pet name for her.

Forrester had never called her that in public before. Was he subtly telling Preston, "Hands off"?

Thus, Preston had come right back with the same pet name?

She looked between the two. Both single guys, both high powered men good at their jobs.

Yeah, they didn't get to be the type of guys they were without having a lot of testosterone flowing through their veins.

They were posturing for each other. Just because that was probably what they'd done their whole lives.

She laughed slightly, couldn't keep the sound from blowing out. "You guys are just too funny." She turned and left them standing there in the hallway, going back into the newser to see if any more details would come out.

She didn't have time for nonsense. People had died. Suddenly, a serious thought returned to her, reminding her why she didn't have time for the bull that could go along with any man involvement right now. She couldn't afford the distraction.

According to Miss Mary, more people could still die.

Because the wrong guy was in lock up.

CHAPTER FIFTEEN

As soon as the news conference ended, Forrester headed toward her.

"Let's walk outside." He waved her away from all the officials clustered in the conference room for the news presser.

The outside door closed behind them, and Forrester continued walking. When they'd rounded the corner, putting the headquarters building behind them, he continued on.

"Forrester?"

He seemed to be thinking, but turned back to her, waving her to keep walking.

Finally, a block later, he seemed ready to talk, casually looking around him as they walked. Checking for anyone listening in?

Then, he raised an eyebrow at her. "I think they are purposefully ignoring any signs that this guy's not the guy."

She knew this side of him, how he'd always liked to think out loud, often coming to a conclusion as they talked. She'd seen him do it with cop friends, too.

But, now, for some reason, he wasn't talking to them. Probably would be politically incorrect to verbalize ideas that went against the Police and Fire Chiefs' official line.

"You remember Roberto, the FBI computer whiz?" he asked.

She nodded. "Worked with you when you were undercover with the Coalition."

"Yeah." He looked behind them again. "He's been checking into some stuff for me while I was held captive in that farce of a news conference." He half-laughed grimly.

At the corner, he turned, looked back toward the police and fire headquarters then changed direction with her.

"This guy they got in jail for all these arsons?" He raised an eyebrow. "He lived a couple of blocks over from Miss Mary's street." He stopped talking for a beat, shooting her a look. "And, he was about one payment away from going into foreclosure on his house. Behind on his property taxes, everything. Lost his job about a year ago, ran out of money."

He turned to face her full on. "He had every reason to burn down his own home. To get out of the mortgage, maybe get some insurance money to tide him over. That's a fire of convenience. Not an arsonist."

"Emmh," she just murmured, waiting to see what else he would come out with.

"Roberto said if we can get hold of this suspect's computer, if he has one, and hasn't sold it, that we'd probably find computer searches on the best way to burn down a home. Or searches showing him studying up on the arsonist's MO."

"Emm," she murmured noncommittally.

He looked down at her contemplatively. "So, what aren't you telling me?"

With a quick check behind them, she turned away from the headquarters building and started walking. Forrester looked back too, then quickly caught up with her.

"What?" he said.

"A source just called me and said that the guy who set the entire block on fire around Miss Mary's house?" She waited for him to catch up to the change in direction of conversation.

"Yeah?"

She had his full attention now.

"The source said that person was white. A white boy, they said."

"White? In that neighborhood?" He blew out a burst of air. "That'll stand out. Urban gentrification hasn't hit that area yet."

"Exactly." She stopped now, with one more check around them. "And, there's something else." She met his eyes.

"Yeah?"

"The night of the councilwoman's fire, I got the feeling one of the neighbors out there saw more than they wanted to talk about. But, that they were afraid. Maybe when they heard about the body being in the building, they decided they didn't want to be the next body found in that neighborhood and didn't want anything to do with the investigation."

"Makes sense."

It wasn't paranoia, an unfounded fear. They'd both seen witnesses show up dead before they could ever get to court.

She could imagine living out on that lonely road of Mary Jackson's house, with few people who would show up to help you if you screamed.

Suddenly, a thought occurred to her.

"Do you think maybe that's why the second fire on that street was started? To randomly kill any possible witnesses?"

He turned to look at her with a dark horror on his face. "Kill anyone who could have possibly seen anything?"

"Hard to believe," she agreed. "But, it kind of makes sense since it was on the same block."

If so, they were dealing with one of the most dangerous people they'd ever run across. And that was saying a lot.

"There's something else, Red."

Man, how she liked it when he called her that. Made her feel like a heroine in an old film noir, the old black and white detective flicks with the tough dame heroine.

It made her feel like a character in her own life. The heroine in her own story.

She just hoped she was a tough dame who survived this investigation into a murderous arsonist.

A shiver ran through her.

Why did she suddenly think that? Almost as if she'd had a premonition.

But, this had nothing to do with her. She just had to be a bit more careful in this investigation than any before.

Cause like she always told Forrester, news just wasn't all that safe of a profession. Kinda like being a cop. Kinda like being a firefighter.

You had to have it in your blood to get out there and

deal with all that was required of you in all of those professions.

"Come back to me, Red," Forrester said.

She realized he was staring down at her.

"Sorry. Got preoccupied."

"I could see that. What were you thinking about?"

"Nothing." She shook off the weird thought. Fear was bound to rear its ugly head in a situation this terrifying. And paranoia. "Just, it's a freaky idea, someone actually doing the things this person is doing. What is he thinking?"

"When we start understanding this guy, we're really in trouble. When we're able to think like him," Forrester repeated the words he'd said to her many times before.

The saying was pretty appropriate for people like them who worked with, around, and investigated some of the weirdest people in the world.

"Do you think we ran into him out there?" She looked up at Forrester.

"Possible. Some of these guys like to hang around and see the action and drama they cause. See fear in people's face."

"Maybe we should ask Roberto to run the video JoJo shot at both scenes through some facial recognition software for us, see if this guy shows up at all three of these fires," she continued.

"Good idea. I already asked Roberto to do that with any video that aired on any of the newscasts." He looked sideways at her. "You know that's all the video we can get our hands on without giving the TV stations a warrant. Takes a while to go the warrant route."

She nodded. "But, if you just happened by my house

and saw an external hard drive laying on the counter with our raw video on it, you could probably just run that over to him. I mean, it wouldn't be illegal borrowing that from a friend without asking. It wouldn't be breaking and entering, you just thought it would be okay. Could apologize afterwards if anyone finds out."

She raised her hands in an imitation of innocence. "I mean, I'm not gonna give it to you. I wouldn't do that."

He smiled darkly and nodded. "'Don't quite recall where I got that information' is also in my vocabulary," he repeated one of her often quoted phrases.

"We're getting to be too much alike, Red."

Then, without preamble, he reached for her, pulling her in, wrapping his arms and his scent all around her.

For a long moment, he just held her, letting her absorb his pheromones, the comfort of his arms with the sense of safety and assurance that everything was going to be okay.

That's one of the things she missed most about him, the feeling he conveyed to her that all was right in the world, or would be shortly, once he got on the problem.

No one had been able to save those women who'd been found in the burned-out buildings, though. How devious was this arsonist to have gotten all of those women alone?

CHAPTER SIXTEEN

"We have got to go on the air with this information about a witness saying the arsonist is a white man." Cassie stood by the desk in the conference room where the news meeting always took place.

"You only have one witness who thought they saw that Cassie. The police are saying they've got their man."

"I don't think they're right."

The news director sat back, crossing his arms. With his expression, he said his mind was made up.

"We're in their back pockets, Jerry, if we just accept whatever they say."

He sat forward, uncrossing his arms. "What?"

"If we just go along with their story, contrary to this eye witness account, what good are we? We have a duty to report what might be the actual truth. Since when do we do whatever the police and fire chief tell us to do?"

He raised a finger. "You forgot the mayor." He gave a wry half-smile.

She didn't smile back. "Jerry. People could die. More people," she corrected herself.

The smile left his face. She'd just lectured to him

like he was a first year journalism student.

"I get that, Cassie. I really do." He leaned forward, and everyone at the table did the same, their gazes sliding back and forth between Cassie and the news director, noting every detail for later when they retold the story.

He met her eyes, with a serious, assessing look that she hadn't seen since he'd first hired her.

He stood to pace. The guy wasn't taking any of this lightly. It was a big burden, trying to decide what information to put out there.

Don't go with the information and the public was at risk. Tell them unfounded claims and you fed a hysteria like this town hadn't felt in a long time.

Crime was usually logical. Go into a high crime neighborhood and you might get your car jacked. Get a divorce, and you stood a chance of your ex shooting you in a fit of passion.

But, this stuff? A prostitute, a city council woman, a radio talk show host?

This was off-the-chart random.

"Look, Cassie," her boss turned to say. "If you can get me one more legitimate source, not someone you prompt to say they don't think that guy is the right guy." He waggled his finger at her.

Then, he sucked in a deep breath and narrowed his eyes. Everyone in the group looked intently at him. "Then, I think it's fair to go on the air with this information."

"I have a very reliable source. Very, Jerry. We need to do this now. We shouldn't hold this information back." This was one of the reasons she'd gone to journalism school in the first place, provide vital information to the public.

"Who is your source, Cassie?"

She'd already refused to say once.

"Don't you trust my judgment, Jerry? Isn't it enough that I say this person is reliable?"

He shook his head.

"I can't tell you, Jerry. I can't. It could get this person dead."

He shook his head, his face reddening, puffing up like a balloon. He was just being bullheaded now, throwing around his weight.

"Ok, then," she said, and got up. "I've got a story to cover."

"Cassie," Jerry called out in a firm, loud voice.

The conference room was silent, everyone waiting, watching the drama.

"Don't you say this on the air, unless I tell you it's approved," Jerry stated flatly.

She turned to leave.

"Do you hear me?" he called after her like she was a little kid.

Okay, maybe she was acting just a bit like one.

She pivoted back toward him, and every eye in the room switched from the news director to her.

"Gotcha, Jerry," she said, more for her own professionalism than to placate him. "Heard you loud and clear."

His face got even redder. He knew she was just saying what he wanted to hear at the moment. He walked around the conference table, stopping about five feet from her.

Chairs swiveled so people could get a better view. One producer half stood so she could see over the people grouped in front of her.

"If you say this on air without prior authorization from a manager, then you're fired."

Fired?

Ok, then.

"Gotcha, Jerry." She pivoted on her heel and left. At least those high heels she wore did a great pivot and walk movement.

Not a sound came from the conference room as she walked all the way down the hall.

She walked all the way through the newsroom, out the back door to the parking lot, and got into her car. Driving out, she dialed Forrester's number.

"Hey," she bit off as soon as he picked up. "Where are you?"

"I'm out in the hood where the first victim of this round of killings, the prostitute, was found. Thought maybe it's calmed down enough people will be more willing to talk. Maybe it's been long enough and they'll figure the guy's moved on out of their area."

She nodded then realized he wasn't going to see the head nod. "Emm," she made a sound.

"What's up, Red?"

"Ohhh," she blew out her frustration and anger into the air. "Jerry," she said the one word that would give Forrester all he needed to know. "The guy is being all logical. He quoted me Journalism 101. 'You never go with only one source.'"

The thing was the guy was right to some degree. He always was.

But, this was different.

"This city will be lulled into a false sense of security by the report of the the arsonist's arrest," she blurted out. "People will go about their business without looking over their shoulders."

Tears formed in her eyes from the frustration and the conviction that she was right to tell the women of Atlanta they might not be safe.

"I'm going to go with it, anyway, in my live shot." It was the right thing to do.

"I guess you never really liked that job anyway?" Forrester half laughed.

He knew it was her dream job, coming home to Georgia, and reporting in a Big Ten market.

"If I lose my job over this? I won't mind telling my next perspective employer why I did it."

Especially if she was right, and she prevented more deaths by reporting the truth on the air. Course if she were proved wrong, no news director in his right mind would touch such a loose cannon.

"Where are you doing your live shot?" He didn't argue over what she was planning to report. He never had.

He'd argue with her about possibilities on cases. But, he'd never tried to tell her how she could report on the story.

"I'm gonna go to that last building that I visited with Hobbs. And don't worry," she cut off the comment she already knew was coming. "I won't go out there by myself. JoJo is gonna be there. He's already headed out. We edited in-house cause I had to argue with these guys so much about it."

Fury blew through her again. Even now, an in-house editor was cutting the last two tracks from her piece. It would be the world's shortest piece of nothing that she'd ever put on the air.

Jerry would be mad about that, too. He'd probably make her feed back another track from out in the field before the live shot.

She tried to distract herself from how angry she was by looking at the sky.

The early sunsets were a lighting problem for JoJo, which is why he'd headed out before her.

"The sunset is so beautiful," she said.

Forrester laughed. He knew what she was doing, trying to get her mind off just how upset she was.

"Are you guys still doing a live shot tonight? What with the Braves baseball game being televised on your station?"

"Yeah, we go on after the game. It's running late which gave Jerry more time to argue with me. I'm gonna turn on the radio and check out how close they are to the end of the game."

She heard the sound of his car door opening, the engine starting. "You're coming over, aren't you?"

"Whatta you think, Red?"

She laughed under her breath. "I think I know you all too well."

"I'm way over on the other side of town, but I'll be there in time to see you do the live shot that gets you fired." He laughed brusquely. "Do you want me to hold you back from saying what you think when he calls? Or will it all be over with but the shouting by then, anyway?"

"Smart ass," she said. Then, she hung up, cause she had to laugh. It wasn't what he said, it was how he said it. He always made her laugh.

She'd missed that. Missed the laughing in bed. As well as everything else they'd done in bed.

This break up with him had been as hard on her as he'd acted like it had been on him.

But, the image of him in bed with another woman had just been impossible to get out of her mind.

"We were technically broken up," she said to herself as she'd done so many times. "You have no right to be mad at him."

But, the reason she'd moved out initially was because she'd needed time. Time to heal, to lick the wounds of anger. And the huge loss she'd felt from...

"Stop it, stop it!" she yelled at herself, then looked around to see if anyone was watching her talking to herself in the car.

At least these days when people saw you talking to yourself their first thought wasn't "crazy". It was that she must be talking on a blue tooth or speaker phone. Or a ear piece they couldn't see.

Not crazy. Though, she kinda was, if you got right down to it. To screw up a marriage with someone like Forrester.

No. He'd screwed it up.

Oh, just face it, they'd both screwed the marriage up. She'd talked back and forth to herself like this the last few weeks since she'd started seeing him so often on the fire stories.

Maybe cause it'd been long enough since her granny had died that her grief was starting to subside somewhat. She didn't burst into convulsive tears whenever she realized her granny was gone for good.

And with the lessening of grief, she didn't need someone to be angry at as much as she'd needed in the first few months.

Looking back now, she could see how she'd been

wrong to take it out on Forrester. But, that still didn't make it right what he'd done.

Sleeping with a woman only weeks after she'd moved out.

But, not being able to reach him cause of that stupid undercover job when her granny had died, that had been the final straw on all those nights alone and all the special occasions he'd missed because of that stupid undercover job.

She'd been practically an undercover widow. As good as divorced, she'd told herself at the time.

"Oh, water under the bridge," she said out loud.

Then, from up ahead, she saw the live truck, parked right where it should be.

She pulled up to it. The live shot wasn't even set up yet. And JoJo wasn't out pulling cable hectically like he ought to be since they were nearing the live shot possible timeslot. If the game went short, they needed to be ready to go live. Where was JoJo?

She got out, walked to the live truck. Not inside. She turned to survey the surroundings.

That's when a glow from the back of the house lit up the darkness that had fallen while she'd driven to the live shot site.

Instantly, a horrible feeling hit her. Flames quickly ran around the edges of the vacant house, getting a head start on destruction before the firefighters could get there to stop it.

"JoJo!" she yelled and ran toward the house. "JoJo!"

CHAPTER SEVENTEEN

She sprinted toward the house, fear propelling her like a jet rocket.

"JoJo!" she shrieked.

Nothing.

"Where are you?"

She ran around the house. The entire back side of the house was going up in vicious red tongues of death.

A wall of red and orange covered the building. But, through it, two dark figures stood out, silhouetted as they struggled. JoJo's enormous frame stood out. No doubt who that was.

But, he staggered back and forth drunkenly as he fought with another person.

The other person, a man, shoved him, and JoJo went down.

"Stop!" she screamed. But the noise of the fire and their distraction as they fought covered up her voice.

The doorway was an immense sheet of fire blocking her from them.

Turning, she bolted toward the front entrance. That man could kill JoJo before she got to him. JoJo was big, but the guy he was fighting had somehow gotten the upper hand.

At the front door, she hesitated only for a second, looking in through the smoke, trying to see if the man who'd fought with JoJo was hiding inside, waiting for her. Damn, she wished she had her gun.

Flames were now licking up the frame of the inside doorway that led to the back of the house.

Terror gripped her. Run into a burning building, with a crazed serial killer inside? Fear of those flames gripped her, like a giant hand clenching and squeezing her, almost stopping her from entering.

But JoJo was inside. He could die if she didn't help him.

JoJo was one of her best friends. He'd been her first photographer when she'd gotten to Atlanta. She'd begun to consistently ask for him until they'd just known to give him to her every day.

They were a team. And good friends.

He had two little kids who needed their daddy to come home. Not to mention a wife who loved him.

Fury gripped her, pushing back the fear. Fury and righteous anger at this person who thought he could take away her friend, Felicity's husband and most importantly, those two little kids' daddy.

She looked around for a weapon. An old two-by-four lay on the ground, probably pulled loose from the porch by some kids or a homeless person.

She grabbed it, took a deep breath, pulled her shirt up over her mouth and nose, and ran into the burning house. Ran for all she was worth, ran for all JoJo was worth.

Smoke pulsed in the room. It swirled snakelike around the door, then upwards, quickly filling the front room. She squinted to get her bearings, then ran straight back.

At the back room, she saw a blurry figure leaning over JoJo. Tying him up?

Planning to leave him to burn?

She ran toward the figure, stopping a few feet away. The noise of the fire, and the thick smoke hid her approach from the man who crouched over JoJo.

Swinging the two-by-four backward, she then brought it forward with all her might. It connected with the man's head with the sound of a watermelon hitting a concrete sidewalk.

The man staggered away from JoJo, falling to one knee. He turned toward her.

Through the smoke, with the flames reflecting off him, he looked like a demon from hell, her worse nightmare. Just a pair of eyes and an open mouth.

Then, the smoke swirled away from him, toward her. She coughed, grasping tightly to the two-by-four in case he rose to attack her.

He lurched forward. On his knees, he was still an imposing figure. If he got those big hands on her, she was done for. And so was JoJo. She swung the two-by-four once again, connecting with his head.

Just as the plank him square in the temple, she got a good look at his face.

Oh, my God. Him?

Forrester saw the glow coming from up ahead, pulsing up through the trees. Instantly, his gut clenched.

He hit his radio. "Officer needs assistance. Officer needs assistance!" he yelled the call that would bring a quick response. "Need fire trucks, EMTs and as many officers as you have in the area. We've got another fire. I repeat, another fire. Maybe with entrapment."

He quickly gave the address as he skidded to a stop by the curb. Then, he jumped out of the car.

Maybe he should have said, "Officer down." That wouldn't be too much of a false call, because he knew that at any moment he could be down. Because with one quick assessing glance at the situation, he knew he was going to have to run into that burning building.

The live truck, Cassie's car. And not a person visible on the street. He pulled his weapon and ran toward the front steps, getting a look into the empty live truck as he angled past it, just to be sure. Though he'd known before he'd looked there would be no one inside.

There was no way they could have missed the flames rising from the building.

He took the front steps two at a time and peered inside the house. Flames crawled up the living room walls.

"Cassie!" he yelled. "Cassie!"

A muffled response came from the back of the house.

Gray smoke billowed through the room like a spectral fog, ready to inhale the spirits of whoever remained in the house, sucking the oxygen from their lungs, replacing it with this killing, carcinogenic cloud.

Adrenalin pulsed through Forrester's veins, making it impossible to feel fear. A blinding rage at whoever was trying to hurt Cassie filled the space where fear would dwell.

He ran into the smoky morass of a house. Flames reached out toward him.

He narrowed his eyes, holding his breath.

Finally, he saw Cassie's red hair shining through the ugly gray. He'd never loved that hair so much as now.

He stepped into the room, looking around for a human threat. Two figures lay on the floor. One covered with a blanket, not moving.

Another lay beside it.

Cassie had her arms underneath a third person's arms, trying to haul them out of the room. But, the figure was immense compared to her. The smoke whirled away enough for Forrester to make sense of the figure. It was JoJo, and he was completely unconscious.

She couldn't drag the dead weight of the giant man out of the house.

"I've got him." He pushed Cassie aside, taking JoJo under the arms. "Get out!" he yelled into her ear.

The fire exploded around the sink. They were all minutes away from dying if they didn't get out. A flashover could happen at any moment, turning them all to embers.

She shook her head and ran to the smaller figure covered by the blanket. Throwing the covering back, she revealed a female form.

Cassie coughed, choking from the darkening smoke. He knew from experience it would be useless to argue with her.

So, he started dragging JoJo's heavy frame toward the living room. His lungs burned. He needed air. But there was only deadly, toxin-filled fumes in this room now.

Cassie followed him, pulling the woman's body with a grip under the arms. How was she still managing to function?

The living room walls were a solid seething mass of

orange and red. The hallway on the other side of the living room oozed oily black smoke.

With a mighty lunge, he dragged JoJo out onto the front porch, and sucked in a gasping lungful of air. That gave him the strength to drag the large, lifeless body down the steps and into the yard far enough away from the house that the flames couldn't make one last ditch effort to jump toward him, claiming their lost treasure.

He turned toward the house. Flames shot out of the roof, yelling in frustration that the humans were getting away. Cassie emerged from the smoked-filled doorway, staggering under the burden of the smaller woman.

He ran to take her from Cassie, throwing his arm underneath Cassie's to support her weight as they both stumbled down the steps.

Cassie gasped, sucking in air as she struggled to exhale the fumes she must have breathed in. Nobody could hold their breath that long.

She collapsed weakly, and he lowered her the rest of the way to the ground. Then, he deposited the other woman's body on the grass. It was a body to him right now, cause he didn't know if she was alive.

All he knew was that Cassie was alive and she might need his help. He dropped down beside her.

"Are you okay?"

She nodded, tears streaming down her face, choking and gasping. She raised a hand, and pointed a finger at JoJo. She couldn't talk but her message was clear.

Check on JoJo.

He pivoted and crawled the few feet to the big man. Leaning over him, he listened for a breath.

A rattling, croaking gasp shook free of his lungs. Not good, but at least he was breathing. Sirens seemed to answer JoJo's desperate attempts to breathe, screaming down the street, with red lights flashing off the trees.

"Thank God," he muttered.

He looked back at the house. There was still someone in there. But there was no way he could get back into that building without deciding to die.

The entire structure was engulfed.

Firefighters jumped off the engine as soon as it slowed. Two ran toward them, holding oxygen tanks with masks attached. They fit one onto JoJo's face then came toward him. But, he pointed them toward Cassie.

Despite her protests, they pushed one onto her face before turning to the figure that lay unresponsive on the ground.

Two other firefighters ran to them. "Anybody else inside?" one yelled.

"Yes," Forrester choked out, his throat so raw he could barely speak. "Back of the house, the kitchen area."

The firefighters looked at the flaming beast, their eyes showing just how serious a decision it was to go inside. One turned and yelled to two men who were unwinding a hose that was fastened to the truck. Those firefighters turned the hose on the front door, flashing the flames with the quenching water as the first firefighters fastened on their breathing apparatus and headed up the front steps.

The firefighters with the hose advanced on the door, shooting water into the building, cooling the room to help prevent a flashover, and clearing an escape route for their buddies. Then, the advance firefighters ran forward into the water-doused doorway.

Other firefighters ran to hook up hoses to the hydrant down the street. They all worked feverishly, knowing the danger their comrades had just accepted to engage.

Going into a burning building, risking their own lives to save someone they didn't even know.

They might never receive a proper thank you from the victim, not even a box of cookies. But, they'd go in after him or her.

Cassie turned toward the flaming inferno, horror on her face. Then, she looked back at the unconscious woman lying beside JoJo.

The first fireman who'd reached them was working on the inert female figure. He'd listened at her mouth, then had shaken his head at the other guy, and began CPR. The other firefighter ran back to the truck for extra gear. Furiously, the first firefighter pumped on the woman's chest.

Just then, a fire ambulance screeched up. The tech jumped out, bolting toward them.

He quickly took over working on the woman. All around them, people were in full force, coming to the rescue of other humans.

This was what was normal, people taking care of people.

Not that monster who'd set this fire with the intention of killing humans.

And probably had. The third figure that had lain on the kitchen floor. Had the killer been successful in claiming at least one victim?

And who was that person?

CHAPTER EIGHTEEN

Cassie stood in front of the camera, outside the burning building, while firefighters still fought the flames.

"You're live in fifteen," a replacement photographer called to her since JoJo had been hauled off to the hospital.

She looked at Forrester, leaning up against the truck. As their eyes met, she smiled and silently mouthed, "Thank you."

He nodded, and his eyes creased in that smile he could give with only his eyes. The mouth wasn't involved. But, it didn't have to be.

Those green eyes said it all.

A producer ran up to her with only five seconds to spare before Cassie went live. "The station was able to get someone at the hospital. JoJo's going to be fine."

"Thank God." Cassie almost collapsed with gratitude and relief. If she'd arrived a few moments later, JoJo would probably have been dead.

Then, the murderer could have turned his attention to her. And they would have found three bodies in that burned-out carcass of a building when some producer finally showed up to ask why they'd missed their live shot.

The station would have sent another reporter out to report on her death. They'd have run a photo of her and JoJo, then they'd have faded to black.

She and JoJo's deaths would have been a reader.

Life's a bitch, then you're a reader, as the saying went in the business.

JoJo would never have had a chance to go home to his wife and two little girls.

She looked at Forrester.

And she would have never had a chance to spend any more time with him.

Did she really want to spend any more time being mad at him?

No. An instantaneous response came from deep inside of her. But, then, that answering little critic said, "But do you really want to go back there?"

To a man who'd lied, who'd cheated on her. Even if they'd been separated.

He wasn't there the night Granny had died.

Because he'd been deep undercover.

Then, when she'd taken her grief out on him, he'd reacted as if they'd never been married and slept with another woman.

After you kicked him out, the pro-Forrester side of her brain jumped in.

Then, through the raucous debate inside of her head, the voices of the anchors emerged.

"Cassie, are you okay?"

She glanced up at the monitor inside the truck, seeing her own face on the live screen. "Sorry, guys, how long was I just standing here like a zombie?"

"It's okay, Cassie, after everything you've been through. I can't believe you're still reporting live. You really should be at the hospital getting checked out."

Out of the corner of her eye, she saw Forrester cross his arms and nod agreement. He could hear the truck's monitor that was turned down low so it wouldn't reverberate in her live shot.

She smiled. For the camera. For Forrester.

"I'm okay," she said. "Better than I've ever been, because I realize I could be dead tonight. And life never tasted so wonderful."

Then, she returned a serious look to her face. "There are two dead people tonight, Victoria. One died in that fire, another from smoke inhalation. And my photographer JoJo Graham almost died."

"We're not confirming the identity of the two dead people yet. Until they notify next of kin. But, I can tell you that I believe the man they have in the Fulton County Jail on arson and murder charges is not the right man."

She heard several gasps in her ear. From the anchors? From producers? She didn't care.

"A man attacked my photographer. I saw the man doing it. He would have killed JoJo if I hadn't stopped him. There is no plausible explanation to me except that this man was the serial arsonist-murderer."

She inhaled deeply. "But, that man is dead now, from the same fire I believe he set. Dead by his own hands."

She looked into the camera and smiled grimly at the audience she knew was glued to her every word. She was their eyes on the scene. They deserved the truth in her reporting. "I believe he was the arsonist and that we are all now safe from that predator."

In the monitor, she could see the anchors staring

blankly at the camera. That wasn't the official city message, it wasn't the official station message. But, it was hers. Because it was the truth, as she saw it.

Whether she had a job tomorrow or not.

Kellogg, the replacement photographer, turned off his camera and looked at her. "If that isn't justice, I don't know what is," he said.

Then, her phone started blowing up with texts and phone calls. It almost rattled off the dash of the live truck where she'd set it just before going live.

Kellogg grimaced. "I wonder who that could be?" He smiled, and stuck out his hand. "Well, if I don't see you again, it was nice working with you."

She laughed as she shook his hand. His expression was so deadpan. Something about photogs. They'd seen so many reporters come and go and so many bad things on the job, they found it hard to take anything too seriously.

Forrester turned and picked up her phone as it continued to vibrate. He glanced at its face as repeated texts flashed on the screen only to be replaced almost instantaneously by the phone number of the station, or as it read, *Those People*, the name she'd assigned it in her phone's contacts.

Forrester held it up and smiled at her. She unplugged her microphone.

"Those people can wait," she said dryly. "I almost died tonight."

Forrester and Kellogg laughed. A producer stood nearby, sent out to help, considering the intense circumstances. She hardly ever left the building, and looked at them like she didn't understand their behavior.

That was okay, though. This was the first time Cassie could ever remember her showing up on a story. She fell into the category of people that photogs and reporters referred to as "people who stay in the building all day."

They were another whole category of people than the people who slogged through the real world out here, where people died and where, as today had fully demonstrated, photographers and reporters put their lives and safety on the line, doing stuff that those people in the building would never understand, never experience.

"I'm calling JoJo's wife before I talk to those people back there. I need to find out how he's really doing."

She dialed Felicity's cell phone, ignoring the phone calls that even now were trying to vibrate through on her phone.

"Helloooo, Miss Cassie," JoJo answered the phone, his tone and words confirming he was okay.

Her voice caught in her chest. Tonight, she'd almost lost one of her best friends in the world.

"You choked up, missy?" JoJo squawked into the phone. "I breathed a lot more of that stuff than you did and got whomped on the side of my head, too. And, I'm still talking."

She laughed then, though a bit wetly. "You are definitely okay, I can tell. I'm coming down there to see you."

"Oh, I think you got more important people to talk to." He laughed into the phone. "We just watched your live shot. I'm sure those station folk are gonna want to see you before you come down here."

"I'm done for the night," she said into the phone,

turning away and walking a few feet from the producer so she couldn't overhear her words and report them back verbatim to the executives that thought they ran the Atlanta news business.

Those people in the building hadn't almost died tonight. But, they had the strongest opinions about everything.

JoJo laughed heartily into her ear. "You can always claim a head injury tomorrow. I'll vouch that the guy hit you up side the head, too."

She waited a minute, then asked. Cause information could save lives. "What do you remember about tonight, JoJo? What was going on before you went into the house?"

JoJo sucked in a deep breath, the sound whooshing through the phone lines. Then, he blew it out again. "Not much, Cassie. Not much. That's what bugs me. I just remember there was fire. And then I was fighting with someone and then I woke up in the ambulance. Guess he whomped me pretty good."

She waited a second to see if he'd add more. "You take care of yourself, you hear."

"Okay, missy." He waited a beat before adding, "You do the same, you hear?" All joking was gone. Tonight, they'd both learned either of them could end up dead by the end of the day. Nobody was safe in this town anymore.

It took her a moment to get a grip on her voice, so she could speak without her voice breaking. But, finally, she pushed out, "Gotta go. Don't want to make any more incriminating statements to another station employee. The producer's already got enough dirt on me."

"You're a hero." JoJo's voice lowered into his chest, as if he, too, was having a hard time speaking. "I don't think they're gonna want to fire one of Atlanta's new heroines."

She didn't know if she'd ever heard JoJo speak so seriously. Well, except when her granny had died.

She'd shared the moment more with him than she had with Forrester. Because she'd been in the live truck with him when she'd gotten the news.

And he had driven her back to her car, telling her he'd call the station for her, cause they'd probably still want to get a live shot out of her even if her closest blood relative on earth had just expired.

She'd gotten into her car and started calling Forrester, trying to get a message to him through any avenue she had for him. And hadn't heard back from him for five days.

Until after the funeral. She'd sat there on the front row, as they lowered her granny into the ground. Even now, the visual of that happening had the power to bring her to tears.

But, she pushed that image back. Because her granny would have wanted it that way. "You've got your life to live," she could almost hear Granny's croaky old voice now. "Get on with it, girl."

She looked back at Forrester. And suddenly, the past seemed just that, long gone.

If she'd died tonight, would she have gotten to the Pearly Gates to hear Saint Peter say, "I bet all that self-righteous indignation doesn't seem all that important now, does it, girl?"

He'd point down to Forrester, walking around on earth. "You could have had more time with that. You

know the Big Boss made him just for you, don't ya?"
He'd raise an eyebrow. "You don't get too many
second chances in life, missy."

Why Saint Peter sounded like JoJo, she wasn't sure.
The same intonation, choice of words, and that laugh.

"I gotta go, JoJo. Just wanted to check that you're
okay."

"I'm more than okay, missy. I'm just fine—alive and
kicking."

She hung up as Forrester reached her. He wrapped
one arm around her waist and waited for her to lean in.

And Saint Peter help her, she did.

Leaned into this living, vital man. With whom, as
long as they were both alive, she might have a second
chance.

She breathed him in, smelling of the fires of hell
they'd just escaped.

She leaned in closer to him and realized that
underneath all that smoke, he smelled like heaven. He
smelled like a second chance.

CHAPTER NINETEEN

He crept around the outside of Cassie's house. The place that should have remained undefiled by that detective.

They were divorced now. She was to be his. Not that blasted detective's. He'd had his chance and blown it.

But, obviously she was a whore. And that whore had the detective back in her bed.

She'd pay.

The detective would pay.

A blind, raging fury swept down over his vision, like a burning sheet of fire.

Only the fires of hell could cleanse her soul. Fire was the cleanser. He would arrange the rendezvous.

He boldly walked to the back window of the house.

A candle burned inside the room. A proper harbinger of things to come.

Slowly, knowing what he'd see, he stepped up to the window.

Between a crack in the curtains, he saw bodies illuminated by the soft glow of the candle's flickering flame.

It would be a much brighter flame's light sweeping

across their bodies before much longer. The cleansing fire of hell he would unleash on the house.

They would be dead before the afterglow of their dirty sex left their bodies.

No. He stepped back. He had a better plan, one that would hurt more. With a pain that cut into the very soul.

They would pay.

He made the vow of righteous condemnation that always started the murder, the raging anger taking hold of him as he silently screamed the words he lived by.

They will pay.

The candlelight caramelized her skin into a heady concoction that he bathed himself in. Her scent washed over him, rinsing away the memory of the lonely nights since he'd lost her.

After the divorce papers had been filed, he hadn't made the same mistake he'd made when she'd first left him. The mistake of thinking any woman could replace her.

The mistake of inhabiting the undercover identity he'd so embraced, of emulating the type of men who slept around, believing that what their women didn't know wouldn't hurt them.

An intrinsic characteristic of his nature had changed.

Something inside of Cassie culled the truth from him. More and more, he found himself unable to lie.

Unable to tell the lies that had always flowed so easily from his mouth when he needed to avoid trouble.

That growing inability to lie to her had told him more than anything that she was his life mate. She made him want to share the realities of his life, good or bad. Right or wrong, he wanted her to know the truth of him.

She looked up into his eyes now, as if she could read all that was flowing through him, the powerful emotions that moved him, drove him to connect with her.

She pushed the last items of clothing from her body, baring herself to him, as if to answer the silent vow he'd made to her.

Nothing between them, not a job, not a lie. And certainly, not the trappings of society, clothes to cover the body.

As she kicked off her underwear, his heartbeat accelerated.

Until it was impossible to think. He could only feel. Feel her skin against his, her heart beating next to his, and then her body underneath his, opening to him, her warmth pulling him inside her very center.

"God, this is what life's about," he groaned just as she wrapped her legs around him, pulling him tightly into her core.

"Oh yes, it is," she murmured.

Then, words were impossible. They merely felt, and stroked, and joined together into one living, breathing, life altering force.

He lay curled around her, his stomach joined to her back, his hand stroking along her arm.

She was sated with him, yet still couldn't get enough of his touch.

"So, are you moving back in with me, or am I gonna

get a drawer over here?" he murmured like it was a foregone conclusion.

She chuckled softly. "Let's not get ahead of ourselves. The ink on our divorce isn't even dry yet."

"So, we can smear it, make it illegible, invalidate it?" He kissed along her shoulder, slowly climbing to her neck, making it hard to think.

Just making it hard, from the feel of him as he pushed up against her.

He rolled her over, sliding into her. In the small amount of conversation they had been able to conclude between bouts of lovemaking, they'd exchanged enough information to know that she was still on birth control, that she'd not had another partner since him.

He hadn't either.

At least not since the woman who'd completely annihilated any possibility for reconciliation as far as Cassie was concerned.

Until now?

Cassie awoke the next morning, and immediately knew something was different.

The smell of man inundated her senses. Not just any man.

The smell of Forrester. That pungent, make-you-want-to roll around-in-bed-with-him-all-day smell.

She'd never been able to get enough of his scent. Just something about it. It had been one of the hardest parts of breaking up with him, not being able to smell him.

But, now, she felt desperate to get him out of there, out of the house she'd worked so hard to turn into a refuge from him. And, the pain he'd inflicted on her.

That's why she'd left the marriage house and set up her own place as soon as she'd decided they were through. But, when exactly had that been?

When he hadn't been there for her when Granny died? That had been the original cracking point. But, then even though she'd said they were through, that hadn't been the end for her.

The real end had been when he'd slept with another woman so quickly after they split up. Because if he could do that, she'd decided, then he hadn't really cared.

If he'd replaced her with another so easily.

Kinda like her dad had replaced her?

That was ridiculous. She wasn't a little girl anymore, hurt because Daddy dropped her off at Granny's house and left her. So soon after her mother had died.

Because he'd met another woman, one who didn't want kids.

It was ridiculous to think she was still repeating childhood patterns, feeling childhood hurts.

But, it had felt like that.

Her granny had died, and Forrester hadn't been there for her, not showing up until Granny was in the ground. Then, when she'd moved out of the bedroom, he'd slept with another woman.

Before she was even out of the house. Had just moved on.

Damn it.

Damn it. Damn it. Damn it.

She was reliving it in her mind. Reminding. That was an appropriate word. Letting it flow through her brain as if it were happening now.

She shook her head as the feelings of humiliation lapped at the shores of her heart again. So many people in the cop world had known about it. Or at least, she'd imagined they had. Imagined they were all talking about it.

And she'd imagined it, for sure. Too many times. So many that it was like a dam in her brain, that only needed the slightest weakness to break and let it all come pouring out again.

She pushed the past back, because she was better than that.

But, here Forrester was, in her bed, with his smell all over the place.

A quick, almost unconscious reaction made her want to get him out of there as soon as possible. Before he could hurt her again?

"You're a grown woman, Red," she muttered just below her breath. He stirred behind her, and she was up, slipping out from underneath his arm, and heading out of the room.

"You certainly are, Red," he said. She glanced over her shoulder and saw him eyeing her body.

A shiver ran through her from that look, that sexy, want to take her now look.

She grabbed a robe, slipping it on.

"Come on back to bed," he growled, an early morning, roughness in his throat that matched the look of him, with a slight beard growth that would scratch against her skin, making sure she knew there was a man in her bed.

"Can't," she said, decisively, wrapping the robe's sash tightly around her waist and cinching it. "Got a story to do."

"You almost died and you can't take a day off?" he said, with a lazy yawn, stretching, his arms raising above his head in a full body yawn.

"I didn't almost die." She needed coffee. "JoJo did, not me."

"Come back here." He reached toward her. She stepped back, even though she was way too far away for him to reach her.

But, that hand tempted her. To let him pull her back into bed. Back into his life?

"I gotta make coffee." She pivoted, getting the heck out of there.

Away from him, lying in her bed with his scent all over the place.

CHAPTER TWENTY

She showered quickly, making sure to lock the bathroom door behind her so Forrester couldn't join her. He'd rattled the knob anyway, playfully, as if he were going to come and get her.

"You know you only got a privacy lock on this thing," he'd said through the door. "I could go find a little screwdriver or a piece of wire and be in within a minute. You got any wire hangers around this place?"

He'd scratched softly at the door.

She'd listened to the playful noise and been tempted to open it and let him in.

But, no. This was the day after she'd almost died.

No matter what she said to him, yesterday, she'd thought she might die. Because she could never have left JoJo to die in that blaze.

The thought of those two little kids at home with no daddy coming home wouldn't have let her flee to save herself. Not to mention how she felt about JoJo. Or at least, she'd like to believe that about herself.

But, the terror rose up in her throat at the memory of those flames snaking around the wall, heading toward the ceiling. She'd been afraid of a flashover.

Had heard of their deadliness, didn't know how long she'd had.

She turned the water to cooler, letting it rinse over her, with all the relief from the heat that singed her memory.

Then, she flipped off the water, wrapped a towel around her hair, then another around her body. And began her quick morning routine.

She blew her hair quickly, put on some makeup, then looked out into the hall to figure out where Forrester was before heading to her room to dress.

A few minutes later, she found him in the kitchen, leaning up against the counter, drinking a cup of coffee. Fully dressed, thank goodness.

He looked her up and down. "All business today, eh?"

"Mmmhmm," she murmured agreement, walking past him to refill her cup. "What are you doing today?"

He waited a beat before answering. "Gonna follow up on that last body. Try to figure out who it was."

"You mean the one that's not Clayton the fireman, right?" She made the mistake of looking over to meet his sideways glance. His eyes narrowed, studying her, with that cop look he got sometimes. Like he was trying to read her. Like he could read her thoughts.

"I bet you just make all the girls confess, huh Forrester?"

He laughed. "What the hell is that supposed to mean?"

She shrugged. "Nothing."

"What are you gonna do today, Cassie?" The question was pointed, direct.

"Me?" She took a sip of coffee and swallowed. "I'm

gonna chase down whatever I can get on Clayton, get a read on him, flesh out the beast. Gonna start up in Knoxville. That's where I understand he's from."

He laughed slightly. "You're good, Red. You already know that much?"

"Yep," she said, answering his laugh with one of her own. They'd always laughed in the mornings. And at night. And just about anytime, really.

Another thing she'd missed besides his scent. And, how he made her feel in bed. And...

He nodded, still studying her.

"Quit looking at me like that, Forrester." She took another sip of coffee, not making eye contact.

"You be careful, Cassie. Don't be alone today."

She snapped her gaze back over to him. "What do you mean?"

"You know what I mean. There's something funny about this whole thing."

She'd felt it too. "That's why I want to find out more about him, give the viewers a picture of who this guy is that sets fires, leaving bodies and embers splashing behind him."

"Oooh, kinda literary," he said. Then, his eyes narrowed, and his face became very serious. "Be careful, Cassie. This thing is strange."

She nodded and looked out the window over the sink. You couldn't let every little scary feeling you got stop you from doing your job.

"Gotta plug on," she quoted her granny, in an often repeated saying Forrester had heard from her many times.

Forrester snaked a hand out, snagging her wrist. The reference to her granny had sounded like a reproach, maybe.

But, she hadn't meant it that way. Just wanted to talk about her granny to someone who'd loved her as much as Cassie had.

"I'm so sorry," Forrester said in a low voice. "So sorry that I wasn't there when she passed. I loved the old gal and would have done anything to be there by her side with you to say goodbye."

Quick tears rose in her eyes, instantly making her entire face hot with the need to cry. She sniffed. "She really loved you, Forrester. I guess we should just remember how nice you were to her when she was alive."

"I guess we could," he conceded in a half-hearted voice. "But, I'd rather kill that bastard Max, for not telling me your granny was low sick in the hospital. I swear that guy just likes to cause trouble."

She nodded. "I know. He came by and hit on me after Granny died." She swore silently. "I think he didn't tell you how sick Granny was in order to put a wedge between us."

He looked her in the eye. "You believe that?"

She nodded. "I do."

"Then, why can't you forgive me?"

She looked at him, and he nodded again. "Cause I slept with that woman so quickly."

She looked away. She wasn't going to answer the almost rhetorical question. But, he waited so long. Saying nothing.

"Yes," she finally said, turning to look him fully in the eye, pulling her wrist away from his touch, that suddenly burning touch.

"That was F'ed up of me, Cassie."

She almost wanted to laugh at how hard he was

175

trying not to curse. Something she'd always hated. Reminded her of her father and his new wife, who'd used curse words liberally, as if they were something most people said in polite conversation.

"Get the F out of here!" her dad's new wife had yelled at her when she'd broken some vase that lady had just loved. More than an eight-year-old little girl, anyway. And, she'd used the full word.

Cassie couldn't even bring herself to think the full F word, it reminded her so much of that time. And those people who hadn't loved a little girl.

Forrester stepped into her vision, cutting off the memories. "That was screwed up of me, Cassie. I can't erase it, though I wish I could."

He clenched his jaw and narrowed his eyes. "But, I can promise you it will never happen again. I went off the deep end when you moved out of our bedroom, started drinking. Pretty heavily."

He raised both hands. "I know that's not an excuse. But, I just felt so alone. I stepped into the role I was playing in my deep undercover life, started drinking even. One night, I stopped by Miguel's. Thought Luke was gonna be there. He wasn't. And instead, I started talking to that bartender. One drink led to another, and then, I went to bed with her."

He'd been easy pickings. But, that wasn't an excuse.

Or was it? She'd moved out of their bedroom, told him they were through. And, he'd acted on it. If they'd been through, it wouldn't have mattered.

But, she'd been acting like a high school girl. Saying things she didn't mean. If she'd just moved into the other room, and made it clear he was going to have to pay for a while, hadn't said she was going to file for divorce and move out as soon as she found a place, it would have been different.

But, more than the sex, it had been the lies he'd told to cover his tracks. She'd have thought she was crazy and paranoid, sensing something was going on with him, if that woman hadn't come over and found Cassie still living in the same house as Forrester.

The shocked look on that woman's face probably had mirrored Cassie's face. Mandy. She had a name. And Mandy had been honest when asked by Cassie, admitted what had happened, explained that Forrester had told her Cassie had left him. Mandy had been apologetic.

But, Cassie didn't hold sleeping with Forrester against her. Because technically, Cassie had told Forrester she was leaving him.

Forrester reached for her hand again. She felt torn between wanting to rip her hand away and run. And letting him take her hand, pull her into an embrace, make all the months they'd been apart go away.

"I started drinking as a kid, Cassie."

She looked up at him. He almost never talked about his childhood. Just that one time the other day when he'd dropped the bombshell about his mother having been in rehab when they'd gotten married.

"I told you how I sneaked liquor from my parents. How they'd have fights sometimes accusing the other of how much they'd drank." He shook his head. "The alcohol helped ease the pain for me. But, it also engrained it in my personality. When I drink, it reduces my impulse control. I'd been drinking when I shoplifted some liquor as a kid. That's how I met Captain Barnett."

The guy who'd become a role model for him.

"The captain was in the store when the clerk had caught me as a fourteen-year-old sticking a bottle in my jeans' front. The captain took me home to my parents rather than arresting me. When he got there, my parents were brawling and drunk in the living room."

He shook his head. "You could hear them all the way up the front walk. The captain didn't say anything to them. Just started coming round, picking me up after school, making sure I went to baseball practice."

He took another sip of coffee. "I didn't go see him for months after you and I split up. Cause I was drinking," he said with a head tilt.

"But, when I got the divorce papers from you, I went to see him, then straight to an AA meeting."

He looked into her eyes, hard, direct. "I haven't touched a sip of liquor since, Cassie." He nodded. "Never again. Not a sip of alcohol, not another woman. Not another woman, as long as there's the slightest chance of you and me. Do you hear me?"

She looked at him and nodded.

"Do you believe me?"

She glanced away. "I hear you." But, did she believe him. On an emotional level, as well as intellectually?

"I am going to make sure you believe me, Cassie. I want you to know you mean everything to me."

He stepped closer, his voice lowering. "I want kids with you, Cassie. I want to take them to baseball games, or softball games if they're a girl." He tilted his head to meet her eyes, and a smile began deep inside of her.

"We could give them a really good life, Cassie. Kinda make up for the one it seems neither of us had."

He met her eyes. "My parents were lousy ones by choice. Yours died, not their fault."

She coughed. "Actually." She turned and paced away from him. Did she want to get into all of this now?

Yeah. Now or never, a little voice whispered. Just say it, just say it. Spit out the hurt that she never talked about.

She turned to look at him. "I'm gonna say something, then I'm gonna leave. I don't want a big scene, okay?"

His expression was hesitant, expectant. "Okay," he finally said softly. As if he knew something big was coming.

"You're not the only one with secrets about their family life. Sheesh, you have to wonder does everybody have them?"

He half laughed. "I'm starting to think so, the longer I live. No perfect families."

She took a deep breath, willing it all the way inside where she hid the secret, pushing air into the ugly fetid space.

"My mom died," she blew out, then sucked in another breath, trying for the strength to say it out loud. "But, my dad—later on, he just left. Took me to my granny's, to be precise. And left me there."

She sucked in a deep breath to fight the pain the words evoked, the memories of that horrible time, then forced out the rest of it. "Because his new wife didn't want any other woman's child in her life."

She smiled sadly, trying to force the sadness from her heart. "I think I reminded her that my father had loved another woman before her. How F'ed up is that?

179

Hurting a child because my stepmom was too small a person to accept my father had lived before he met her."

A sigh came from Forrester's mouth. She didn't dare look at him. Didn't want to see the impact, feel it again in her own chest, the pain that little girl had felt. Being replaced by another woman.

The shock rattled through her. Like Forrester had moved on so quickly?

But, that was different. She'd kicked the marriage to the curb, called it garbage, and said she was through with him. She'd left him.

But, it hadn't felt different, she realized. Losing Granny, being all alone in the world again, while he'd been off, who knew where, had felt just like when her mother had left her.

And then, Forrester so quickly sleeping with another woman, had felt as horrible a pain as that little girl had known.

"Damn," she said out loud. "Are we all destined to live our childhoods all of our lives? Are we imprinted and unable to get past it?"

She laughed harshly. "I always think I'm so smart. Me, the big reporter lady."

Reporter lady?

Like Miss Mary had called her. Suddenly, she remembered something Miss Mary had said.

"I've got to go," she said, meeting Forrester's eyes.

"Okaaay." He shook his head, lifted his hands, clasping them together into one large fisted bunch, then exploded them out. "Boom. Drop that bomb, then leave."

Suddenly, old childhood wounds seemed so

insignificant compared to all that had been going on recently in the current world.

"Childhood hurts are one thing. But, someone was going around hurting people in a very real sense. I need to go out and report on that. Investigate that. Understand that."

He nodded. "Yeah, me too," he said quietly then narrowed his eyes on her. "When am I gonna see you again, Red?"

The use of *Red* said he'd accepted the quick turnaround of mood.

That was good. Because all she could think about now was the man who'd wrecked havoc on the city of Atlanta, setting fires to homes, almost burning people to death.

The flames that had almost trapped Miss Mary, almost burned JoJo to death, flashed over in her mind, creating a firestorm that raged with a fury.

CHAPTER TWENTY-ONE

"Was he a mean little boy?" Cassie held the microphone in front of the mouth of a neighbor who'd lived next door to Clayton when he'd been a little boy. A guy who looked to be in his eighties.

"No. Actually, he wasn't," the old man said. "Never would have figured him for a murderer. Had a soft heart, for hurt kitties, dogs, kids littler than him."

He shrugged and narrowed his eyes. "Then, later— when the bullying started." He gazed away into the trees behind his property. "He changed."

"Bullying?"

"Yeah, my kid told me how he was pushed around by the other boys. He used to set fires as a kid. Kinda like he was letting off steam."

"Really?" she prompted, always finding it better to use just a few words, keep them talking without ever really realizing they were opening up.

"I'm thinking that's how he got his rage out over the bullying, through the fires." The old man laughed without much humor. Darkly, as if seeing the pattern now that would turn into arson in a grown man.

"Big ones?"

He barked out a raspy laugh. "One got out of hand.

My whole garage went up." He shook his head. "Thank the Lord my car weren't in it."

"His daddy whipped him up good. I could hear the hollering all the way over to my house. And the fires seemed to stop." He raised one grizzled old hand and pointed a finger into the air. "Always thought it was so ironic, cuz his granddaddy was a preacher. A fire and brimstone preacher." He cackled like that was a good joke.

"Guess he took the fire and brimstone part a bit too far?" Cassie wrinkled her eyes like she got the joke.

"Yeah. They were a big old family, went to church to hear granddaddy, then all got together for Sunday dinners. Sometimes over at Clayton's family home. Sometimes they all went to the other cousins' houses. Fire and brimstone." He cackled again. "Never really held with the fire and brimstone preaching, myself. Got too skeered as a kid, sitting there, listening to the preacher talk about hell."

He shook his head. "Too scary. Guess little Clayton was following in the footsteps of his granddaddy with the fire part of the fire and brimstone. Neighbors used to joke Clayton would grow up to be an arsonist or a firefighter. 'Thank golly, it was a firefighter,' people used to say."

The old man's cloudy gray eyes met Cassie's. "Guess we was wrong. He grew up to be both."

A shiver ran through Cassie. "Are any of his family still around here?"

The old man rubbed his chin. "No'm, they moved away, like so many people do these days. Clayton's parents went on down to Florida. The granddaddy, well, he passed on to his great reward. The others? Can't remember what happened to them."

She nodded. "When did Clayton's parents move away?"

"Oh, a long time ago. Went down to Florida somewhere. Can't remember."

"Thank so much. You've been a big help." She handed the microphone to JoJo.

"Oh, missy?" He stopped her with a wave of his hand. "I remembered me something about his family. Seems like he had a cousin down Atlanta way."

"A cousin?" She focused on his face, willing more information from him. "Do you remember a name?"

"No'm. It plumb escapes me at the moment." He looked off at the sky.

Cassie waited, but it became clear after a bit that he wasn't going to remember anymore. So, she gave him a card and left.

As she and JoJo walked back to the truck, they looked at each other. "Wow," they both said almost in unison.

"We've got to find some of his other family," Cassie said.

"Oh yeah," JoJo said. They always thought alike.

"You feeling okay after your encounter yesterday, JoJo?"

"Great. Great. I could probably drive by now."

"Do you remember any more details about last night?"

JoJo just laughed.

"I'll take that as a no." She shook her head, the keys to the SUV securely deposited in her pocket. She patted them. "I'll drive. You just shoot today."

They'd taken an SUV rather than a live truck for the long haul up to Tennessee and back. JoJo had refused to take any time off. He didn't want to miss any of the action any more than she did.

They were both newshounds, adrenalin junkies, all those things that made up good firemen, policemen. And yeah, news people.

That was probably one of the reasons she and Forrester had been so right for each other. They were both the same type of driven people.

They were right for each other till they weren't, she reminded herself.

The curling memory of last night swirled through her, with a heat that would warm the heart of any arsonist. Forrester singeing her nerve endings with the fire that had blazed through and around them.

Would she ever stop remembering them together?

She got into the car, slamming the door, forcefully. JoJo arched his eyebrows at how hard she shut the door, then walked around to the back of the SUV.

As JoJo put his gear away, she typed an update into her phone, pressing send back to the station before JoJo was even in the passenger seat.

"Let's haul some rear, girlie," he said.

She laughed. It was funny cause be always drove so carefully. "We want to put news on the air, not be the news," she repeated his often used phrase.

"No. I beat death yesterday. I'm feeling immortal." He laughed jovially.

"Don't use up them lives too quickly," she returned. "Working in news, we always have to keep a few in reserve. How many you down to now?"

He laughed dismissively. "I got a few left in my

pocket, I'm sure. He patted his shirt pockets. "No, wait. This might be my ninth. Forgot about that time in Birmingham when that old hillbilly yelled at me, "Get off'n my property you stinkin'... He looked at her and laughed, with a little tilt of the head.

"The N word?"

JoJo nodded. "Of course, he used all the letters in the word, not just polite white people's abbreviation. Then, he took a shot at me."

"Oh gosh, JoJo. Just when I think I've heard all your stories." She started the engine. "It was the N word that ticked you off, right? Not the gunshot?"

He laughed. "You know me well, girl."

Forrester kicked up his feet onto her coffee table, shooting her a look for permission.

She waved toward the table without saying a word. They'd both shared the philosophy that houses were to be lived in. Furniture was meant to be comfortable.

The only pieces she was particular about were the few she'd taken from Granny's house. But still, those pieces had already seen long, hard use. And if they'd survived as long as they had, she felt sure they'd survive her use.

"We kicked the other news crews' butts with the portrait we had of him, since they only got his name when it was released by the police just before the five o'clock news."

"We got more for tomorrow." She tapped her head. "Keep dropping little nuggets into the pieces, drawing the public on." She took a swig of the non-alcoholic beer Forrester had brought over. Said he couldn't give up the taste, or the coolness of it running down his throat.

"I've been looking for other family. I've run a quick Internet check and can't find anyone here in Atlanta, though the old guy seemed to think Clayton had a cousin down here. He said he had some family in Florida, but I haven't been able to find them either."

Forrester's eyes were fixed on her as she talked, making her itchy, overly aware of him.

Were they going to talk about last night?

No. She needed to keep the focus on her story, the investigation. This was one of the biggest stories of her career. It was huge.

Not to mention, just so damn interesting.

"It is so unbelievable that he was an arsonist as a child," she blurted out.

Forrester smiled with his eyes.

"Nothing ever surprises you, does it, Forrester?"

He looked at her, directly, intensely. "Are you kidding, Red? Everything surprises me. I still cannot believe the things people dream up." He shook his head, looking off into the distance, musing.

Was he getting ready to tell some story from undercover. He never talked about that.

Probably since it had contributed to the end of their marriage.

"That's why I got into this business, cause people are just so damn interesting," he mused.

She waited. That was usually how she got anything out of him, wait, and let him have dead air to fill up.

He looked at her sideways, as if to say he knew what she was doing. They did know each other pretty well.

"I've got Roberto doing his computer genius stuff.

He'll find something for us." Forrester nodded sagely.

"The old Tennessee guy said Clayton was never mean as a child, was kind to animals, kind to little kids."

"Really?" He leaned back in his chair, drumming his fingers on the beer bottle. The non-beer bottle, she laughed to herself.

"What?" He shot her a look.

"Nothing." He wasn't the subject of the conversation. She didn't want to veer over into casual conversation. Especially not about him, his ways, his anything.

"It doesn't fit the pattern of a serial killer, to be sweet and kind to little animals and kids, does it? You know cause you'd be nice to women, too?" She took them right back to the reason she'd let him come over in the first place.

"No, it doesn't." He leaned his chair back onto two legs. He always liked to grab a straight back wooden chair from the old wooden table in her dining room. Liked to work the chair, sometimes straddling it. Other times, he sat in the usual way, and rocked it back and forth on its legs. Like now.

The guy couldn't just settle into a chair and relax. Unless he was between cases, which was rare.

It was like the body movement released tension, helped him think.

"Maybe," he said, bringing the chair back down onto all four legs. "Maybe he just killed people who came up on him when he's doing a fire? He only offs people who are a direct threat to him?"

"Like JoJo finding him?" She took a sip of the non-beer, and began peeling the label off the bottle. "Maybe."

Then, she shook her head. "Something feels very un-random about those killings, though."

"I know, right?" He leaned the chair back again.

She laughed slightly, and he just shot her a glance.

"Do you see a pattern in any of those killings?" He looked at her, leaning forward, resting his elbows on his knees.

"I do," she said. "Except for JoJo, which probably was an accident, coming up on Clayton. Wrong place, wrong time kinda thing." She tilted her beer bottle back for a sip then sat the beer onto the coffee table.

"They were all women." She began counting off, holding up one finger. "And it strikes me odd, that there is something maybe alike about them." She held up a second finger.

"Me, too." He pushed the chair back onto its back legs. "The first and the fourth in this string were prostitutes."

That hadn't been officially confirmed, but she'd suspected it by the way the woman was dressed. Not just hoochie mama style, but something a bit more over the top.

Forrester raised an eyebrow. "That's not for official consumption yet, her being a prostitute."

She nodded and he took a sip of his beer then lowered the chair. "After the first, I thought they were gonna continue to be prostitutes. Like what happened a few years back, with those two dead prostitutes. But, when the next victim wasn't, then another wasn't, I started thinking what's alike?"

She waited. Wanted to see if he'd come up with the same correlation as she had.

He arched an eyebrow at her. "Say it."

189

"Say what?"

He leaned forward. "What you're thinking."

She looked away from those intense, direct eyes. Those clear green eyes that had gotten a confession from so many just by continuing to look into the suspect's eyes.

"You know," he prompted.

"They all seem to have something to do with sex. Something to do with being a *bad girl*?" She laughed at the phrasing.

"They were all *bad girls* of a sort," he agreed. "He was punishing them for going against the good girl rules."

"Prostitutes," she said, and nodded. "The ultimate rule breaker of the good girl rules."

"A high profile *homewrecker,*" Forrester emphasized the word. "The radio personality."

Homewrecker? A quick little reminder of the woman Forrester had slept with kicked her painfully. Hell, their home had already been wrecked. By her, if she really admitted it.

She'd signed on for marrying a cop. She'd already known what living with a cop would be about. But, still, she'd held it against him when he'd been unable to get home to her in her time of need.

Hell. Don't go there, she closed her eyes and yelled at herself to shake herself out of the repeated pattern of the first few months of their breakup, when the loop had played over and over in her brain.

She looked up and realized he was watching her, reading her.

"What's the council woman got to do with them?" she asked, even as the connection to the other women popped into her head. She held up a finger. "The city council vote to grandfather in those strip joints over on Cheshire Bridge Road."

"Yeah." He nodded.

She leaned forward. "Remember how the cops and the neighboring businesses all wanted the city council to run those people out of the neighborhood. And she was the deciding vote to allow them to stay if they were already in business."

He just looked at her, letting her talk, as if he knew this was her way of thinking. Talking it out.

A thought popped into her head. "Do you think maybe a cop's involved, too? Like maybe they helped give Clayton the idea or something. They were the ones who really wanted those people out of there."

"Why would you even think that. You think I'd do something like that?" He looked at her, tilting his head, his eyes serious like he meant it. But he didn't, was just provoking her, trying to get a rise out of her. Knowing sometimes that was the best way to shake up her way of looking at something so she got a new angle.

She looked back at him for a minute, then just laughed. "No. I can't see you trying to run strip clubs out of business."

"What's that supposed to mean?"

She shrugged. "I just don't see you having that much of a problem with nekkid ladies."

He took a sip of beer to hide his smile. But, his eyes, with that giveaway smile in them still showed.

Damn! The guy was just so hot. That look about him, like he was living every minute of his life. He was just so damn alive. And vital.

Made her feel alive to be around him.

He lowered his beer. And those eyes fixed on her. He stared at her for a long moment, the smile dropping away.

She looked down at her beer, carefully continuing to work the label, trying to get it off in one piece. Anything to get her mind off of him and those eyes.

The way they'd looked at her while they made love last night, as if he was memorizing her.

A shiver ran through her. The way he'd touched her, as if imprinting the memory of her on him for life, as if he'd take those memories with him to his grave. And into the next world.

He leaned further forward and reached for her hand.

But her phone vibrated on the coffee table to her right.

She jumped from the sound, then quickly grabbed it, before he could see the name or the number. She checked the incoming number.

"I gotta take this." She stood up, heading toward the back porch before she hit the connect button. "Hey," she said, as she opened the back door.

"I didn't catch you at a bad time, did I?" Preston's voice sounded casual, like it was nothing. But, he wouldn't be calling her about nothing.

"No, it's okay."

CHAPTER TWENTY-TWO

"Hello," Cassie called into the nearly dark house. "Preston?"

Why had she agreed to meet him at this time of night? It wasn't late, but dark had fallen, and there were too few street lights, making Miss Mary's neighborhood seem like a cemetery.

A ghost town populated with the ghosts of all the people who had lived out their lives on this once bustling street. Along with the ghost of the city council woman.

A shiver of awareness of how alone she was out here ran through her.

"Yeah, it's me. In the kitchen," Preston's voice came from the back of the dark house.

She stepped into the burned-out hulk of a house, the charcoal scent pinging her nose with a pungent tweek.

She used her cell phone as a flashlight to keep from brushing her clothes against the walls. Silently, she edged through the building, unable to stop imagining it as it must have been the night Councilwoman Betty Farber was brought here.

Before the fire was set.

The assignment desk knew where she was. She

pushed back a shiver of anxiety with that reassuring reminder. She was only feeling the nerves anyone would experience in this horrible place.

Preston stepped out into the hall flashing a large light onto the floor. It lit up the house like a beacon, his face illuminated in its back glow, spectral shadows molding his features into something frightening and unfamiliar.

"Hey, thanks for coming out."

"Sure." She nodded. "I told JoJo to call me in a few. Said I might need to shoot an interview with you. Told him he didn't need to come on over. But, he probably will anyway, just the way he is. Overzealous. Always wants to be the photographer that gets the exclusives."

Preston's eyebrows raised, and surprise crossed his face.

Could he read that she was lying, that suddenly, she wanted him to think someone might show up at any second. She ran her fingers over her phone. Maybe she should text her assignment editor to go ahead and send JoJo or another photog over.

She'd told the assignment editor to expect a phone call or a text from her every fifteen minutes or to call the cops. Had texted her right before she went into the building where she was meeting Preston, but hadn't told the assignment editor who she was meeting.

You just couldn't trust that information to get out into the newsroom mix. Once one person knew who your source was, it could go the circuit in no time.

But, she could be dead or gone by the time cops got the phone call from the desk that she was in trouble.

She had never felt nervous around Preston before.

That he might hit on her, yeah. But, not that he might hurt her.

Kill her?

Was she a bad girl? Had she violated norms of society?

Not many. A bit of binge drinking back in college. Thank goodness, she'd had girlfriends who'd always made sure she got home safe.

But, then she'd quit that. Had settled down and worked to get her degree and achieve her dream job. Knew there was very little economic help coming from her almost non-existent family.

Always known she had to make it in life on her own.

No. She wasn't a bad girl.

Hadn't even slept with anyone since her divorce.

Did sleeping with your ex-husband count as bad? No. Once married, always married in a way. The preacher had waved his hands over them and consecrated their sex. A preacher trumped a civil servant stamping and certifying their divorce papers.

Preston stepped back into the kitchen, leading her forward with the light. She shaded her eyes from the blinding glare, and Preston dropped the beam further down.

"Sorry," he said, his voice echoing through the building.

"No problem."

"It's eerie out here in the dark, huh?" He looked at her, his eyes flashing black.

She just nodded, and suddenly, the worst feeling swept over her. Had this been how the women had been lured to their deaths?

By a trusted official?

A panic came out of nowhere. This was ridiculous. She didn't need to be afraid of the battalion chief.

Still, a sudden urge to run pushed up out of her stomach. Would the predatory need to chase erupt if she did so? If she needed to be afraid of Preston?

Some innate survival instinct prodded her to rush back to her car, lock the doors and get as far away from this place as possible. But, that was crazy cause the danger was past.

The killer had died at his own hands. Life could get back to normal. Still, here in the dark where a woman had died, it was hard to disregard the scary clawing hands that scratched at her nerves.

Get him talking, a little voice said inside her head, a voice that sounded very much like her granny's.

Even now, coaxing her, leading her in the right way.

"So, what'd you want to talk to me about?" she piped out in a cheery, conversational tone, as if he'd called her and they were having this talk while she was safely at her desk in the newsroom.

He looked at her with an odd expression, as if her forced cheerfulness was obvious. "I an inside scoop I'm only going to give to you. But, first," he shook his head. "I really want to personally apologize for my associate, Firefighter Clayton Randolph. Please tell your cameraman how sorry I am for what happened to him."

Cassie nodded. Hobbs was turning into the person she knew again, his expression empathetic, caring. "It wasn't your fault."

"I feel responsible. Like why didn't I see he was capable of that. I'm disappointed 'cause I had high hopes for the guy." He bit his bottom lip.

"Don't," Cassie said. "I've heard that kind of talk

from countless people surrounding bad guys before. Don't beat yourself up for seeing the best in him."

Hobbs looked back up at her and smiled.

Her cell phone vibrated and she looked down at it. A twitch in Hobbs face said he didn't like the interruption. But, she needed to respond since she'd told the desk to check in with her.

It was a text from the assignment editor, *You okay? Need me to call the cops?* A smiley face after that.

Did she? How close to the truth was this meant-as-a-joke question?

The killer was gone. Still, alone out at in this neighborhood at night, you couldn't be too careful. Her nerves were on edge after all that had happened the last few days.

Not just yet. Contact me in two minutes, she texted back. That two minutes comment would catch Smiley Face Woman's attention. Might even prompt her to send a photographer swinging by to check on her.

That assignment editor was older and savvy, not like the young green ones who might overreact, call the cops to come with sirens on for no reason. Scare away a source forever.

She looked up to Preston's questioning gaze. She laughed, self-consciously. "My desk checking up on me. Can't be too careful these days."

"Good idea," he said, but his tone said he was affronted, that she thought she had to take precautions against him.

Heck, if she'd brought Forrester along, she could imagine how that would have gone over.

"You had something you wanted to show me?" All she really wanted right now was to get out of the dungeon of a building, charcoaled walls as black as any medieval torture chamber.

And everywhere, the scent of death, as she'd think of the smell from now on.

Hobbs studied her for a moment, every long second of which the chill inside of her grew colder. There was something so vacant about the way he stared at her.

Eyes empty, devoid of human feeling.

Slowly she edged backward, ready to turn and run screaming if he did anything. Why was she thinking like this?

His hand reached out, and her mouth opened involuntarily, a shriek forming in her gut. Before the scream could erupt from her throat, he pointed behind her.

Her stomach released, and with it the shakes started, her arms and legs feeling weak and wobbly.

She turned to look where his extended finger indicated. A closet. An old pantry, maybe?

"The cops missed something," he said, his voice low and gravelly, the texture scraping across her nerves. "I thought you might like to know about it. Maybe say something on the air about the shoddy investigation."

That was why he'd gotten her out here? He had a bone to pick with the way the cops were running their investigation.

It was a joint operation, firefighters and cops. In fact, the GBI, the Georgia Bureau of Investigation, were even lending a hand.

But, it was the cops he wanted to highlight?

"Who's handling the investigation on the cop side, do you know?" Preston asked.

"Forrester," she said blandly. As if he didn't already know.

"Well, I found something over here in this old closet." He walked toward it, and just as he did, her phone lit up with a text.

"Call cops now?"

Two more minutes please, she texted back.

Preston's eyes rounded with irritation when she looked back up at him.

"Sorry," she said. "Someone's always contacting me from back there when I'm on a story. Someone always wants to tell me something."

He jerked his head back toward the closet and opened the door, with a bit more force than necessary. He jagged a finger toward the floor.

Something about that dark confined space alarmed her. She could be shoved into it, and the door jammed shut. Was there enough material here to burn again?

If she were in that closet and a fire started, would the firefighters find her before the smoke did?

Her diaphragm puffed in and out with ragged, quick short breaths that never got enough oxygen into her lungs.

"What's in there?" She wasn't going inside to find out. Wasn't going anywhere near the closet.

He turned to look at her, his face angry and twisted now.

Why? Because she was standing back, keeping her distance from him and the closet?

"A pair of panties," he said.

"What?" This fit into the sexual line she and Forrester had been talking about. Bad girls often lost their panties.

She almost stepped forward to see. But that black, gapping hole of the small, confined space yawned at her with an avaricious hunger.

"They're in a plastic bag," he said quietly, his voice low, almost as if to entice her to step closer to hear him better.

"What?" She heard her voice rise in amazement at his disclosure. Or in fear for her life? Was she talking too loud, too quietly? Suddenly, it was impossible to monitor herself beyond the pounding in her blood that pulsed adrenalin through her entire body as if prepping her for the fight of her life.

"Hello?" A male voice rattled through the house. Cassie jumped at the sudden noise.

"Who's in here?" a sharp, barking authoritative voice commanded an answer.

"It's us. Who's out there?" Preston barked back.

"Police," the voice rapped again. "Identify yourself then show yourself with your hands exposed."

"Cassie Meyers," she said.

"The reporter?" the man said, something about his voice familiar.

"Yeah."

"Who's the man with you?"

"Preston Hobbs, Battalion Chief," Preston bit off in an angry, impatient tone. "Who are you?"

"Hobbs?" The male voice in the hall came closer. His voice had a laugh to it, like this was all so funny.

A man stepped into the reflected flashlight glow, his own flashlight adding to the already well-illuminated kitchen light.

It was Max, the homicide detective who seemed to hit on her every time he saw her, even though the last she'd heard, he was still technically married to his second or third wife. She couldn't keep track.

"Detective," Preston drew out the word like it was an insult. She'd never realized Preston thought so poorly of the cops.

Maybe since they'd failed to find the guy who kept murdering people and burning buildings that Preston's guys had to risk their lives over?

That would be a source of irritation. He'd wanted to show what *shoddy work* the police were doing.

She just waited, watching to see which of the two men could lift his leg the highest.

"You guys missed some evidence in here," Preston started the leg lifting match.

"Really? You mean it wasn't already burned up cause you guys didn't get the fire out quick enough?" *Round one to the cops.*

"Well, we got it out so you guys could find the last dead woman this guy got away with murdering. Maybe if you worked every scene like dead women were important, you'd have caught him before he had a chance to kill the radio announcer." *Round two to the firefighter who goes for the gut.*

"What evidence do you have here that we missed?" Max bit off the words like he was done playing.

"A pair of women's panties in a plastic bag." Preston jabbed a finger toward the closet.

"What the hell?" Max stepped forward. "I thought they collected those."

He already knew about the women's underwear?

Forrester had also known, certainly, if Max did. Forrester had held back that information from her.

CHAPTER TWENTY-THREE

The scene was alight with cop cars, crime scene investigators. And yes, a few media representatives.

At every news desk in Atlanta, ears were tuned in listening for any calls that might be about the arsonist-killer.

The news crews lined up behind the yellow tape, itching to get closer, always pushing it as far as they could. Just like she would have done, if she were on that side of the tape.

Seemed like she was on the wrong side of the tape too often, in this string of crimes. She liked to report on the news. Not be the news.

Forrester pulled up in his car, and unfolded himself, walking past the other news people. As they asked him questions he gave them a wave and a quick word. "Don't know much. We'll have a statement for you later."

Then, he proceeded underneath the yellow tape.

"I see you're already here," he said to Cassie. Kinda like he wasn't surprised.

"Yep," she said.

"Max said you know about the panties." Forrester looked at her with an arched eyebrow.

"Yep."

"Can I ask you to keep that under your hat?"

"Yep." But, the raging fury she felt almost made her yell at him right here, right out loud, so everyone could hear her.

He turned so his body blocked her from the view of the other reporters and photographers. "You're ticked off."

He said it like a statement, not a question.

She turned full face to him, her eyes narrowed, her breathing labored. "How could you tell?" she said levelly, though it took a lot of restraint sometimes to not yell at your ex.

Like now. When he had farmed her for information but held back himself.

"Just say it," he said, patronizingly. "Get it off your chest."

"Okay." She sucked in a deep breath. She was not gonna yell at her ex-husband, here in front of everybody.

In slow measured tones, she said, "You already knew about the panties."

He nodded, his eyes never leaving her face. "I did."

"I told you everything about Clayton that I found out up in Tennessee. But, you held back some very important information."

He nodded. "I did."

The short, concise acknowledgements could work two ways. This was how it had always gone when they'd gotten into fights. It would start out this way.

But, it didn't always end this way.

She remembered the last screaming match they'd

had. Her screaming actually. He'd just gotten quieter and quieter.

Which had made her increasingly furious.

She sucked in a deep breath. That was then, this was now. He was her ex-husband. Not her husband.

And she was going to start treating him accordingly.

"Look, this one-way street of cooperation is over," she said tersely, her voice low so no one else could hear them.

"Will you keep the panties information under your hat?" he repeated quietly.

That was what he wanted to talk about? Not that she felt betrayed, played?

Fine.

He tilted his head, meeting her eyes. "Cops have to hold some information back. That was something only we knew. We could have used that to find out if the person we might have caught was the real killer."

Made sense, of course. There was a set of rules he had to follow in order to do his job.

But, it still ticked her off.

She nodded and turned away. "I need to ask JoJo if he's gotten all his shots. We're going live for the late news show."

"It's the All Cassie, All The Time News Station?" Forrester quipped lightly. He was stroking her ego.

"Not gonna work," she shot back, and took a step to go around him toward the microwave van another photographer had brought out to meet her and JoJo, since JoJo had come straight from home.

Forrester snaked a hand out, taking her by the forearm. The touch singed her skin, electricity arcing through her entire body at his nearness.

She turned so that his hand fell away. He looked down at her, his eyes carrying even more heat than his touch.

"Am I gonna see you at your place after this?"

Images of the two of them, locked together, naked, skin awash with the touch of the other, flashed through her mind.

If they were alone, she'd probably yell at him. She needed time to decompress, process everything that had happened. "No," she said.

Disappointment flashed in his eyes. Hurt, even.

Then, something beyond him caught her eye. A car full of people pulled up in front of Miss Mary's house. People piled out of the back seat, and one young male ran around the car to pull open the front car door.

He held out a hand, helping Miss Mary get to her feet, and step out of the car. The young teen waited, while she put her arm through his, then walked toward Miss Mary's house with her.

"I hope they don't think they're going in there," Forrester said shortly.

"I'll tell them they can't," she cut in. "I want to speak to her anyway." She waved Forrester off and hurried toward the group.

Loud tones from Miss Mary's group voiced dismay at the state of the house. "No way, Granny, you're not gonna be able to move back in there."

"Oh yes, I am," Miss Mary stated definitively, her tone undefeated, defiant. "Big Pappy and I lived here all our lives, raised our chil'ren, even a few grandchil'rens here. I'm fixin' it back up and moving back in."

"Not till you're sure they caught that crazy fire man,

Granny," said the tall teen who still had Miss Mary's arm through his. "Be sure he was the right guy."

"That's right. Not gonna give that man a second chance to burn me up. Case that man that died wasn't the right one."

A lot of nods and emmhmmms indicated they all agreed.

"Miss Mary," Cassie said, smiling at the old woman as she approached the group.

"Miss Cassie," the old lady cackled. "Here's my hero, chil'ren. She done rescued me out of my burning home."

She grabbed onto Cassie with her free arm, pulling her in for a long hug. The teen patted Cassie's back.

Other family members stepped forward, putting hands on Cassie's back.

It almost felt like a religious moment, a laying on of hands, with all of their love encasing her, pushing back all of the dangers and fears that lurked in the dark.

She'd remember this moment tonight when she was trying to get to sleep, when the images of all those dead women ran through her brain.

When the fire that had licked around her and JoJo, and the dead councilwoman and radio talk show host, lit up her brain so she couldn't drift away into unconsciousness.

Last night, she suspected the only thing that had allowed her to sleep was the exhaustion she'd felt from making love with Forrester. And being physically spent from the adrenalin release and the terror during the fire.

What would she do tonight?

Remember this moment, with all the love the family was sending her way.

Finally, Miss Mary pulled back, and the family stepped away, heading toward the house.

"Don't cross the yellow line, the cop asked me to tell you," she called to them.

"I need to get my family bible out of there," Miss Mary said, with a note of desperation. "It's got all the dates and names of the births and deaths in the family."

"Can't believe you forgot that, Granny," one female teen said.

"Your granny was a bit distracted," a woman said, that Cassie immediately knew must be Miss Mary's daughter.

"Yep, but she's right," Miss Mary said. "Can't believe myself I forgot it."

"One of the firefighters or the police will come and help you get out what you need, Miss Mary. And, of course, you're gonna need an inspector to come and see that the property is safely repaired before you can move back in."

"Okay, well ya'll go ahead and get a look at it," Miss Mary said to the family. "I want to talk to my girl, here." She took Cassie's arm, nodded her head down the way, and she and Cassie walked away from the family.

The road was lit by the glow of the lights set up for her upcoming live shot and the headlights from a CSI van that had come out to officially take the panties into evidential custody.

If evidential custody could still be declared after the delay between the fire and their discovery.

As they walked along, a little man crept out of the cover of darkness.

"Eddie, is that you?" Miss Mary coaxed, in a soft tone, as if calling a stray dog.

The man sidled up, as if he might have to dodge away from a blow at any moment. A quietness, an almost-not-there quality, hung on him. He didn't make eye contact with either of them, his head down, his shoulders slumped. Like he was trying to be invisible.

Cassie wanted to reach out and pat him, reassure him that the world wouldn't hurt him. But, she knew it already had.

The man had suffered too much, that wounded, scared look in his eyes testified, to ever believe any false reassurances.

She'd come back with food and blankets for him.

Maybe get the Atlanta Homeless Alliance to check on him when the weather got too cold. Looked like the arsonist was burning up all the sources of shelter he'd probably relied on for years.

"Hey," a voice from behind her yelled. JoJo ran toward them, and Eddie shrank even further into himself, looked as if he was measuring whether he had time to run back into the dark or should just try to look invisible.

JoJo measured the shrinking man with one look. A black man probably about five foot, six inches, if he'd stood up straight, which he wasn't, but even then he would have been shorter than Cassie in her shoes, with graying hair, his clothes old and dirty, as if he slept on the ground a lot. And skinny like a stray dog. His clothes hung loose on his small frame, as if he'd shrunken inside of them, if they'd ever fit him, looking more like thrift shop castoffs.

"It's okay, little man," JoJo spoke in a quiet voice,

the one she'd heard him use on his kids, his tone reassuring, non-threatening. "I ain't yelling for you."

He patted the guy on the shoulder, and Eddie flinched.

JoJo looked at Eddie for a moment, then at Cassie. "There's another fire. I think they've got another body." He took off running to put his gear back into his SUV so they could go. From here, she could see the tech breaking down the live truck.

Cassie flashed a look at Miss Mary. "Gotta go."

"You go, sweetie. But you and me, we gotta talk." She tilted her head toward Eddie. "Eddie was out here that night, too. Think he maybe saw something."

The shriveled man looked away, still pretending not to be there. The way he leaned toward Miss Mary though said they had a relationship. That he trusted her.

Cassie smiled at Miss Mary, with a bit of the expression edging toward Eddie. Not too much, not enough to scare him, and make him think she was going to demand anything of him. Just enough hopefully to reassure him he was safe with her, too.

His eyes looked toward the ground, but she could see that he was taking her measure. While still trying to seem like he wasn't there.

Something in his expression said he'd seen something, knew something about the fire.

The next story would have to wait a minute. She looked toward Eddie. "Did you see something that night, Eddie?"

Eddie's gaze flickered up toward her for a moment, then fled away. "Yes'm. I saw Death come for that woman. It were Death that come to take 'er home."

Death?

That was a correct statement all right. She waited for more information, but none came. Eddie just seemed to collapse into himself even more.

She nodded. "Thanks, Eddie. That's very helpful." She smiled at Miss Mary like she'd gotten a lot out of that statement. But, heck, she'd gotten nothing. They all knew death had come for the woman.

"The cops probably would like a statement from you."

"No. No. No." Eddie began to shake his head back and forth almost convulsively. "No. No. No."

"Eddie don't like the police. He thinks they're gonna lock him up."

Eddie continued to swing his head back and forth, like a pendulum on a very short rope. She'd probably gotten all the information out of Eddie that anyone would get. And that hadn't been much of anything.

"Ok, then. No police. But, thanks for the help, Eddie. Thank you, Miss Mary. I've got to go." She nodded and took off toward her car.

As she ran toward JoJo's SUV, she noticed Max and Forrester near Max's car. They were almost chest to chest. And the expressions on their faces, as they spoke to each other? The way they each jabbed a finger toward the other?

Something bad was going down. What, she didn't have time to find out. There was so much history between the two, it could be almost anything.

Work related? Personal?

Could be any of that.

CHAPTER TWENTY-FOUR

Cassie and JoJo got to the scene just as the firefighters were unraveling their hoses, since the scene wasn't that far from Miss Mary's house. The desk had done a good job, getting Cassie and JoJo rolling to the call so early.

A policeman must have spotted the fire and radioed it in so the news desk had picked it up even before the firehouse was alerted. That was all she could figure as to how they'd gotten here so early. Two large firefighters strapped on breathing apparatus, preparing to go inside to check the house for entrapment victims.

God, what would they find inside the home? Cassie gulped air, flashes of the crazed fear she'd felt trying to drag JoJo from the fire and trying to bend the burglar bars that had trapped Miss Mary inside her burning home consumed her mind.

A shudder ran through her.

"It's okay, girl. The firefighters are here," JoJo said, as if he could read her mind. She gave him what she knew was a wobbly smile as he pulled into the curb far enough away from the scene that he wouldn't be blocked in by fire engines that came later, or interfere with their firefighting.

Max and Forrester weren't there yet, their fight probably having delayed them. That and the fact that they knew they couldn't do anything with the scene before the fire was brought under control.

JoJo jumped out of the SUV, grabbed his tripod and camera, clipped his stick mic onto his waist, and ran toward a piece of ground not too close to the house that he would get chased away by the firemen, but close enough that he could get great video and maybe they would run the yellow tape just inside of him, making a better deal for later arriving photogs.

The guy always went into a zone when he was shooting, only noticing what had to do with his story. One of the best news photogs, without all the uptight bull some photogs got into, trying to make sure everyone knew just how smart they were.

This fire was different than the other fires lately. It was in a nice neighborhood, where the yards were tended to, the houses freshly painted, and well-to-do urban dwellers resided.

Some of the people lined up outside watching the firefighters arrive probably were woken up from a good night's rest. Others had been settling down to watch the evening news before they went to bed.

It was just a whole different vibe from the usual neighborhoods for the arson fires.

Cassie sidled up next to JoJo. "This can't be related to the arsons," she said.

"I know. We jumped the gun on this one." He shrugged. "Oh well, isn't the first time, won't be the last."

She laughed. "Right. The desk heard *Fire* and went crazy."

JoJo made a face. "Actually, this was my bad call."
Yours?"

He nodded. "That battalion chief, Hobbs?"

She waited for the rest of the story.

"When he heard the fire call go out over the radio, he jumped around like a cat had bit his ankles and ran to his SUV. Just thought something was big by the way he acted. So, that's why I started us rolling this way. Lucky he had the radio turned up pretty loud so I could get the address."

The red lights from the many fire trucks flashed across JoJo's face, revealing an embarrassment that was rare for him. The guy had good instincts.

"Happens to the best of us," she said. "But hey, maybe that's the story. Everyone is jumpy these days. You hear *Fire*, and everyone automatically thinks the worse."

He chuckled. "That could be your tag. 'Luckily, Rebecca, this time there was no body inside. But, still when the fire trucks start rolling, nobody knows what will be waiting for them. Even the firefighters,'" he intoned in a deep voice.

She laughed. "Think I'll use it."

"Knew you would." JoJo turned back to his viewfinder.

The sound of cars screaming down the road caused a simultaneous jerking motion in the body of the crowd, as everyone turned to look. Two detective fleet cars flew toward the scene, blue lights flashing.

Neighbors in robes and sweat pants, whatever they'd thrown on when the trucks rolled onto the street, grabbed dogs and kids, pulling them out of the way of the cop cars.

Cassie stepped onto the grass, instinctively getting out of the way herself. She glimpsed Max and Forrester through the windshields as they pulled to a stop.

Why were they in such a hurry now? They'd stood around jawing at each other at the previous scene.

Now, they were endangering neighborhood pets and children?

JoJo had already turned his camera to video the blue lights coming up the road. He stayed on the cops as Max jumped out first, blasting toward the house as if he were the first firefighter on the scene.

A large firefighter stepped in front of him, grabbing him by the shoulders, bringing him to a halt. "Hey, buddy. Wait till we get it under control."

Behind him, the flames flared up as if answering the firefighter's threat with a fierce reply. The house was going up in a fierce show of firepower.

"Let me in there!" Max yelled, struggling to get by the giant firefighter. But, he was outmatched by the firefighter who broke through doors for a living.

Max had become a guy who mostly used his brain.

"That's my girlfriend's house, asshole!" Max yanked free from the shocked firefighter.

Max ran toward the house. Another firefighter joined him on the front porch, kicking at the door until it gave. Smoke poured from the door, a black snake that writhed toward them.

Another firefighter ran up behind Max, pushing him out of the way, and the two firefighters, breathing gear in place, headed in.

Max followed them, but seconds later stumbled back outside, heaving, coughing, eyes squeezed shut, tears running down his face.

Cassie looked over at JoJo. JoJo was intently getting it all on video.

Forrester ran forward with a bottle of water and put his hand on Max's shoulder. Then, he turned up the water bottle and poured it onto Max's face.

Max held his face upward, accepting the cooling water on his eyes. He coughed a few more times, then grabbed for the bottle, swigging water down between strangled coughs.

She'd never envisioned Forrester and Max helping each other before. But, they acted like a team, one giving what the other needed.

Maybe their bluster had always been competitive cop stuff. All these guys were such A type personalities that they were bound to clash.

Also, Max hitting on her since the divorce hadn't helped any. Even if Max was married, and apparently had a girlfriend on the side.

Nice to know she would have been batting cleanup on a wife and a mistress. Second mistress? Were there special lowered expectations to go with that? With even being a mistress? How did someone ever decide to take second place in life, after a wife?

Cassie hoped he'd at least lied to the woman, and that she'd been deceived. Hadn't agreed to this indignity going into the relationship.

Don't be so judgmental, she lectured herself. Maybe the girl only considered it a hookup, thought of him as a sex toy she used then sent home to his wife.

Cassie knew she was just trying to distract herself from the reality in front of her. Because in a few moments, it might not even matter what the woman had thought of Max or expected of him.

She could be dead.

The fire glowed in the night, almost beautiful, if it weren't for its deadliness.

A crackling orange engulfed the building's roof, swirling upward in a fiery tornado. Black smoke mired itself into the orange flames, giving depth to the colorful mass.

The fire swirled heat toward them, warming Cassie's face.

"Oh, God, I hope she's out of there," she murmured.

"Yeah," JoJo answered, getting shots that would be Emmy worthy. Though JoJo wouldn't take the time to enter them into the Emmy review process himself. No, that would be up to Cassie to fill out the paperwork and make copies for the producers to review.

JoJo only cared about getting the video. She heard a quick intake of breath from him and focused her attention on the house.

Smoke billowed from the front door, spitting out a firefighter. Like a Darth Vader character, his face covered by a mask, the breathing apparatus strapped to his back, he was nearly unrecognizable as a human being. But, he carried a figure over his right shoulder that was all human.

A nearly naked young woman hung like a dead cat over his shoulder, her skin pale, her body limp. No apparent signs of life from where Cassie stood.

Cassie gulped in air, as if breathing for the woman. She wanted to run forward to assist her.

But other firefighters did run toward him, helping to lay the inert figure down onto the ground.

Cassie leaned around, trying to catch a glimpse of the woman's face. "Oh," a gasp spurted from Cassie's mouth before she firmly placed a hand over it, to prevent any further emotional outbursts.

Silver duct tape covered the woman's mouth and nose. Her hands were duct taped together, behind her back, as well as tied with rope. Her feet were also bound together with the powerful tape and rope. That woman hadn't had a chance of escape.

She looked dead. A horrible feeling swept through Cassie, that a young, vibrant woman could be wiped off the face of the planet so easily.

Was she dead, beyond help? Maybe she could still be revived.

The firefighter who'd brought her out, leaned down on one knee and yanked the duct tape from her mouth and nose, tossing it aside.

A Fire EMT ran up, carrying a large bag. He crouched down beside her and began working on the lifeless woman.

"No," Max moaned, trying to get to her, but Forrester held him back, putting his body in his path, leaning into him. "You'll just be in the way," Forrester coaxed, his voice gentle.

Was he really speaking to Max that way?

The Fire captain ran up beside the small group hovering around her, assessing the situation with one glance. "Work her!" he yelled. "Work her like you never worked anybody."

The tech continued with his intent work as if the captain hadn't said anything, pulling items out of his bag. He was probably used to working with a lot of dramatics going on around him.

"We need her to tell us what happened," the captain muttered, as if he realized he'd just come out of character, had responded like a civilian. He yanked a knife off his hip, and cut the tape and rope to free her hands and then her feet.

Cassie glanced back at JoJo. In the little monitor on the side of his camera, she saw what he was shooting. He'd changed his angle of shooting, pointing the camera where it would catch the people working on the woman, but not her face.

"Good, JoJo. Good framing."

He shot her half a glance and nodded. Horror glimmered around his face, though he said nothing.

Max moaned, pushing against Forrester's hold on him. "Katie, it's Max. Wake up, Katie! Wake up!" he called.

"Someone broke into her house the other day," Max said in a strangled voice. "I said not to worry about it. That there was no chance of them coming back. I should have installed an alarm system for her," he wailed in a shocking display from anyone. But from Max?

The smart-assed flirt, who seemed to feel any woman was fair game for his good looks?

At least, he seemed to care for the woman he'd been sleeping with on the side.

The woman's face was unresponsive. So young, so beautiful. She didn't deserve this.

Nobody deserved this.

The woman lay as if just waiting for a hearse to haul her off to the morgue. A horrible feeling swept through Cassie that somewhere tonight a mother was going to get a call no parent should get.

Maybe she had a father, too. Brothers, sisters? Who

knew how many people would be affected. Little nieces or nephews?

Grandparents, uncles, aunts?

With this one death, despair, horror and anger would fan out, spreading grief to so many.

It just wasn't fair. She felt her hands clenching, the rage inside of her looking for an outlet.

Not fair. Not fair, the words beat like a tattoo in rhythm to the work the tech was doing on her. He fastened wires to her chest, called clear, and gave her a shock.

An ambulance arrived, and a tech jumped from it, running to the crowd gathered around the woman.

"Nothing," the firefighter said to the new EMT. "Gave her one round with this thing." He waved at the device still attached to her. The ambulance tech reached into his bag and pulled out a syringe of something, which he then injected into her. Then, a couple of other firefighters ran up with a gurney. They loaded her up and headed her off toward the ambulance.

Cassie knew they'd keep working her feverishly until a doctor pronounced her. Nobody wanted that woman to die.

Everyone wanted to defeat the monster who was snatching away the women of Atlanta. They wanted to beat him at least this one time.

No one would feel safe now. She'd prayed that Clayton was the only killer. But he either had a partner or there was a copycat killer who'd picked up where he'd left off.

And, it wasn't just poor, forgotten neighborhoods being attacked now. If the monster would go into this neighborhood with their security cameras and alarm systems, he'd go anywhere.

Why this woman? Why her?

Cassie's brain ran at a sprinter's pace.

She and Forrester had begun dissecting the victims. Two prostitutes, four if you counted the two from years before, a councilwoman who'd voted on the wrong side of the moral line, maybe the monster would figure. A radio talk show host who'd had an affair.

Now, another woman having an affair with a married man.

It was like the film *Fatal Attraction* that had scared men decades before, as her granny had laughed and told her about when it was on television one rainy afternoon.

"Scared a lot of men into keeping it in their pants," Granny had cackled.

Was this guy was trying to do the same with women, now? A moralistic terrorist? Trying to terrify women into being "good girls"?

A raving anger raced toward Cassie's mouth. She wanted to scream, "Who are you to judge, you monster? Who put you on this planet to dole out the death sentence to women who don't fit your image of a proper female?"

She realized she was heaving, her breath coming in ragged pants, her hands clenching and unclenching at her sides.

JoJo looked over at her and nodded his head in silent agreement. He was envisioning his daughters, his wife, his sister, his mother even, passed judgment on by this jerk.

A shiver ran through her. Was the monster out there in the dark, laughing at the pain he caused, taking pleasure in the punishment he'd meted out?

Was he looking at her even now, judging her behavior, planning punishment for her?

She looked around the crowd, looking for someone with evil glinting out of his eyes, a sadistic pleasure in the pain he could cause. But, no one looked out of place.

Only firefighters, police, and people who looked like they lived here, huddled together into small groups, disbelief and fear on their faces.

She noticed a man grab his teenaged daughter and pull her closer. One mother shook her head violently when her daughter pointed down the street, as if she wanted to go stand with her friend.

The terrorist had achieved what he wanted. Everyone shrunk closer to the light, away from the dark where evil and death might lurk.

Cassie turned, almost involuntarily, toward the dark edges of the scene. Was he still lurking out there in the dark?

She shivered violently, the cold sinking into her very center. When would he strike again?

Where?

Who would be his next victim?

CHAPTER TWENTY-FIVE

Cassie collapsed onto her couch. She'd been awake more than twenty-four hours.

Her life was turning into a laboratory experiment. And she was the mouse.

A voice narrated in her head, "After thirty-six hours without sleep, the subject will become jumpy, nerves rattled almost beyond endurance. If it goes on much longer, the participant may begin hallucinating."

How long until that happened?

She kicked off her shoes, put her feet on the couch. And felt herself sinking away. There was nothing she could do to stop it.

She was going to sleep. With her last bit of willpower, she leaned over and clicked her phone to silent. Though she probably wouldn't have heard it anyway.

A loud rapping exploded like machine gun fire in her head. She jumped up and looked around, almost expecting the SWAT team to break into her home.

The rapping returned, loudly and insistently. Someone was at the front door, and it probably wasn't the SWAT team. They wouldn't knock anyway, they would just barge in. If the SWAT team came to mind first at an alarming noise, she'd been on too many police stories. Too many SWAT situations.

You could silence your phone but apparently not your front door. Who the heck was out there anyway? Who dropped in unannounced? Someone wanting her to sign a petition or buy something? Probably.

But, the rapping continued. Damn them, she ought to just open the door and scare them to death with the way she probably looked.

Still, after years of being on the news, an instinct kicked in to make herself presentable.

She staggered to her feet, and into the bathroom to check herself in the mirror. That hair was a mess.

She grabbed a wide-toothed comb and tried to make herself look human, not like some wraith from the depths of hell. Though that was how she felt.

She should have just gone to the door that way. That'd teach them to go around knocking on strangers' doors.

She stuck a bit of toothpaste in her mouth, then rinsed her mouth out.

"Now, maybe they'll just run screaming away," she said to her reflection. "Rather than having a full-fledged heart attack on my front porch. Too much paperwork involved in that, having to talk to the police. I just want to scare them away, not kill them. Then, I want to take a shower," she muttered as she headed to the front door.

Another loud knocking caused her to jump.

"Hold your horses, I'm coming!"

A familiar voice said, "Good thing, too. Your neighbors are starting to look over here."

Forrester.

She should have looked out the window before she went to all the trouble to comb her hair. She could have just hollered out the window for him to go away. She'd been too sleepy to even realize it was probably him.

But, her hair was combed, her mouth rinsed out. Might as well give him what for, for failing to cooperate fully in the information sharing.

She was just sleep-deprived enough to tell him exactly what she thought.

She flung the door open. "Why aren't you home sleeping? That's what any reasonable person would do after all this time."

He shrugged and pushed past her into her living room.

"Uh, my house," she reminded him.

"Sorry," he muttered. "Just saw a couch and was drawn to it." He arched an eyebrow.

She laughed slightly. Hard to stay mad at him when he joked like that. Besides, he really did have cause to hold back information about the panties.

There was always something the cops liked to keep back, to use to figure out if the guy who confessed was really the murderer.

Or to trip up the guy who denied blame.

Forrester collapsed backward onto her couch, kicking off his shoes. He held up a hand toward her, beckoning her to him.

And heck if she didn't go.

She lay down beside him on the couch, wrapping a

leg across his, one of her arms across his chest, and tucking her face into his neck.

The smell of him almost undid her, making her want to get both their clothes off and repeat everything they'd done yesterday, and more.

She was like an addict. Once she'd had a taste of him she wanted more and more.

Her brain had nothing to do with it. Because she knew they didn't have a future. The past had shown her that. If all she wanted was a roll in the hay, why not take it?

Don't think so much, her body begged her.

But, her curiosity overcame her lust.

"Tell me about the panties." She sat up, swinging her legs back down to the side of the couch.

He let his hand fall free of her and also sat up. "Since you already know about them, might as well."

He ran his fingers through his hair. He looked toward her kitchen. "Got any food?"

She nodded. "Scrambled eggs and toast okay?"

"Your speciality," he said with a nod and a rough laugh.

She got up and he followed her into the kitchen. "I'll do the toast," he offered as she pulled out a bowl and some eggs.

She broke half a dozen into a bowl, added milk, and some spices, then began scrambling, looking at him with a nod to start talking.

"I don't know where those panties came from at the house you and Max and Hobbs were at tonight."

"What? Max acted like he'd seen them before."

Forrester shook his head dismissively. "He was acting for Hobbs. Didn't want him to be able to say we'd missed something. Blamed it on shoddy CSI techs. Basic 101 Pass-The-Blame-Down-The-Line technique."

Cassie shook her head, sprayed some PAM onto a skillet, then turned on the stove. After a moment, she poured the eggs into the pan, and began stirring them.

"So, no panties preserved in a plastic bag were noted at the councilwoman's location?"

"They may have been there, but nobody noticed them before, to my knowledge. Don't know how that happened. Gonna make it kind of hard to bring them into evidence. A defense lawyer can go to town with that."

She nodded. "If the panties don't fit, you must acquit."

It felt like old times, cooking together, talking over cases together.

What had gone so wrong that she hadn't she been able to forgive him when he hadn't been there for her when Granny had died?

Because she'd just felt so abandoned? Like when her parents had abandoned her. Was everyone doomed by their childhood. Did even sweet little girls and boys, with sweet, normal families turn out with baggage from childhood?

Out of the corner of her eye, she caught him watching her.

A spark of want responded in her as his eyes swept up and down her form, taking in every curve in her figure.

Noting additional curves?

Maybe she had comforted herself with food just a bit

too much. Food as a replacement for the sex she hadn't been getting?

And for all the sorrow of losing Granny. And for missing him, she finally admitted to herself.

"I've gained a bit of weight," she acknowledged, as if saying it would take the sting out of any judgment by him. Say it before anyone else could.

"Looks good," he murmured. "You needed a bit of meat on your bones. More curves in all the right places." He tilted his head toward her backside, then glanced back at her chest, then up to meet her eyes, heat flaring in his gaze.

Damn. She hadn't meant to encourage that line of thought.

"The panties," she reminded him. She turned to take two plates from the cabinet, feeling his eyes on her backside the whole time. Her a-little-bit-bigger backside.

She turned to meet his eyes, then took the skillet and dumped the eggs onto the plates, giving him a heck of a lot more. Would she even be able to eat in front of him after her comment about weight gain?

He dumped two pieces of toast on each of their plates, then reached into her fridge for jam and spray-on, no-calorie butter.

Just making himself at home.

Something about it felt good.

She grabbed a cup and poured herself some coffee, then took her plate and headed to the dining room table. More formal, less intimate.

As if that would help.

He settled in across from her, taking a big bite of eggs, then closing his eyes and moaning. "Missed your eggs," he said.

She laughed. "What's to miss? They're just eggs."

"Yeah, but you made 'em." He opened his eyes, fastening them on her with a heat that pierced her straight through and through.

She'd need to go the Grady Hospital Burn Unit before this was all through. Or see the surgeon who attended to all the shooting victims who were cops.

Could he save a pierced heart?

She narrowed her eyes at him. "The panties?"

CHAPTER TWENTY-SIX

Just the sound of the word panties on her lips got him going. To places he didn't need to be going.

She was making it obvious she'd pulled back. Or was she?

She'd let him into her house. Into her body, even. The memory of that scorched through his mind for a split second, making it impossible to concentrate on crime cases.

If she said the word panties again...

"The underwear," she said this time. "Is that better? Make it easier to talk about?" Her eyes narrowed with humor.

"Yeah, actually. Whoever gave that item of clothing that name should be shot. *Panties.* Sounds like something you need to slide down a woman's thighs. Not like a simple clothing protector."

"Ouch," she groaned. "Clothing Protector? Don't think you needed to go there."

He narrowed his eyes back at her, feeling the connection of their humor. What he'd missed most about her. Well, almost most.

"So, this guy seems to be taking souvenirs in the form of women's underwear." He wagged his head, thinking for a moment. "That was careless of him if he did leave those underwear at that scene, cause it seems like it would be pretty important to him to take them."

She nodded. "Most weirdos like him want something to remember their killings by, I hear."

"Women's underwear," he drew out the word. "So personal, something they've worn next to their sex. Would have their own unique musk on them."

She shuddered. "Grossing me out."

He tilted his head at her. "You want to talk honestly about this stuff or not?"

"I do. It's just imagining this guy with all those panties in his possession."

He nodded in agreement. "Yeah, everything about it is bizarre. Never met a killer I could understand though. And when I start understanding them, I know I'm in trouble."

She took a sip of her coffee, and he couldn't help but watch her. It had been so long since he'd had this sort of contact with her. Sitting around talking over a home-cooked meal.

And it was blowing his mind. Could they just ease back into the relationship? Cause that was how it had been the first time, an inevitable slide toward togetherness.

They'd found themselves unable to spend much time apart, gravitating back to each other at every possible opportunity.

He looked down at his plate and shoveled in a mouthful. To keep himself from saying anything that would ruin it, that would be premature, causing her to think too much about the situation.

They just needed to slide toward each other naturally.

His phone vibrated on his hip, and he took it off, looking at the face. "Gotta take this." He nodded at her and got up, walking out the back door onto the little deck.

He could feel her watching him as he shut the door. But, he had to be able to talk freely without her figuring out what he was asking about.

She was good that way. Only a word here or there, and she picked up on the meat of the matter.

"Hey, Roberto. Whatcha got?"

Neither he nor Roberto cared for small talk, only wanted to get to the info.

"Your firebug's cousin?" He waited a beat, as if knowing the impact his next words would bring. "Clayton's cousin is Max."

"What? And Max said nothing about it?"

Roberto said nothing for a moment, as if knowing Forrester needed a moment to process the news. His brain felt buzzed, as if the circuits were overloading.

Forrester sucked in a gulp of air, then moved on. "I would have thought Clayton's cousin would be a firefighter, if he were in any of the public safety fields."

He could almost hear Roberto shrugging through the phone. "Maybe Max worked as a firefighter before he became a cop?"

His turn to shrug. "Never heard that," he verbalized.

"Doesn't mean it didn't happen," Roberto added what Forrester was thinking. "I'll keep checking into him. Hey," he bit off, sharply. "What's this I'm hearing about Max's girlfriend being the latest victim?"

"Yeah," Forrester acknowledged what Roberto's tone said. "Pretty f'ing unbelievable, huh?"

"Sheesh, you got that right."

They said nothing for a moment, each weighing the impossible thought behind that fact that they couldn't help thinking.

Roberto said it first. "Are all these other women just collateral damage so he could off his girlfriend, get her out of his life? Maybe she was making noise about going to the wife?"

"Pretty big f'ing waste if that's true. All those beautiful women."

"I'll say," Roberto added. "And me without even one woman in my life."

"You?" He said it like it was unbelievable. "The big Latin lover that you are?"

"Yeah, right. After that bullet to the jaw, all I've been doing is reconstructive surgery and visiting dentists to get my teeth back right."

Neither said anything for a moment, knowing just how close to death Roberto had come on a drug bust gone way bad.

"You sound good though," Forrester said.

"I feel good. Hey, on another note about the case. Did you hear Max's girlfriend officially was pronounced at the hospital?"

"No." Forrester let out a burst of air in disgust. "They were still working her when they took her away from the scene. You can't help but hope."

"Heard they're questioning Max down at the station."

"Yep. They're keeping me way far away from there, knowing our personal history."

"Yeah, a defense attorney could make hay with that one. 'Didn't you almost punch each other, one time, Detective Carson?'" Roberto imitated that overly unctuous, yet biting tone that was a good imitation of what Forrester had heard from defense lawyers as he sat on the witness stand testifying about cases.

"You're pretty clued in to what's going on in our department," Forrester said.

"Yeah," Roberto muttered. "The guys couldn't call me fast enough when all this started coming down with Max. They figured if anyone would want to know it was me."

"Emm," he murmured agreement.

His cousin Luke had told him Max had hesitated on a drug bust that went way bad. Roberto was one of the first to encounter the bad guys. When the bad guys came out shooting, Max had held back just long enough for Roberto to take one through the jaw.

A shot that had almost killed him.

Of course the guys would pounce on the opportunity to tell Roberto everything about Max's current situation. None of them could stand the guy anymore.

Dislike of the guy grew on you. Naturally, as you got more and more exposure to him.

"I know you've heard they found panties at one of the scenes," Roberto said matter of factly.

"Yeah."

"And, I heard they found a bag of panties in Max's car when they checked it in. Were putting him on administrative leave since he was so personally connected to the murder, so they took his gun, his badge, were checking in his car. And found a bag of frigging panties."

"What?"

"Oh, yeah. I thought you would have heard by now."

"What?" That was all that could work itself out of his brain. Women's underwear had been found in

Max's car? And he was the cousin of the firebug?

His phone made a little chirp, telling him a text was coming in. "Hold on," he said to Roberto.

He read the text. "They want me to go talk to Max's wife."

"Oh, man," Roberto laughed with a groaning sound mixed in.

"Yeah. Right?" Man, that wasn't gonna be fun. "I guess we should all start referring to her as his second ex-wife from now on."

"Yeah, sooner or later, you can add ex to any woman he ever marries, I'm figuring." Roberto laughed. "Better you talking to her than me, man. Don't envy you that."

"I wonder how much she knows. Not looking forward to telling a woman her soon to be ex-husband will be featured on the next newscast crying and nearly falling on the ground over the woman he was having an extra-marital affair with."

Roberto made a darker sound, no laughter this time. "Or that he's the prime suspect now in a string of serial murders that he used his firebug cousin to cover up? Found with a bag of women's panties in his car."

"Yeah," Forrester said. "Not a fun part of the job at all."

Max—a serial murderer? He'd always given Cassie the creeps, coming around her, sliding his hand down her arm, and such.

He'd been able to look at her at times since the divorce and just see the creeps she was feeling when that jerk was close to her.

Had that awareness kept her from being one of Max's victims?

Chapter Twenty-Seven

Cassie stepped out of the shower, toweled off and did the basics of hair. She dried it quickly because she knew she wasn't gong to last long before falling into bed.

The cumulative lack of sleep was catching up with her. She wanted to get back out on the street and work the story.

But, first she needed a nap. She didn't know how Forrester was still standing. And how he was going to cope with talking to Max's wife.

She laid some clothes out, pants, a shirt. Then, she went to the underwear drawer. She always got her clothes ready when working on a big story. Didn't want to get a phone call about a really big development and go running out half naked.

Once she'd gotten to a story and realized she hadn't put on a bra. She'd had to keep her arms crossed over her chest nearly half the day.

She grabbed the first pair of underwear she saw, slipped them up her legs, and pulled them into place.

The sudden image of all those women having their panties taken off by that creep murderer flashed through her mind. Had he done it while they'd still been conscious?

Putting even more terror in their minds?

Were they already bound and gagged, knowing what was probably coming? After the first two had made news, the women had to have known what their fate would be.

She shuddered, then deliberately tried to pull her mind away from the dark image. Tried to remember how JoJo had figured out what her problem was that day with no bra.

He'd called her risqué. "Risqué Cassae", he'd started saying. "No Brassiere Casseriere."

He'd kept on with variations until they'd both been laughing, with Cassie joining in on coming up with new names for herself.

She grabbed a bra, then, determined not to repeat that mistake, and put it on backwards, snapping it, then turning it around to fit onto her body.

She grabbed a pair of loose yoga pants, donning them, then grabbed a light T-shirt. She walked to the bed. But, heard the sound of a car outside, then seconds later, knocking on her front door.

She looked out the window and saw a car she didn't recognize. Picking up her purse, she checked for her gun.

It was against company policy to have a gun on station property but she'd gotten so spooked lately that she'd begun carrying it anyway, making sure it was well hidden in her car when she went to the station.

Heck, the job was so dangerous, they ought to issue every one of the field crews a gun when they started. "Here's your station ID. Here's your gun."

But, she'd been a good little girl, following policy, refusing to take a gun with her to work, even when Forrester had insisted she needed one as much as he did on his job.

"Hell, I'm not a good girl any longer." She pulled the gun out. "Let some bastard come after me, and he's getting it."

Luckily, she and Forrester had practiced together often back when they were married. She'd kinda thought it turned him on to see her with a gun.

So, sometimes, just for fun, she'd suggest they go shooting. Could always depend on a good time when they got back home.

She tucked the gun in the back of her yoga pants, praying it didn't slide down her leg cause the waistband wasn't that tight. On second thought, she tucked it inside the waistband of her underwear as well.

Patting it to be sure it was securely in place, she walked to the living room.

Another knock almost made her jump out of the yoga pants. Her nerves were rattled from lack of sleep.

And a stranger at her door.

She padded quietly to a side window where she could get a look at whoever was standing on her front porch.

Preston Hobbs?

As if he felt her watching him, he turned to make eye contact with her. The shock of meeting his gaze rattled her even further.

He smiled. Such a natural smile that she felt reassured. He probably just wanted to shoot the breeze, talk over the shocking recent discoveries.

Still.

She didn't want him in her house. The memory of the time he'd come up to her after the news conference flashed through her head, with the uncomfortable feeling he'd given her, sliding his hand up her arm.

So intimate. As if he thought something was developing between them.

Well, there sure as hell wasn't.

She raised her head in an acknowledging nod. "Around back," she said through the glass, tilting her head toward the side of the house.

She didn't want to open the door, with him right there, have to push him back to get out onto the front porch. Didn't want to be in that close contact with him, have him look down at her while she pushed past him. Might even have to touch him to get by.

Walking toward the back door, she grabbed a spare key from a table beside the television and slid it into her bra.

She opened the back door, setting the knob so it would lock behind her, and stepped outside just as Preston came around the corner. The outside daylight felt good, felt safe.

Leaning against the deck railing, she smiled at him. "What's up?"

"Did you hear they're arresting that detective for the murders?"

"Arresting him?"

"Yeah. They're taking his DNA, charging him with tampering with evidence until they can get back the results of the DNA. They're thinking they're gonna get a match with all those panties they found in that bag in his car."

Wow, Preston really had the inside scoop.

"Crazy," she said noncommittally. Forrester wasn't going to be able to pin on her that she'd given away any facts.

"Do you think it was all so he could get away with killing his mistress?" Preston walked up the stairs and leaned back against the railing opposite her, as if settling in for a long talk.

"I don't know. What do you think?" Turn the question back around on the other person, an old interviewing technique she'd learned early on in her career.

"What do I think? To start with, I think he's crazy." He laughed, with a laugh that said you couldn't make this stuff up.

He was right. But, she thought that a lot in her line of work.

"Very astute observation, Dr. Freud," she said. "Shall we call Dr. Jung for a backup opinion?"

"Jung? You're talking above my pay grade. Everyone knows about Freud but I'm not all that familiar with the Jung guy." He looked at her, his eyes narrowing. "I noticed him hitting on you a couple of times, that detective, that Max."

The guy did notice things. She'd thought that about Preston several times since she'd gotten divorced. Had him come up and make comments to her about things that most people wouldn't notice.

He'd been out there the night she'd shown up at the fire scene without a bra. She'd felt him slide his gaze down to take in her shirt front. Then, he'd looked quickly away.

That was when she'd noticed she didn't have on a bra. And that it was plainly clear to anyone who'd been as close to her as the battalion chief had been that night.

She'd done a quick look back over the night, wondering how many people had noticed, just thought she was the type of reporter who would show up on a scene with no bra.

Skanky Cassie, was one of JoJo's nicknames that night.

Preston hadn't commented, but she'd felt the heat in his eyes as he spoke to her, known he was thinking about that glance down at her chest.

He'd noticed Max hitting on her? But, had never said anything until now?

When they were alone. When she was wearing such light clothing, with an almost implied intimacy in its at-home feel, clothes you'd wear around the house with your boyfriend.

A shiver ran through her, that he might be imagining the two of them like that.

"So, why'd you come by, Preston?" she said, attempting a light tone but feeling like it sounded forced. "Not that it's not always nice to see you."

He looked down at her, his eyes rounding at the subtle confrontation.

He took a breath, looked away, toward the wood line behind her house. "You ever see any wildlife back there? Any rabbits? Coyotes? A lot of people in these areas have seen them, I hear. Just enough woods back there that they run along through them till they get to that wildlife sanctuary about a mile from here."

He knew her area pretty well. But, that was to be expected. His area of fire coverage extended to this area.

"No. I haven't seen any coyotes. But, a few rabbits.

Hope no coyotes come and eat them. I kinda like 'em. Although my neighbor just over there hates them, says they get into her garden."

Preston laughed like they were making normal small talk. Like this was normal, him coming by uninvited, unannounced.

And he'd avoided her question about it.

He turned his gaze away from the wood line, fastening it on her. Like a coyote fastening a rabbit in its gaze, just before it attacked.

CHAPTER TWENTY-EIGHT

Cassie pulled the curtains back half an inch to watch Preston drive away. Thank God her neighbor had come out into her backyard, starting her gardening routine, and had looked over to see Cassie and the battalion chief on the back porch.

Cassie had waved at her like everything was fine. "You're not still having problems with those rabbits, are you?"

When the other woman had said she was, Cassie had used it as a chance to get off the back deck and walk over. Preston had no option but to follow her.

While they were still by her neighbor, Cassie had made her excuses, said she had to get some sleep.

Then, she and her neighbor had watched Preston walk away. Together. Cassie had stayed right beside the woman while the chief walked back around the house.

Her neighbor had looked at Cassie with a cocked eyebrow. "Beating 'em away with a stick, huh, Ms. Available?"

"Work stuff." Cassie had laughed, like it was normal for a work acquaintance to just drop by.

But, it wasn't.

Cassie let the curtain drop. Her nerves were so

rattled now, that she'd never get to sleep. Might as well get to work.

Forrester had gone to talk to Max's wife. She'd give him some time to talk to the wife, then she and JoJo would go over. If JoJo wasn't sleeping.

He had it coming. They'd both been up way too long. She'd wait for him to call her.

Might even have to get another photog to fill in if Max's wife agreed to an interview.

Until then, she'd just get information. That was sometimes all she got anyway on such a sensitive story.

She went to the mirror, put on some moisturizer, letting it sink in while she dressed. Then, she slapped on enough makeup to look presentable and headed out.

Once in her car, a feeling came over her. She needed to work the Max angle of the story. But, there was something underneath her skin, just begging her to go in another direction.

To go get some feedback from someone who might have nothing to do with this story at all.

———————

Forrester walked through the doors back to the area where they were interviewing Max.

He squinted his eyes as he looked through the two-way mirror into the room where Max sat, hunched over, his forearms leaning on the table, muttering to himself.

"The guy's losing it," the police chief said out loud to the group of cops surveying Max through the glass. It was a pretty big deal when the police chief himself would come down to get involved in the investigation.

But, nothing had gripped this town like the fear this killer had brought to Atlanta.

His wide-ranging selection of women, and leaving them to die in burning buildings. The image of women waiting to burn to death was a horrifying one that kept many women awake at night, he figured.

Cause it sure as hell kept him up.

That was all anyone wanted to talk about. The radio talk shows, the television news.

Politics had been put to the wayside for once.

Republican, Democrat, Tea Party loyalists, liberal tree huggers. All they cared about now was finding this killer.

"Hey, you're here." The police chief fastened his gaze on Forrester, turning toward him. "He wants to talk to you."

"So I heard." He shook his head. "Why would he want to talk to me? The guy hates me."

"So I've heard," the police chief mimicked his words back to him. It was pretty bad if the police chief had heard about petty rivalries in the detective unit.

Rivalry? That was too nice of a word for what Max and he felt for each other. When had it begun for real?

Oh, yeah. When Forrester and Cassie had split up. And Max had seemed to think he was going to be her next ex-husband.

He'd already despised the guy, strongly believing he'd let Roberto get shot. Some said he'd hesitated long enough for Roberto to catch a bullet just cause he didn't like the smart-mouthed young Mexican American.

Or was it because Roberto had a way with the girls and was stealing some of Max's thunder when he was around?

Women were Max's thing. And, he'd already shown

he could be vindictive in a way that could get somebody killed.

Of course, there'd been no proof he'd allowed Roberto to get shot. Just enough conviction on everybody's part that the guy had been run out of the SWAT team and any involvement with the task force.

No one would work with him.

Not with a man that'd let you take a bullet if he just didn't like you.

Forrester looked through the glass at the man.

Was he also a cold-blooded woman killer?

The chief narrowed his eyes at Forrester. "Go work him. Get us a confession. Let's put this thing to bed. Use that hatred he has for you, if you have to. Say anything you need to, that you're gonna be his wife's baby daddy."

The chief's mouth tightened and his voice sounded like he was chewing gravel, it was so hard. "Put that bastard away forever, detective."

Forrester turned and walked through the door that put him face to face with Max. He knew cameras were running, recording every word, every nuance of facial expression.

Max knew it too. And the guy hadn't lawyered up? What was he thinking?

Max looked up at him, but his expression didn't change. The guy was seriously worried. And still, he'd asked for him.

"What's up?" were the first words he said to Max. "Why'd you want to see me? Want me to be your last victim before they lock you up for good?"

"Right." Max gave a dark laugh. "Let 'em get it on

video tape too." He motioned toward one of the cameras with his head.

Forrester leaned up against a wall. He really didn't want to get within swinging range of a maniac. If that's what Max was.

He was a cop and hadn't been charged with murder yet or he'd have been handcuffed and manacled so he'd never get a shot at hurting anyone. But, they were still playing the game. Hoping to get something on tape they could use.

Max leaned forward across the table, making eye contact with Forrester, for the first time without a hint of malevolence that Forrester could remember in a very long time.

"I didn't do this, Carson." He narrowed his eyes. "If you really think about it, you'd know that."

Forrester just waited. It was a tactic that usually worked for him. Let the suspect fill up the silence. Amazing how much talking people would do if you let 'em, sometimes circling back around until they'd tripped their own selves up.

"Heck, I bet you already think it feels funny."

Forrester looked down at his nails, flicking at a rough spot on his cuticle. The thing was, it did seem weird. Max liked to sleep with women, not kill 'em.

"So, where'd those panties they found in your car come from?"

"Hell if I know. Someone's trying to set me up. Why would I be so stupid?"

"I always ask myself that about criminals," Forrester answered. So many of them went to such lengths, put such effort into their criminal enterprises, that he couldn't help but wonder how successful they'd be in the business world, if they just stayed on the up and up. "Keeping souvenirs of the murders in my work vehicle? Are you kidding me?" Max sneered. "Maybe you're obsessed. Want to touch them throughout the day, those nasty, silky panties? How the hell do I know what drives a maniac?" He turned a hard gaze on Max.

"Why'd you want to see me?" he growled.

Max sat back, breathing in and out several deep, ragged breaths that sounded like they had to hurt sawing out of his lungs. Then, he gulped in a breath and looked up at Forrester. "Cause as much as I know you hate me." He waited for Forrester to somehow acknowledge the truth in that statement.

Forrester purposefully kept his face blank. This tape would be viewed over and over by the guys who reviewed him. And then showed in court, and seen on TV news. It would all be made public eventually.

He wasn't giving the guy anything.

He just stared him down, with no expression, no acknowledgement of what they both knew to be true.

Finally, Max just nodded. "You hate me. But, you also understand what makes me tick, and the fact that I would never do these things. I would never do anything that would lock me up in a cage for the rest of my life."

"Yeah, you're too smart for that, aren't you Weber?" Forrester used the most insulting tone he could manage, summoning up every bit of disgust he'd ever felt for the guy. "You could kill women and get away with it. Or so you thought."

He edged closer, bringing even a higher level of rudeness to his tone. "But, I guess you really weren't. You thought you could kill all those women, and then make your girlfriend look like a victim of this faceless murderer."

He leaned forward, towering over the sitting figure. "How stupid are you, that you thought we would never figure out that your cousin was an arsonist? How'd you get him past the polygraph entrance test at the fire academy, Weber?"

Max's face faltered. The sign of a suspect about to cave?

"How much did you have to pay to get that taken care of, huh?" Forrester beat on the subject while Max was off balance.

"He was just a kid when he did those things," Max said. He looked away. "I didn't think they'd care about that at the academy."

"It would still have shown up on the polygraph. I understand there was nothing."

"Really?" Max looked at him with a sudden dawning in his eyes. "Maybe you should look at who administered that polygraph test?"

Forrester leaned back against the wall. Feeling as if Max had shoved him against the wall. The thing was, the guy was right. They'd overlooked a basic piece of police work. Everyone had just been so happy to have caught a killer.

Twice now, had they just accepted whoever was ready at hand as the killer?

The homeowner who'd just planned to burn down his own home for the insurance? Clayton? An arsonist firefighter?

Maybe Clayton had just covered up the murders, been a convenient ally for the real murderer?

He looked at Max, and Max nodded, leaning back,

with a satisfied smile. "You can still hate me after this investigation is over, Carson. But for now, go find the real killer."

Forrester looked at Max, with that self-satisfied, smug smile, and wanted to put a fist through the guy's face. But, as much as he knew he disliked the guy, he also knew he was right this time.

The real killer was still out there, stalking women.

CHAPTER TWENTY-NINE

Cassie knocked on the door and waited. Finally, the curtain beside the front window moved, and Cassie lifted a hand, waved and generally tried to look non-threatening. A friendly little smile.

It always helped being a woman. Men weren't threatened by you, women weren't afraid of you. She got doors opened for her a lot more than the guy reporters.

Even when she'd first come to town. The guys usually had to wait until people knew them better from seeing them on television.

A marked news vehicle helped, too. But, times like this when she was just on a fishing expedition, not turning a story for the next newscast, and not in a marked car, it helped being a woman.

Preston's ex-wife, Dorothy, opened the door. "Cassie," she said, a hint of surprise in her voice. They'd seen each other at Public Safety Awards luncheons once or twice.

Police and Fire combined their awards into one big event once a year. The so-called hero awards and other commendations were given out then. Sometimes, Fire and Police personnel would get awards for the same event since often they worked hand in hand on many scenes. So, a couple of times Fire and Police had joined their awards banquets.

"Come in. I'm surprised to see you. Aren't you out working on this story about the killer?" Dorothy waved Cassie inside.

It was a homey little bungalow-style house. Probably built in the 1950s, from the look of it. Wood floors, smallish.

Not like the McMansions that were so often favored in the new construction in town.

"This is cute," Cassie said. She didn't want to launch into the real reason for coming right off. Ease into it. Cause it was gonna get weird.

"Thanks." Dorothy smiled but Cassie could see the questions behind the smile.

Why are you here? Haven't seen you once since the separation. Hardly knew you before it.

She couldn't blurt out her questions about Preston. Why hadn't he picked up on Clayton's comings and goings? Had he had any funny feelings about the guy?

She'd paged Preston twice before swinging by his old home. The guy had fallen off the map, it seemed. So, instead she was going to pick his ex-wife's brain for clues to Clayton's behavior.

Sometimes you got more from the person who lived with someone than from them directly.

"I have a house kinda like this house myself," Cassie continued in a casual tone. "I like this bungalow style."

"Yeah, not too big, not too small. Just right." Dorothy waved her back to the kitchen. "I was just fixing coffee. Want a cup?"

"Yeah." Over a cup of coffee felt right, kinda like

two friends talking. She just needed to probe without really saying too much.

Dorothy started the coffee pot, then leaned over and opened the door to a small crate. A puppy ran out, and Dorothy caught it quickly. "Oh, no you don't. Potty first." She smiled at Cassie. "Be right back."

The coffee perculated as Cassie sat at the table waiting. How was she going to ease into her questions?

The back door opened, and Dorothy walked in, setting the puppy on the floor. Then, she walked to erect a little gate that would keep the dog inside the kitchen with them.

"Can't let him roam the house until he's fully potty trained." She looked down at the pup with an affectionate smile.

"He's so cute." Cassie waved her hands up and down at him in the universal puppy language saying, *Let's Play.*

The puppy batted his feet on the floor and began jumping in time to Cassie's hands as she bounced them up and down.

"I see you've had a puppy before." Dorothy laughed, and the puppy turned to her and licked her ankles. She picked him up, cuddling him under her chin.

Yeah, Cassie could see fighting with the ex to keep that puppy. "What type is he?"

"A Pekingese. Had one as a kid, just love their personalities and their cute little faces. So, I finally got me another." He wiggled and she set him back on the floor.

Cassie leaned down to waggle a few fingers at the puppy again and he bounded toward her, bouncing up and down, back and forward, striking his little feet on the floor again. "What's his name?"

"Rover." Dorothy laughed as she said it.

"You could have named him Spot." Cassie smiled at her. She had the feeling they'd have been friends if they'd actually gotten to know each other.

But since their husbands worked in different departments, their paths didn't cross that often. Cops hung with cops and firefighters hung with firefighters. Well, now they could be friends if they wanted.

Dorothy looked at her, her eyes turning serious. "Why are you here?"

Cassie gazed back at her for a long moment, then decided to tell the truth, or a part of the truth. "I have some questions about your ex."

"He's still technically my husband. We're still married. He won't sign the papers, keeps holding onto them. Still wants to show me who's boss."

She shrugged. "Guess we'll have to go to court then. I'm not gonna have people saying Dorothy Hobbs' husband is running around with every woman in town. Gonna change my name back as soon as I can."

Cassie held her breath, waiting for more.

But, Dorothy got up, poured two cups of coffee and set them down on the table, pushing Cassie's toward her.

"He was a big womanizer?" Cassie finally prompted.

"Oh, yeah. It's really what ended our marriage. I was just not gonna stay with a man who was with a new woman every time he left town. Would go away to some of those fire training sessions, or that big conference they hold out west for media training. He always went to that cause it was in Las Vegas."

She blew out a burst of air. "He has big political aspirations. Said he made a lot of *contacts* there."

"Contacts?" She rolled her eyes. "That was what I was afraid of. Always expected him to come back with some STD."

She shook her head, dismissively. "I'm not some political wife, where I'm gonna be *standing by my man* at the podium, while he admits to the entire world he's humiliated me and betrayed me."

"But, that's where he was headed, into politics. Talked about it all the time." She fastened her gaze on Cassie. "Those men in political offices, they always seem to apologize more to the public than to their wives. Have you noticed the haunted look in all those women's eyes?"

An intense jag of pain shot through Cassie. She remembered that moment when you realized your husband had just *done* a woman who wasn't you, had an extramarital affair or a one-night stand. And they expected you to get over that? When she first found out about Forrester, the image would pop into her head over and over.

She pushed the memory from her brain, cause this wasn't about her. And looked down at Rover. "Well, at least you got the house and dog."

"If I can keep the house." She laughed raggedly. "The mortgage is pretty high. Maybe I can get a roommate." She smiled at Cassie. "You know anybody nice needs a place to live?"

Yeah, Cassie immediately liked her. "It's tough being divorced. I know."

Dorothy reached across the table, laying her hand on Cassie's. "I heard about you and Forrester. I'm sorry."

She squeezed Cassie's hand, then slid her hand back to her cup, but kept her eyes on Cassie as she took a sip. "I would never have figured you guys for splitting up. He just seemed so in love with you."

Cassie took a sip of her coffee, looking down at the puppy, anything to distract herself from thinking about Forrester and their split.

"I used to watch him at those awards luncheons," Dorothy murmured. "He would just gaze at you, like you were the only woman in the room, in the world."

She shook her head. "And here you guys are divorced. I guess you shouldn't envy anyone cause you never really know what's going on inside their marriage."

Rover jumped up on Dorothy's leg and she laughed, leaning over to pick him up, nuzzling him with her face.

Rover struggled to get down, though he'd just begged to be picked up. Cassie laughed at the scrunched face of the dog, as if he were being held against his will, tortured.

"You should get yourself a dog," Dorothy said. She set the puppy on the floor and threw a dog toy for him. "I got this little fellow the week after we split up. I haven't been lonely a minute since."

A shiver ran through Cassie, a dark, warning sensation that spread through her entire body. She looked up at Dorothy.

She knew what the answer would be, but still, she asked it. "Didn't you already have a dog when you and Preston split up?

"Nope." Dorothy shook her head, sadly. "No dog. I always wanted one, but Preston thought it would be too messy. Really, the thing was, if it wasn't about getting ahead in his job, Preston didn't have time for it in his life. So, first thing I did was get me a dog. Correction," she said with a laugh. "I got me a puppy. I've have dogs before, when I was a kid, but never a puppy. They should come with a warning label. Caution, go back. Extreme ankle biting ahead."

She laughed again as the puppy bounced toward her, as if he'd known they were talking about him.

No dog. No dog for her and Preston to fight over at the breakup. Then, she hadn't scratched his hand. Or, at least not for the reason Preston had said.

Maybe he was just embarrassed about the fight? She'd come to talk about Preston's clues or hints that he thought something was wrong with Clayton. But, Preston had become the main topic of conversation.

"Was your breakup rough?" she said, watching the laughter fade from Dorothy's eyes.

"Nope." She shook her head, her expression flat. "Like he didn't even care. Just packed up and left when I asked him. That's why I'm surprised he won't sign the papers."

Her eyes narrowed. "Preston has other ways of getting even with you. If I had a sister, he'd probably try to sleep with her to get back at me. That's more his style. I don't have a sister, thank goodness. I wouldn't wish him on my worse enemy."

"That bad, huh?" The thing was, Cassie would have thought any woman would have been lucky to have her own ex-husband, Forrester. He'd been a wonderful husband.

Well, until the end when everything had gotten all screwed up. Literally.

Was she like Preston? Getting back at Forrester

through means besides fighting for not being there when her granny died?

When who she'd really been mad at was God for taking her granny, even though she'd lived out a full length of years.

But, she'd still been so mad at Forrester.

Moved out of his bed, said she was gonna divorce him, then gone emotionally berserk when he'd turned around and slept with some woman. Why shouldn't he have? She'd said they were through.

Guess you shouldn't say something like that unless you meant it.

"What?" Dorothy broke into her thoughts. And Cassie looked up at her, almost having forgotten where she was.

She realized her own feelings must have been all over her face. She sucked in a deep breath.

"I was just thinking about my own split up with Forrester. Kind of ridiculous when I think back. He was deep undercover when my granny died. Granny was like my mother, really."

Dorothy's eyes softened. "That must have been hard. Did you have to go through it alone?" She reached across, putting her hand on Cassie's again.

Oh, yeah, she would have liked to have been friends with her. Maybe they still could be.

"Pretty much alone. I sent word through the supposed network to Forrester. But, he never showed till almost a week later. Said he'd never gotten word." She shrugged. "I didn't care. I was furious by then. When he got home, I hardly spoke to him. Moved into the other bedroom, said we were through and that I'd be filing for divorce."

She'd made sure to stay gone as much as possible, working overtime.

When, he'd slept with that bartender? Then, she really had been gone. For good.

Cause, she'd realized she couldn't live in their home without him. With all the memories of him and the two of them as a couple that their home contained.

"Wow, that must have been hard on him."

Hard on him? "It was hard on *me*."

"I know. I know." Dorothy patted her hand. "It just seemed like he really loved you. Divorce is hard on everyone."

She scoffed then. "Except Preston, apparently. He probably just went back to some woman he'd been with the night before when he was," she air quoted, "working."

Cassie met her eyes, and felt the pain the woman still felt over her failed marriage. "Do you know that for sure, that he was cheating? Or did you just get a feeling?"

"Believe me, when a woman gets a feeling, she's probably right." Dorothy got up and refilled both their coffee cups. She set the coffee pot back on the warmer, then sat down, pushing Cassie's cup across the table.

"I had more than a feeling." Dorothy looked Cassie in the eye, with an intense hardness, and took a sip of coffee before saying, "I had plenty of proof. I found panties."

A convulsive wave of cold swept through Cassie, chilling her from the inside out. Chill bumps broke out on her arms.

"Panties?" she whispered, barely able to get the words past the iceberg in her throat.

Dorothy raised an eyebrow as if she thought the whisper was about the enormity of the cheating. "Yeah. The guy kept panties, if you can believe it? I went out to his work SUV one day when he was over here packing up some of his stuff. I was looking for a favorite lipstick I thought might have fallen out of my purse. Just kept wondering where it could be."

Her face paled a bit. "When I stuck my hand underneath the back seat, way back far, thinking maybe the lipstick had rolled back there." A sheen of tears rose into her eyes. "And pulled out his little trophies, his mementos of his conquests? Different sizes, different types of underwear. So, I knew it wasn't just one woman."

She shook her head, blowing out a gust of air that sounded like it ripped straight from her heart, it was so ragged. "Who does that? Like he was just so proud of himself. Keeping panties. I thoguht, why? So, he could panty sniff later?"

"How gross of a human being is that?" She shuddered. "And that thing was my husband."

She took a long sip of coffee, her throat working to get it down, the muscles visibly straining. "At least, I don't have to say that anymore," she choked out. "Or soon I won't, if he ever signs the papers. Or if I just have to get my lawyer to push forward without his signature. I am through being his little puppet."

Cassie wrapped her arms around herself in shock. She needed to call Forrester, let him know.

But, there might be more she could get out of Preston's wife, more helpful information.

Should she blurt out what she thought? No, something told her that if Dorothy knew that she'd close down. As much as she seemed to despise her ex, nobody was this vicious unless they still had feelings.

There might be a little bit of her that still loved him, still hoped he would come begging back to her, promising never to cheat again.

"How long had the cheating been going on?"

"It happened over in Birmingham once." She grimaced. "I found panties there, too."

"That's why we moved to Atlanta. I wanted to put some distance between that woman and us." She shrugged, and laughed bitterly. "As if there weren't attractive women in Atlanta. That woman wasn't the problem. Preston was the problem."

She took a long sip of coffee. "I don't think he can help himself. It's like he just seems to build up to it." She rolled her eyes. "I don't think it had anything to do with him loving me or not."

"What do you mean builds up to it?" Cassie waited, already knowing it was the tension that a serial killer felt, the need to kill again. She eased her cell phone out of her pocket, hid it below the table where Dorothy wouldn't see it and began texting Forrester.

She typed, I'm at Preston's ex-wife's home. Call me immediately. I have something to tell you.

"It's funny cause he would start ranting and raving about how nobody has morals anymore," Dorothy said. "You know, he was the grandson of a preacher? Really almost more of a daddy to him, since Preston's father ran off with another woman, abandoning him. Then, his mother took to the bars, drinking and carousing, according to Preston. Can you believe the irony?"

"No," Cassie whispered, suddenly seeing the psychological profile that would forge someone who was able to do the things Preston had to have done.

"Yeah, the guy used to beat Preston, saying 'The hell if I'm going to raise two sinners. You won't turn out like your sorry daddy.' As if he could beat the evil out of Preston. Beat the hell out of him, literally."

Dorothy looked off into the distance. "It was like Preston would almost channel him when he got into a rant, like one of those old-fashioned fire and brimstone preachers."

Dorothy shivered. "Used to scare me to hear his granddaddy preach when we'd go over to Alabama. Imagine growing up with that, and then the beatings on top of it."

"I think he just rebelled against that and the feelings would build until he would go out and cheat." She looked at Cassie with a question in her eyes. "Does any of that make sense? I know it's crazy, but still kinda making sense, huh?"

Crazy all right. But not for the reasons Dorothy thought. The guy was making moral judgments on those women he killed, bringing the wrath of the Lord down on them.

Using his very human hand to smite them.

Beaten as a child, he'd learned that harsh physical punishment was the penalty for transgressions. And he'd grown up to punish these evil women. He'd given them the death penalty.

"Clayton was the grandson of a preacher, too," Cassie said, searching Dorothy's eyes for clues, to see if she'd suspected a connection between Clayton's fires and Preston.

"I wonder if that was why Preston took Clayton under his wing," Dorothy mused in a distant voice.

"Cause they could relate, both from that fire and brimstone background. Preston met Clayton when he was down visiting Clayton's cousin Max. Max brought him to the safety awards dinner once. Preston took a liking to him, convinced him to come down here to the academy."

"Do you think he saw Clayton's tendencies to start fires?" Cassie looked at Dorothy, searching her face for clues. Had Preston groomed his assistant to aid him in covering up his murders from the very beginning?

"No, but that is ironic, huh? Raised on fire and brimstone, then dying by fire. And probably facing a long afterlife of fire and brimstone, too." Dorothy laughed harshly. "Who could believe that? I haven't been able to reach Preston. I think he's hiding out, licking his wounds over his protégé. Or just worrying about how it will reflect on him, more likely." She harrumphed with a disgusted sound.

Cassie had all she needed to know. Forrester and the other cops could get the rest.

She pushed back her chair, standing up. Dorothy looked up at her with disappointment. "Oh, sorry. Guess I got too heavy, huh? Nobody really likes to hear these sad stories. Should have kept it light."

Dorothy opened a little crate and popped Rover inside, closing the door. "Using a crate for potty training," she said with a smile that didn't quite hide her sadness.

Cassie reached for her, pulling her into a tight hug. Then, she pulled back and looked earnestly into the woman's face. "I'm sorry about what you went through with Preston."

She gazed at her, hoping later, when the truth came

out, Dorothy would believe what she was about to say. "And later, when the investigation into the killings is all over, I hope we can spend time together. I think we might be able to become good friends."

Dorothy's eyes softened. "I'd like that. I don't have many friends." She smiled.

Cassie hoped she remembered that when she knew the truth of what had come out of their talk.

"Keep that in mind, no matter what happens in the near future."

Dorothy tilted her head, a question in her eyes.

Cassie couldn't answer that now.

She had to stop a killer, a killer who even now could be stalking other women.

The focus was off the killer, everyone believed he was in jail. Women's defenses would be down.

The true killer would have free reign. To punish. To kill.

CHAPTER THIRTY

Forrester looked through Clayton's personnel file, flipping through page after page before finally finding the results of the polygraph.

"The actual graph itself isn't in here?" he looked up at the battalion chief who ran the training academy.

"It should be." The chief leaned over and leafed through the file. "That's weird."

"Actually kinda what I'd expected." Forrester picked up the written report of the polygraph, all that was needed to actually pass the training. "Who ran the polygraph?"

The chief took picked up the file, flipping through it. "Preston Hobbs."

A chill ran through Forrester. "Preston?"

"Yeah, he was the battalion chief in charge out here at the time. He probably just wanted to keep involved in every aspect of the academy, giving the polygraph. The guy's a control freak, ya know."

"Did Hobbs do that a lot, give polygraphs?"

"For a while he did. Went and got certified. Ran the tests. Said it would cut back in costs. Then, he gave it up. Said he had too much on his plate. Just when all the real budget cutbacks came along and we could have used the money elsewhere, we had to spend it on polygraphs."

Had Preston done it just long enough to get his firebug through the academy? When had he discovered Clayton's tendancies to arson. Had he then just brought him along as someone to cover up his murders with fires? Someone to eventually take the fall for them?

But, Preston apparently wasn't done murdering after Clayton had died. Why had he gone after Max's girlfriend? Just cause he hated Max so much?

Was it because Max had been hitting on Cassie, getting between him and a woman he seemed to have become interested in?

A chill shot through him. Someone had sent Cassie all those tips about the fires, allowing her to get exclusive early video and a jump on the stories.

Had to be Hobbs.

Then, he'd enticed her out alone to spots where no one could find them. It had only been luck that Max had gone back to that burned-out house and found Cassie and Hobbs together there.

He pushed back from the table, knocking his chair over in his haste to get out, yanking his phone from his pocket. The battalion chief looked at him, his eyes rounded.

But, he didn't have time to explain.

He had to find Cassie.

Cassie and Dorothy walked toward the front door. A slow clicking in the lock stopped them both in their tracks. Dorothy's mouth dropped when the door pushed open.

"Preston," she gasped.

A pulse of fear shot through Cassie. Should she run, pulling Dorothy with her? Dorothy stepped forward, anger emanating from her pores.

Preston stepped across the threshold like he lived there, coming home after a day at work.

"What the…" Dorothy's voice rose in indignation. Preston locked the door behind him. When the lock turned, Cassie's heart clenched in an odd imitation of the sound of the mechanism clanking shut.

A scream formed in her gut, but she held it back. Flight or fight? The predator must be feeling the same warring sensations, attack now, or wait a bit to catch his prey off guard.

There would be no off guard with her. She knew what he was capable of. She just needed to get herself and Dorothy out of the situation. Somehow.

"I told you to leave the key when you left," Dorothy said, self-righteous anger lacing her tone. "This is not your home anymore."

"Really?" Arrogance and derision filled Preston's voice. "*My* name's still on the mortgage. *I* am the one making the payments. Who are you to say it's not my home, Goddess of All Things? Legally, it still is my home." He sneered at her. "Mine more than yours."

"Well, we'll see what a judge has to say about it." Dorothy stepped closer, jutting her chin out. "My lawyer says…"

Preston clamped his hand onto her face, cutting her words off, and pushing her to the floor with one mighty shove.

Cassie gasped as Dorothy let out a cry, falling hard, then recovering enough to scuttle back like a crab, putting distance between herself and Preston.

Cassie reached into her purse. She had to get her gun out.

Preston was faster. He pulled a gun from the back of his pants and pointed it at her.

Cassie silently cursed at herself. She should have pulled her own gun the moment she saw his face coming through that door.

But, they still had a chance. He hadn't seen her gun. She leaned forward, giving Dorothy a hand to get up. Dorothy stood but pulled back, whimpering, her gaze fixed on the gun.

From the kitchen, the puppy made a whimpering sound that sounded amazingly like Dorothy's. Preston sneered.

"Guess you got that dog you'd been nagging me for. Does he go to the bathroom all over *my* floors?" He looked around. "That type of thing could bring down the resell value."

He laughed harshly as if he'd just made a really funny joke.

"Let's go see your puppy," he said in a commanding tone, not like he was asking them to do it, but telling them to.

He pointed the gun at Dorothy, but took Cassie by the arm, gently almost, turning her toward the kitchen.

As he turned Cassie, the patch on his uniform shirtsleeve caught her attention. He still wore the patch of the firehouse they called The Squad.

The Squad, the name for the specialized group of firefighters who performed all sorts of difficult rescue missions. From rope rescues of stuck, high-rise window washers to ditch cave-ins, they had training that could save lives in situations that might lead to further deaths if not conducted carefully.

They'd go in to rescue firefighters who'd been trapped inside burning high-rises. Other firefighters often joked when they showed up on scenes, "Oh, get out of the way. Here come the heroes."

But, when they were trapped inside a burning inferno, Cassie was sure they seriously referred to the squad who came in after them as heroes.

Preston had been captain at Firehouse Four and proudly still wore its patch.

The patch was an ominous thing, a skull wearing a fireman's helmet.

Death came for those women, homeless Eddie's words floated back to her.

That skull patch looming in the smoke must have looked like death to the homeless man who'd spent many years hiding from danger, finding shelter wherever he could. Homeless Eddie lived in a world full of danger, a world where the little man had no real safe haven.

If someone remembered seeing Preston at the arson scenes, no one would think anything of it.

People often got their memories confused during emergencies. If they said they saw a firefighter, people would think they were just confused on their timeline.

Terror flooded up into her mouth, the same terror that Eddie must have felt. Death had come calling in the form of this firefighter, the man who falsely wore the heroes' patch.

"Go on," Preston shoved Dorothy again. What did he have in mind for them?

As they rounded the corner to the kitchen, Dorothy

gasped. Smoke seeped underneath the back door, clouding the puppy's crate. "Rover!" Dorothy shrieked as she stepped over the dog gate and ran toward the little dog.

Preston kicked the gate aside dismissively, dislodging it from the wall.

Dorothy opened the crate and pulled out the puppy who hacked and coughed, wheezing for air. The pitiful, strangling sounds were horrible, like the puppy was choking to death.

Preston laughed dismissively. "Might as well leave it in there, will make it easier on it if it just goes to sleep now."

Dorothy whirled, rage on her face. "It's not an *it*. He has a name. He has a life. And he's mine."

Preston shrugged. "Good. You two can go together then, two creatures I have no use for. Dogs and bitchy women. No bitches of any species allowed."

Dorothy looked at him, her face blank. Then, understanding dawned and terror crept across her face. "It's you. You've been killing all those women?"

"I haven't." He sneered. "They did it to themselves. They made the choices that brought down the wrath of God. I am but the hand that smites them."

Dorothy looked at him for a second, then back at the smoke coming underneath the backdoor. "We have to get out of here."

"You're not going anywhere. You're going to meet God's judgment here in the house where you broke our marriage vows."

"I did? *You* cheated on me. You broke the vows to keep yourself only unto me."

"Don't quote scripture to me." He shook his head

slowly, patronizingly. "I never slept with another woman. You're the one who didn't trust your husband. You broke the sacred vows you made to God to take me as your husband until death do us part."

He smiled. "Well, I intend to see that you keep those vows. It will be until death do us part. *Your* death. When you get to the pearly gates, technically, you'll still be married."

He raised a shoulder. "I'm doing you a favor, really. Now, maybe you won't burn in the fires of damnation for all eternity."

The way he turned a phrase, justifying murder, was so evil, so diabolical.

"You're the one breaking one of God's most important laws," Cassie spit out. "Thou shalt not kill."

She pointed an accusing finger at him. She had to do something to distract him from the rage that was building toward Dorothy.

Even if he turned his wrath toward her? Wrath? Now, she was using biblical phrasing, like him. As if God had anything to do with what this man thought or did.

Maybe if she distracted him, it would buy them some time. Time for someone to see the fire out back before Preston killed either of them.

Or maybe, she would be able to pull her gun at some point.

Cause, sure as the fires of damnation, she wasn't going out without a fight.

A really big fight. He'd have to knock her out before he tied her up.

Dorothy set the puppy down on the floor. "Get out

of here, Rover." She picked up a dog toy from the counter and threw it.

Rover ran for it, running through Preston's legs. "Filthy thing," Preston roared, jumping, as if trying to keep the dog from touching him, like he had bacteria he would release.

Preston lost balance, falling against the counter with his gun hand.

That was Cassie's chance. She reached for her gun, pulling it and pointing it at him. "Drop it! Drop it, now!"

He looked at her with fury in his eyes, then started to point the gun back at her.

She fired, straight into his abdomen. With a loud groan, he slid to the floor.

"Come on!" Cassie kept her gun trained on Preston. She pushed Dorothy away from Preston, toward the back door. "Get out."

Dorothy moaned. "We can't go that way. It's on fire."

Cassie glanced at the back door. Heavy smoke poured underneath the door, and through the curtained window, she saw the orange flicker of flames. She coughed as the smoke curled through the air. Coming for her, coming for all of them.

They had to go past Preston.

She pulled Dorothy toward him, but the woman pulled back, quivering and muttering, "No. No."

So, Cassie went first, stepping over him, and pulling Dorothy by the wrist behind her. Just as Dorothy stepped over Preston, he reached out, grabbing her legs, bringing her down on top of him.

Then, he put the gun to her head. "I guess we'll go

wherever we're going together, babycakes. Husband and wife 'til death does us unite?"

"Maybe that should be the new marriage vows." He struggled up, keeping Dorothy in front of him so Cassie couldn't get a clean shot at him without possibly hitting Dorothy.

The smoke was getting heavier. It filled her nose and mouth and she began to cough. The puppy scampered back into the room, oblivious to the danger.

"Get out, Rover," Dorothy commanded, desperation in her voice. She began to sob. "Poor little thing doesn't deserve to die. He never did anything wrong."

"He doesn't matter," Preston choked out, coughing and sputtering from the smoke. "Animals don't have souls. He doesn't matter."

"So, you're taking away all the life that he has?" Dorothy wailed. "If he doesn't go to heaven, then his time on earth is all he has. How can you take that away from him?"

Preston jerked her closer. "I didn't do it to him, you did. With your sinful breaking of marriage vows."

Dorothy began to sob then, as if she knew she had no hope. She was dealing with a maniac.

Cassie could read the self-doubt in her eyes. How hadn't she realized her husband was such a monster? She was blaming herself.

Sirens shrieked outside, help screaming toward them.

Preston tipped his head to the side. "We don't have much time left now, wifey. They're coming for us."

"Swing low, sweet chariot," he began to sing in a deep, baritone voice. "Coming for to carry me hoooome."

The gospel song was a twisted, macabre imitation of a Sunday morning church service. In this setting, it was nothing but a threat.

Desperation grabbed Cassie's insides, squeezing, wringing them free of any oxygen that she could get from the smoke-shrouded air.

"Looked over Jordan and what did I see, coming for to carry me home," Preston belted out into the smoky air, a joyful voice that turned Cassie's stomach. "A band of angels coming after me, coming for to carry me home."

He gazed down at Dorothy. "They're coming to carry both of us home, Dorothy."

She whimpered, trying to pull away from him, but he pulled her closer, speaking into her ear. "I'm not afraid to meet my maker, Dorothy. Why are you? I've lived a righteous life, enforcing his word here on earth."

Cassie looked into his eyes, and saw every Sunday morning bible lesson she'd ever learned twisted in his brain into the right to pass judgment on others.

A perverted killing specter of a human being. The smoke swirled around them, and for just a moment, Cassie felt she was in hell, meeting the devil.

A blond-haired, blue-eyed devil.

Just then, a loud bashing at the back door caused Preston to struggle to his knees and turn around to point his gun toward the door. Suddenly, his back was exposed.

Cassie stepped up, putting her gun close to his temple.

And fired.

The noise from the gunshot rang through her own skull as if the bullet had penetrated her head.

Dorothy screamed, a distant sound through the ringing in Cassie's skull. The sound of a crashing noise at the back door also penetrated the ringing.

The door gave and flung open. Forrester stood outside, a fire extinguisher in hand. He took one assessing glance into the room, then blew the sides of the door with the fire extinguisher.

After clearing the doorframe of fire, he ran in.

Dorothy and Preston lay crumpled together in a blood-covered heap. Preston had taken her down with him, falling onto her, pinning her.

The woman screamed long, nonstop, hysterical screams. Her hands flailed in the air like pinwheels, trying to get the body off of her.

The fire flared up again and Forrester turned to blow more foam around the back door.

Cassie pulled Dorothy from underneath Preston's body. But, Dorothy continued flailing her arms as if she didn't realize she'd been freed from the weight of her husband's bloody body.

Forrester dropped the fire extinguisher and grabbed Dorothy by her wrists. "Let's get out," he said into her face, loud, insistent, commanding. His voice seemed to bring her back to herself, because she stopped fighting.

Flames licked around the back door, with an ominous crackling sound. They'd only been beaten temporarily back by Forrester's fire extinguisher.

He pulled Dorothy toward the front door and she went. With Forrester's other hand, he gave Cassie a directing touch that got her moving.

But, a small bark penetrated the ringing in her head, and she looked down to see Rover at her feet, clutching his dog toy, inviting her to throw it again.

The little dog was oblivious to how close they'd all come to dying, being the lowest to the ground, he'd been spared the worst of the smoke effects. Cassie picked him up and carried him under her arm toward the front door.

A crazy burst of happiness filled her. They'd survived a nightmare. She laughed as she stumbled out, passing firefighters rushing in, long poles in their hands, equipment on their backs weighing them down. Like it was an everyday occurrence, they rushed into the burning building.

"He's in the kitchen!" she shouted as they passed her, and pointed the way for them.

But, she already knew that nothing could be done for the man. She'd put a bullet into his brain.

She stumbled outside, choking from the smoke. Behind them, the house exploded into flames.

He'd set the fire at the back, but must have poured accelerant on all sides. A shudder ran through her as she thought of her and Dorothy trapped in that burning house with a maniac.

She cuddled the puppy to her chest, letting him lick her face, as if nothing had happened.

She had to get herself one of these. A little being just happy to be held by her.

Then, she turned. Forrester handed Dorothy off to an EMT and was now rushing toward her.

CHAPTER THIRTY-ONE

Forrester stood in Cassie's living room, waiting for the other shoe to drop. He'd known she had something big to say from the moment their eyes met after he'd taken Dorothy to the ambulance.

She'd held her peace until after all the reports were taken, all the police interviews were done, and she'd done an on-air piece about what had happened inside Dorothy's house.

She must be exhausted, cause she looked like she could hardly keep her eyes open. But, a nervous energy buzzed about her.

Like the words were just aching to get out.

"Say it," he prompted her. Better to get it over with now.

Cause the dark look in those hazel eyes said it wasn't good, what she had to say.

"I almost died today," she stated flatly. She pointed her finger back and forth between them. "We almost died today."

"No." He shook his head. "We cheated death today."

"Death being Preston Hobbs?"

"It came in that form," he agreed. "Better to look at it like you survived, lived to die another day." He grinned, trying to bring her back from that dark space that seemed to clutch at her.

He reached for her, wanting to pull her close and comfort her. The average person didn't deal with the types of things she'd experienced in the last week.

She pulled back, shaking her head, turning toward the window, opening it and letting a cool breeze blow through the room.

"You're in shock," he said.

She turned to look at him. And nodded. "I am." She walked closer to him, then stopped while they were still separated by several feet.

She didn't want him touching her? Was this it? The moment when she killed the possibility of them?

Had today put everything into sharp focus, that they'd just been playing at the possibility of rebuilding a relationship?

"You know you probably shouldn't make any big decisions while you're still in the throes of the trauma you experienced and witnessed today." He shook his head. "Hell, this week. Most people will never experience in a lifetime all that you've experienced this week."

She smiled slightly, as if waiting for him to finish.

Then, she'd hit him in the gut?

"You were a hero." He ticked off on his fingers. "You were a hero twice with Miss Mary and JoJo." Then, he raised a third finger. "And you saved Dorothy." He tilted his head, raising a fourth finger. "And you saved yourself. You were almost a victim. But, you saved yourself as well as Dorothy."

A bigger smile slid across her face. She cocked her

head, and a bit of pride showed on her face. "You know, I never thought of it that way."

Maybe he could also change her mind on other matters.

Like them? And a possibility of a future for them. A restart of their marriage vows?

"Not to mention," he continued, determined to send as many good feelings splashing through her veins as possible. "All the possible victims Preston might have killed if you hadn't stopped him."

She narrowed her eyes and pursed her lips. "We can stop talking about me now."

Time to talk about them?

Man, he wanted to delay that moment. Cause he had a bad feeling.

"We could have died today," she repeated. "I could have died. You could have died. This thing could have turned out so horribly."

She held up a hand to keep him from protesting, then sucked in a ragged, deep breath.

Gathering her strength to bring it? To say that what had seemed to be awakening between them was over? It was a mistake to go back over that same ground again?

Because you didn't get a divorce lightly. And you didn't lightly start up with the person you'd already been unable to stay married to.

God, he didn't want to hear her say those words that would kill his hope for a new life for them.

He reached for her, pulling her against him, covering her mouth with his, using whatever means necessary to remind her of what they'd had.

The passion, the heat, the love. Because they'd had all of that.

Before life had gotten in the way, strangling the love that had been very real.

It hadn't been his imagination, all the love and passion that had flowed between them. The other day when they'd made love, the feelings had been every bit as powerful between them as they'd ever been.

They could have a life together again. If he could just remind her, before her mind completely sealed the vault on all those feelings.

She let him kiss her for a long moment, a moment that felt like it could win them a reprieve, win them a second chance.

Finally, she pulled back, looking up at him with passion-hazed eyes. "We could have died," she breathed the words more than saying them.

The words exhaled softly, penetrating his defenses. She wanted to say it. He had to let her.

No matter that it felt more painful than any bullet to the gut could have, any knife to the heart. Her words would kill a piece of him that he'd never be able to revive again.

No other woman would touch that piece of his heart that was hers. No matter how long he waited for his love for Cassie to disappear, he knew it would never be the same with any other woman.

Nothing would ever feel the way they had felt together.

Ever. Period.

He didn't even want to think ahead to all the dark, haunted nights he would experience without her.

Just survive this moment. The way they'd survived moment to moment so many times this last week. Surviving the fire that they'd dragged JoJo out of.

Surviving the moments that Hobbs had held a gun that could so easily have killed either of them.

They'd survived. And he'd survive this too. No matter how much it felt like facing death, thinking of a future without her.

Cassie tried to gather the words that would erase the hurt. Would tell him her thought process. And help him to understand everything.

"Forrester, when I thought that one or both of us might have died today, I realized that there might not have been any more chances."

She took a deep breath. "We're young." She gestured back and forth between them, the movement more to help dispel some of the nervous energy thrumming through her veins, than for any descriptive purpose.

"And being young, you feel like so much of life is ahead of you, endless chances. If you get it wrong now, well, you've still got a lot of time to get it right."

She shook her head, turned and paced a moment before turning back to look into his eyes, those green eyes that always sparked something within her, a desire to touch, to connect with him, either verbally or physically.

Those eyes held the essence of him.

"I love your eyes," she blurted out. "When I think of never being able to look into them again…" She shook her head in disbelief of that possibility.

"I almost lost all of that, Forrester. You or I could have died, with me losing any more time with you."

His eyes widened. With a hint of hope showing in them? What had he thought she was getting ready to say?

He gazed at her, steadily, waiting.

"I was so angry when Granny died, Forrester."

He nodded, his green eyes flooding with empathy.

"I was angry at everybody. The entire world. I had lost my granny." She squeezed her hands together, determined not to cry again.

"And then, I didn't come home for a really long time," Forrester said, his voice husky, deep.

"Exactly," she said with a nod. "You gave me a really good target to shoot all that anger at. I mean, I know you've told me you didn't hear through the channels that Granny had died."

He nodded.

"I think Max did it on purpose," she said. "I think he is very capable of something like that."

He just nodded again.

"So, even though I knew on some level it wasn't your fault, I didn't care. It made the pain of losing Granny easier to bear—to be angry instead of sad." She looked at him with a question in her eyes, wondering could anyone really understand that crazy behavior?

"I get it," he answered.

"Do you?" she said with a laugh. "Cause I didn't for the longest time."

He just looked at her, waiting for her to continue. Was that hope in his eyes?

"Today, when I thought all the tomorrows might be gone, any time I could have spent with you, I thought what a waste." She shook her head. "What a waste of time. I wonder if everyone on earth knew that tomorrow wasn't coming, would they stop their pettiness, vindictiveness, their whatever that keeps them from connecting with others?"

He reached for her then, pulling her to him, with a strength that bonded them into one body, his arms banding around her, fastening them together so tightly. That she thought they would never be able to be separated again.

"Does this means what it sounds like?" he whispered, pushing his face into her neck.

"If you can forgive me." She pulled back to see those green eyes, to read his reaction.

A wet sheen covered them, just before he smiled. "I may need some more apologizing. What say we take this to the bedroom."

She laughed, lightness spreading through her, literally and figuratively, as he swept her up in his arms and carried her to the bed.

He deposited her on the bed gently, then fell into the bed with her, rolling onto his back, as she wrapped herself around him.

He gathered her close, his scent spreading around her, reminding her of all the nights they'd shared together, all the mornings they'd awakened in the same bed.

She wanted that again. Time with him, for as long as she lived.

But, no matter how much she wanted to make love to him right now, the reality of so many nights with so little sleep began overriding her physical need for him.

Forrester nuzzled into her neck, and she laughed, throatily, feeling his mouth find the sound, following it as it trailed all along her vocal chords.

"I want to make love," she said, sleepily, finding it hard to push out the words.

"We can do that." His mouth became more urgent, exciting sensations throughout her.

"But, I don't know if I can," she murmured, afraid she'd fall asleep before they even finished this conversation.

He pulled back, fastening those green eyes on her like a beacon of hope. "That's all right," he said, passion infusing his words. "Sounds like we have all the time in the world. All the tomorrows that both of us have on this planet."

She smiled into those eyes and knew it was the truth. They had all the time in the world.

And all of that time would be spent loving him. No more wasting any chances, taking time for granted. She knew what she wanted to do with the rest of her nights from now until forever.

Sleep with Forrester, love Forrester.

And from the way those green eyes looked at her, be loved by Forrester.

"We have all the time in the world," he murmured, gazing down at her.

Those green eyes simmered with passion, with love. With a heat that spoke of all they could share in this bed.

Maybe she wasn't that sleepy after all.

The End

Read Mick's story

Targeted to Kill

A Men of the Badge Novel

Romantic Suspense at its best, with a keep you up all night reading intensity. Sometimes redemption and second chances at love come with the worst circumstances. Guilt and grief were copartners in the death of Mick Hampton and Becca Jefferson's love. Now, FBi agent Mick Hampton must stop a horrific attack on American soil as well as save the woman he has loved for most of his life.

The undercover operation to stop the attack takes a dramatic left turn when Mick's former fiancé is kidnapped by the terrorists.

Is Becca Jefferson's kidnapping a matter of simple revenge? Or do the terrorists know more than Mick thinks they do?

The operation becomes a desperate attempt to survive for Mick and Becca, while still preventing the murder of countless innocent civilians.

Love is the prize if they survive.

Read Weston's story

Tempted to Kill

A Men of the Badge Novel

The chemistry between Alisa and Weston could be as deadly as the drugs that are readily available in the dark underworld of sex and drug trafficking in Atlanta.

An undercover cop, Weston's job is to "blend in with scum," and go after the big guy in the drug ring. Protecting Alisa as she searches for her missing teen sister could jeopardize the mission as well as his and Alisa's ability to keep breathing.